character,
driven

CHaracter, Driven

DaViD LuBar

TOR·
TEEN

A TOM DOHERTY ASSOCIATES BOOK

NEW YORK

CHARACTER, DRIVEN

Copyright © 2016 by David Lubar

Reading and Activity Guide copyright © 2016 by Tor Books

A Tor Teen Book
Published by Tom Doherty Associates, LLC
175 Fifth Avenue
New York, NY 10010

www.tor-forge.com

Tor® is a registered trademark of Tom Doherty Associates, LLC.

The Library of Congress Cataloging-in-Publication Data
is available upon request.

ISBN 978-0-7653-1633-2 (hardcover)
ISBN 978-1-4668-5269-3 (e-book)

Our books may be purchased in bulk for promotional, educational, or
business use. Please contact your local bookseller or the Macmillan Corporate
and Premium Sales Department at 1-800-221-7945, extension 5442,
or by e-mail at MacmillanSpecialMarkets@macmillan.com.

First Edition: March 2016

Printed in the United States of America

10 9 8 7 6 5 4 3 2 1

For me

CONTENTS

cHaracter, Driven

intro [DUCTION | SPECTION | version]

THANK GOD FOR Alexander Graham Bell. If the phone hadn't started ringing, my crazy-drunk stepfather probably would have finished beating me to death with his belt. As it was, I felt pretty sure I'd lost an eye. And at least three teeth.

Half blind, I took advantage of the distraction and rammed him with my shoulder. I'd never fought back before. But this was different. Until now, he'd poked, slapped, and grabbed me in painful ways, and gut-punched me more times than I'd like to remember, but he hadn't done any lasting damage. At least, not physically. This morning, he was out of control. Crazy mad. I wanted to tell him there was no reason to be angry. But it wouldn't have mattered. I wasn't even sure I could form words with my mangled mouth, or force those words past the rage that clouded his mind. So I rammed him the instant the first ring of the phone drew his attention.

He staggered back, crashing into my dresser. Between one

heartbeat and the next, I debated and rejected the idea of diving out a second-story window. The front door was my only option. His footsteps smacked the floor behind me as I raced down the hall. I grabbed the stair post and swung around, hoping to reach the first floor before he caught up.

I misjudged the depth of his fury. I hadn't gone more than three or four steps when he tackled me. He must have dived from the landing. We tangled and tumbled, then crashed to the floor with a sickening snap. I was on top of him, faceup, my back pressing against his chest, unsure which of our bones had been broken. I had a feeling that, for the first time in history, the classic parental lie—*This will hurt me more than it hurts you*—had actually come true. I also had a feeling my life was about to change in drastic and permanent ways.

Do I have your attention? Good. That's crucial. Grab the reader with the first sentence. There are ten zillion books out there, and no special reason to pick up this one.

Of course, at this point, there can't be any book, because I've just started writing these words. But, somehow, you're reading them. I realize this could cause confusion. Let it go. It's not good to think about the order of creation for written works. It's sort of like that time-travel paradox where you wonder what would happen if you went into the past and shot off your grandfather's penis before your father was conceived. There's no easy way to think it through.

Paradoxes aside, as much as I may have grabbed you with the violent, action-packed bone-breaking opening, I've created a problem. If I start out with a gigantic lie, you might not stick with me. Nobody wants to explore new lands with an untrustworthy guide. But I'd hate for you to leave so soon after we've met. So here's what you need to know to take this trip with me:

I don't have a drunken, sadistic stepfather. I have a blood-related dad who probably gets drunk three or four times a year. He's an accountant. I've never had my face cut by a belt buckle. Never been knocked down a flight of stairs. Never been saved by the bell. Got both eyes. Got all my teeth. Damn fine teeth they are.

I'm screwing up the sequence here. I should have introduced myself first. I'm a guy. I'm eighteen. As of today, actually. Happy birthday to me. If you want to sing along, I guess you'll need to know my name.

Call me Cliff. The most voracious bookworms among you will instantly wonder whether I've offered this name as a reference to some famous fictional Clifford, Heathcliff, or Clifton. Nope. I am not a reflection or echo of someone you've already met. Cliff happens to be my name. But that doesn't mean it lacks metaphorical echoes. By an accident of birth, I am well named for this story.

Think about it. . . .

cliff
precipice
edge

There you have it. I'm Cliff. Cliff Sparks. At the edge. On the verge. Dangling.

At this point, you're probably wondering whether I have a story to tell. Will I face life-changing challenges in a dramatic quest to triumph over seemingly insurmountable obstacles? Will I come of age, reach my dreams, or discover the meaning of life? That would be awesome. Though not every book tells a story. There's another route from opening sentence to satisfied sigh and the terminal snap of a closing cover. That would be a character-driven tale, where I pull you along because I'm so fascinating and charismatic that you'll follow me even if there are no plot threads to grasp. Nice trick if you can pull it off. Sadly, I'm not that guy. If I had an abundance of follow-me charm, I'd have come of age by sophomore year, at the latest.

But I really want you to stick with me, so here's my offer: I'm going to tell you a story. But it doesn't start today. I'm going to take you back to April 16, nearly two months before this very moment, which we think of as the present. (I think I just foreshadowed a flashback.) We'll leap together to the past, for the best of reasons.

I'm going to spin a tale.

And it will be so enthralling that you'll get sucked right in. You'll not only suspend your disbelief—you'll tie a rope around its neck and hurl it off a cliff, then give the other end of the rope a mighty yank, perfectly timed to snap disbelief's scrawny vertebrae like a fistful of dry pasta.

I'm going to sweep you along in my tale spin. Soon enough, you'll forget about this rambling start. You'll forget we've gotten so intimate. Until the next time I burst from the page and raise your disbelief from the dead, hauling the rope back over the cliff so we can both contemplate the decomposition. But either way, no more lies. You can rely on that. And on me.

Yes, sirree—I'm going to suck you right in. Because this is one sweet-ass mother lode of a gripping tale. Here we go . . .

SHE WALKS IN, BEAUTY

VENUS IS THE morning star.

As is Jillian.

Let me explain. My school day starts with Calculus, which is a form of math designed to convince people they want to be History majors in college. Our teacher, Mr. Yuler, doesn't talk much. He'll write a problem on the board, then sip coffee from his ever-present mug and walk the aisles while we work at our desks. If you're stuck, he'll uncap his pen and circle something he feels you should contemplate. It's not a bad way to start the day, since, between my after-school jobs and my crazy idea that I should make at least a half-assed effort to do a half-decent job on my homework (which multiplies out to a quarter-decent-ass-job), I generally get less sleep than I need. It would be hard to keep my eyes open for a lecture during first period.

So there we sat, twenty-eight zombified students, all good enough with numbers to have taken the college-prep track through math. I was eventually college bound, I hoped. But I needed to take a year off and save up before I could do anything more than catch some classes at County. Dad lost his job again last year, and Mom had her hours cut at the Maple Lane Bakery. She'd worked there since the first time Dad lost his job. We were keeping our expenses low until things turned around.

But let's get back to Calculus. I think, somehow, I felt Jillian's presence before I heard her footsteps or saw her appear in the doorway, where she stood clutching a slip of paper and looking very new to the world of Rismore High School.

There are some things that stab each of us in the heart: a perfect sunset, a flag-draped casket, an unexpected encounter with a favorite childhood toy. Each—the beautiful, the tragic, the nostalgic—grabs part of our spirit in some way.

Jillian had been assembled from a kit of parts labeled WHAT CLIFF LOVES. To describe her, to even hint at the color of her hair or the curve of her lip, would be to reveal too much of my soul. Instead, I'll let you craft your own Jillian. Think of the kit you've labeled WHAT I LOVE. Make her, or him, in that image, breathe life into her form, and place her here at the classroom entrance, inspired. Take your time.

Got it? Great. Let's move on.

I sat, entranced, as Jillian entered the classroom. I stole glances, and risked several longer stares in her direction after she'd taken her seat. But I knew the reality. She'd never notice me unless I had the misfortune to suffer a memorable death in her presence. Something involving spontaneous flames would do the trick. For the moment, I wasn't tempted to pursue that approach—or departure. I really didn't want my encounter with her to be a short story, or a long obituary.

Jillian took the only available seat, three rows to my right, and one row ahead. Most of the guys were staring at her, either boldly or through a series of covert glances. As were the girls.

Nola Lackmore, who sat immediately to my left, cast an appraising eye in Jillian's direction. I would have loved to hear her thoughts. Do pretty girls—and that was Nola for sure—think bad thoughts about gorgeous girls? Abbie Striver shot an escalating sequence of disapproving glares toward Jillian, as if it were a transgression to be attractive.

Both my best friends were in this class. Robert, two seats to my right, shook his hand in the universal gesture of someone who has touched a hot surface. I couldn't see the reaction, if any, from Butch, who sat in the left rear corner.

Lucas Delshanon, directly to my right, let out a half-sighed half-muttered, "Whoa . . ." I couldn't think of a better word.

Ahead of us, Jillian seemed unaware of the attention. Or maybe she was used to it and chose not to admit awareness.

That was the moment when I spotted an opportunity. Mr. Yuler opened the door of the small closet in the back of the room. He rummaged inside for a minor interval, like someone trying to find the last nub of pepperoni in an overstuffed deli drawer. Then he closed the door and let his shoulders slump in defeat.

I knew exactly what had just happened. Jillian needed a textbook. But the cupboard was bare. I raised my hand in anticipation of Mr. Yuler selecting someone to run over to the other Calculus teacher's classroom for a copy. The instant he noticed me, I said, "Want me to check with Ms. Percivel?"

He didn't seem surprised that I was a half step ahead of him. In reality, I was a whole journey ahead. When I returned from my quest, I'd get the chance to weave my way through the crowded room and give the book directly to Jillian. She'd thank me. Our fingers would touch. I'd flash her a smile, letting her see my great teeth up close, and say something classy like, *No prob.*

No. Too slangy. *No problem?*

Yeah. That was better.

"Thanks," Mr. Yuler said.

"No problem." I flinched as I realized I had just fired my one silver-tongued bullet. I couldn't repeat myself. That would make me seem shallow or unimaginative. No problem. I'd think of a better reply by the time I got back. It was a long hall.

I headed down that hall, past the cafeteria, which was just beginning to emit aromatic hints about the species of today's fried protein, and along the new wing, toward Ms. Percivel's classroom. Happily, despite my fears of learning otherwise and being forced to return empty-handed, she had an extra copy of the Calculus textbook.

What to say? I ran possibilities through my mind, testing them in a full fantasy enactment of the moment when I gave Jillian the book and she thanked me.

My pleasure . . .

Not bad. Slightly too refined. I was sure I could do better. *The pleasure is all mine. . . .* No. Too wordy. Unless she was a fan of old Jane Austen stuff.

I held up the book and searched the front cover for inspiration. It showed a broad ethnic diversity of students at undiversified desks, hunched over papers, happily solving the problems of integration. No inspiration there.

Maybe I could make a clever calculus reference? I could say, *Aaaaaaaaaaaaugh!*

I did say, "Aaaaaaaaaaaaaaugh!"

It wasn't clever, and it had nothing to do with Calculus, but it was pretty much the response that's hard-wired into most of us when we plummet unexpectedly. My right foot had just come down not on solid flooring, but on the edge of the steps leading into "the Pit."

Yeah, there's a fucking pit in the open area on the other side of the hall from the cafeteria. It's used as a gathering place for small-group activities, and as a death trap for the unobservant. It has two steep steps that also serve as seats, running along all four sides. I was so busy staring at the book cover and trying to think of what to say to impress Jillian, I'd walked at an angle along the corridor, right into the Pit.

I came down hard. The book went flying. My right hand smacked the floor of the Pit, breaking my fall. It felt like I'd also come close to breaking my hand. I lay there, taking stock of my injuries. I'd smacked my right knee pretty hard on the edge of the bottom step. And my chin. I ran my tongue across the back of my teeth, hoping not to find anything loose. There was a slight metallic taste of blood in my mouth, but nothing felt chipped or broken. I seemed to have escaped with less damage than a fall like that deserved. Lucky me.

I looked around as I crawled to my feet. Nobody had seen me. That was good. The fallen get mocked. It's the law.

Have a wonderful trip!

Nice of you to drop in!

Down goes Cliff!

Crap. I hurt all over. Knees. Hands. Elbows. Chin. Pride. I retrieved the book and limped back to class, my palms throbbing as the numbness of impact gave way to the sting of injury. I winced in pain as I opened the door and hobbled across the room.

"Here," I said, handing the book to Jillian.

"Thanks." She flashed a smile that should have melted away all my pain.

"Uhhhh . . . welcome. Problem. I mean, no."

Great. I had the articulate wit of a bear coming out of hibernation after bingeing on fermented fruit. I clamped my mouth shut before it could spew more nonsense.

"Yeowch!" I eased the clamp as pain shot through my bruised jaw.

Jillian's smile morphed into a puzzled stare.

It seemed like a good time to retreat. I slipped back into my seat, which, between the crowded classroom and the stiffening of my injured joints, wasn't easy.

I already fell for you.

Damn, that would be a totally perfect line, if she'd known about the fall. Witty. Charming. Especially if delivered with a bit of a self-effacing grin. It would have been awesome.

No. It sucked. All my lines sucked. I had no game. As I sat there, drowning in the flood of lost opportunity and imagining the various shades of blue, green, and purple that would soon blossom on my palm, my past dating life flashed before my eyes. It made me want to fall off something much higher than the Pit, or find a pit much deeper.

MADDIE, 'BOUT YOU

MY DATING EXPERIENCE (I almost need a specifically singular form of "experience" to capture the scarcity of it) began in seventh grade. Actually, back then, I guess I was predating. I mean, "pre-dating," not being a predator. Though, on second thought, I guess "predator" sort of describes my strategy. On third thought, maybe I should just tell what happened and let you categorize it.

I'd had a crush on Maddie all through middle school. I think it started, or solidified, the time she yawned. She was sitting next to me in Algebra. It was a large and leisurely yawn. She arched her back and raised her arms in the sort of posture one would use while putting on heavy headphones. But it wasn't her back or arms or even her gaping mouth that ensorcelled me. It was her breasts. As her back arched, those breasts seemed to lag slightly behind the rest of the parade, following her movement but telling the world they had their own free will to do what they wanted as they pressed against the pale brown fabric of her button-down shirt. I could picture her bra cradling them. Coaxing them with gentle upward tugs. *Come on, we're all moving together. Don't be nonconformists.*

This was not an image conducive to balancing equations. The breasts continued their public display of uncivil disobedience during Maddie's return from the extreme edge of lumbar contortion. Eventually, her whole body was realigned in an erect posture. As was part of mine. I waited breathlessly for the next round trip along mammary lane. I even let out an exaggerated yawn of my own, in hopes of priming the pump. And I told myself I had to make Maddie my girlfriend. Breasts that breathtaking needed authorized admiration.

I plotted. I schemed. Maddie was in an Episcopal youth group. I joined it, even though I wasn't an Episcopalian. It was fun. We sang a lot of folk songs and gathered cans of food for the hungry. None of the activities allowed me to catch Maddie's attention. But there were other opportunities to pursue her. She belonged to the Y. I got a membership. She acknowledged my existence when we crossed paths during open swim or coed volleyball, and actually didn't try to flee when I engaged her in conversation. I grew bolder. I decided to ask her out on a date. I didn't phrase it that way, of course. It was more like, "You wanna get something at the diner?"

She agreed.

Looking back at the actual event, I can now see that she spent most of her time scanning the area, as if hoping to spot someone more interesting who might take her on a real adventure, or at least sport her off to a better restaurant and better conversation. It was sort of like having a meal with an owl.

I muddled my way through seventh grade, managing two

more pseudo-dates. I didn't see Maddie over the summer, but I saw her every night, in my fantasies. In early August, a friend, Charles Araby, invited me to go down the shore with him. His aunt had a place. It wasn't near the ocean. It was on an inland waterway. But one night, in the middle of our week there, we took a bus, and then another bus, which delivered us to the boardwalk.

Like most Jersey boys, I was no stranger to the boardwalk. But I'd never been there without my parents. I was especially eager to try my luck at the games, because my dad would never let me play them. He said it was like throwing away money.

I skipped the milk can toss and the basketball game. I could tell those were pretty hard. Then I saw a game I figured I could win. It had stuffed cats that you knocked down with baseballs. In retrospect, the cats were 90 percent fur. Picture a pencil made much wider by the addition of six inches of insubstantial fuzz on each side. Now think about trying to hit it dead center with a misshapen baseball from ten feet away.

The rules were simple: Knock down three cats with three throws, and you win a stuffed animal. There were bears and dogs among the prizes. There were fish. And, lining one side wall, hanging by their tails in all their four-foot velveteen glory, were rows of snakes dyed in bruiselike shades of green, blue, and purple.

I want to win a snake for Maddie.

I can't explain the origin of the obsession. I'm sure the bears and dogs were cuter. I'm sure the fish were more whimsical. Maybe my young mind saw something symbolic in the snake. Maybe I'll drop the serpentine search for symbolism and get back to the boardwalk.

I paid for the three balls. My first throw missed. So did my second. In a world where mercy is an actual component, in a kind and caring universe that doesn't want to see fragile middle schoolers snared in the sticky web of false hope, I would have missed my third and final throw, as well, and skulked off toward the roller coasters. But the universe took a dump on me and had a giant laugh. My third throw hit a cat and knocked it down.

Knock one down, you win nothing. Knock two down, you still win nothing. Knock three down, you win Maddie's heart. And maybe her breasts.

I tried again for the trifecta.

And again.

I was like a lab rat pressing a lever for a jolt of sugar water. I'd hit one cat out of three. Or maybe two, separated by a miss. But never three. Far too soon, I went through everything I'd brought, except for a scattering of pocket change. My entire vacation fund was lying in the bulging pocket of a game barker's change apron.

I handed over my last dollar, in the form of two quarters, four dimes, and two nickels, and took possession of the three baseballs. I hit a cat on my first throw. I hit one on my second throw. I gripped the final ball, knowing I was destined to miss, because when the universe takes a dump on you, it doesn't follow up the fecal splatter with a hug and a kiss. It follows through with a steaming stream of piss. I looked at Charley. He was a ball player. I looked at the guy running the game. He was disinterested.

"Can I let my friend throw the last one?" I asked.

"Nope," the guy said.

Had it happened three or four years later, when I was less daunted by authority figures, I would have been capable of presenting a variety of arguments to support my request. The only signs on display were for NO LEANING and DEFLECTED BALLS DON'T COUNT. There was not a word about the illegality of sharing. But I didn't have the courage to argue.

Knowing I was about to be both broke and humiliated, I threw the third ball.

And I hit the damn cat dead center, knocking it flat on its back to complete the trio of prostrate felines.

Choice!

I had my snake. It was a stunningly cheap carnival creation, colored a shade of blue that doesn't appear anywhere in nature, or even in good art. It was stuffed, by the feel of it, with straw and gravel. None of that mattered. I had my snake and I had my fantasies of presenting it to Maddie.

I won this for you. Nah—it was easy. Glad you like it. Yawn . . .

There wasn't much point in staying on the boardwalk. I was broke. Charley was nice enough to offer to pay my bus fare.

It started raining during the first part of the ride back. It started pouring before we got off the bus. There was an old shelter at the bus stop. It was a concrete building with a single wooden bench inside, barely lit well enough to keep us from stumbling into one of the walls.

Charlie and I went inside to await our second bus.

The rainstorm swelled from strong to torrential. Water rose on the floor of the shelter. There was a drain in the middle of the floor, but it was clogged with candy wrappers and other scraps of litter. I sat there, lost in heroic fantasies.

"Your snake," Charlie said, pointing next to me.

My snake—Maddie's snake—was right by my side on the bench, where I'd put it. But it dangled to the ground. The tail sat immersed in six inches of dirty water.

I retrieved it, but even in the dim light of the shelter, I could tell it was ruined.

There I sat, in the wet gloom of the Spartan concrete shelter, with an empty wallet, crushed dreams, and a soiled snake.

I imagine Charlie laughed, though I don't believe he tormented me with any prolonged or harsh mockery. Either way, that's not important enough to remember. If he did laugh, I doubt it bothered me. I was too damaged to feel anything external.

If you believe that things happen for a reason, I guess this happened to teach me something. The problem is, you can extract a dozen different lessons from the incident, ranging from *Don't try to impress girls* to *Watch where you dangle your snake.* The other problem is, when it comes to life's lessons, I'm not a fast learner. I could provide proof of that, but I've dredged up enough bad memories to hit my quota for the day, and to test your willingness to let me stray from the story.

For now, inexplicably and yet inexorably (whatever the hell that word means), we are back at the moment I wedged my pain-racked, impact-bruised body into my seat in Calculus class—returning to my previous present, presented as that which has already passed.

FALLING BEHIND

WHEN THE BELL rang, I lingered in my seat and watched Jillian leave. Right after I stepped into the hallway, Robert grabbed my shoulder hard enough to leave a bruise, pointed ahead of us with his other hand, and said, "Now *that's* a perfect ass."

Robert had been placed on earth to spoon-feed irresistible straight lines to even the least imaginative of us. The obvious response would be, *No, Robert. You're the perfect ass.* Or a subtler version, such as *It takes one to know one.* I could also have gone totally crude with, *And it gave birth to you, Robert, you piece of shit.*

Given that he was pointing at Jillian, who glided down the hall ahead of us with the grace of a fawn, I decided to do the gentlemanly thing and backfist him in the solar plexus. I have a weak backfist, but Robert has a weaker solar plexus.

"Oof!" He doubled over but didn't crumple. "What was that for?"

"Sexist, inappropriate comments," I said. Even though I'd punished him for his words, he spoke the truth. Jillian did look as amazing from behind as she did from the front. Or the side. But there's a huge difference between thinking about someone else's anatomy and speaking those thoughts out loud.

A biblical voice in my mind intoned: *Thou shall not commit adulatry.* Though I don't think that's a proper word, or commandment.

I picked up my pace. I didn't want Jillian's perfect posterior to move out of range of my adulation.

"He's right, though. It is a nice ass," Butch said. She slipped her hand through my arm and matched my stride. I winced as bolts of pain danced through my elbow, but I didn't pull away. Butch rarely makes physical contact.

"Here's the plan," she said. "You get to know her. Use all your awkward, boyish charm to captivate her. Then introduce me, so I can steal her away with my girlish charm. Okay?" She grinned and fluttered her eyelids.

"I'll give it some thought," I said. I could feel my shoulder muscles tighten at the words "steal her away."

Butch is a little twisted, but in a good way. She has the largest collection of fake skulls I've ever seen, alternating on shelves all around her bedroom with My Little Ponies and Hello Kitties. She gave herself the nickname "Butch" toward the end of sophomore year. She felt it was ironic on several levels, and thus a perfect fit. We've been friends since fourth grade, back when she called herself Princess Bethany. That was followed by Calamity, Mrs. Frodo, Peach, and Yakitori. None of our teachers has ever used any of her nicknames. They all call her Penelope, which she hates. Or Penny, which she despises. I suspect she's about due for another change. I can't wait to see what she comes up with. I have a suspicion, and a fear, her next nickname will be made up of nothing but numbers, hand gestures, and glottal clicks.

It's interesting that we usually start out describing people's hair, and not their hearts. In Butch's case, I guess they were equally amazing. Her hair was long, halfway down her back, and so light, it was almost white. If the school ever put on a stage version of *The Lord of the Rings*, she'd snag an elf role for sure. Robert, on the other hand, had just recently decided that a shaved head, which he'd sported since freshman year, was not his style, so he was currently cultivating emerging growth and a long-term plan for dreadlocks. His family had been pretty much starving in Jamaica, so he was painfully skinny when he came here. He hasn't bulked up much, but at least now you'd need an X-ray machine to count his vertebrae.

What else is worth mentioning? Robert's going to Rutgers next year to study business. Butch is going to Syracuse to study theater. Robert is about four inches taller than I am. Butch is a head shorter. I am exactly as tall as myself. Except when I slouch.

As for Butch's admiration of Jillian's posterior, that was probably a joke. Butch has a boyfriend, Judah. He's a sophomore at Princeton, so she doesn't see him all that much. But she's against "gendertyping," as she calls it. And she likes to play with people's minds. So her comment wasn't surprising. She also has a black belt in aikido, and a framed certificate from the Universal World Temple of Hecate, giving her the power to officiate at wedding ceremonies. If she weren't real, she'd make a great character in a novel, though probably not this one.

self, aware

HOLD ON. SOMETHING just hit me. You know what Robert and Butch look like, but I'm still a shadow. I probably should take a minute to describe myself. The problem is, I have no desire to offer a superficial laundry list of my features, traits, and tics. But you need a hook on which to hang my voice. How to convey this description? I could look in a mirror and report what I see. But I fear resorting to that cliché would reflect badly on my skills. There are subtler, more admirable choices available. I could stroll past the piano, if we had one, and gaze at last year's family holiday photo, if we had one, noting the ways in which my features borrow or diverge from those of my parents, Samantha and William Sparks. Or I could boldly state a description without worrying about context, convention, or motivation.

Yeah. I could do one of those things. And it would work well enough. But I'm eager to give you the truth. And the truth is, nobody sees himself clearly in a mirror or photo. It's not possible. As the poet Robert Burns said, in more words than this, and probably in a virtually impenetrable Scottish accent with the reek of oatmeal-stuffed pig stomach and peat-smoked whisky on his breath, it's a gift to see ourselves as others see us. A gift most of us lack. Happily, I am in possession of that very gift. Last year, on the first day of English, our teacher, Mr. Piccaro, had each of us write descriptions of people seated nearby.

So, I have copies of my written description courtesy of the aforementioned Abbie Striver and the not-previously-mentioned Jimby Fasborne. I'll tell you more about them, later. ("Later" because I don't want to slow the narrative flow with interruptions, any more than I want to burden the prose with parentheticals. "More" because this isn't a short story. This is a freakin' novel of length, depth, and substance. Unless I lose interest or decide to skip a bunch of stuff.) For now, here I am, as seen by other eyes, sliced open and splayed out like an AP Bio specimen, gutted for your viewing pleasure and scrutiny by means of something mightier than the sword. Here's what Abbie wrote:

> The boy [okay—I'm intruding here, but just to point out that she never even uses my name] sat slouched at his desk in the typical unhealthy posture of an aimless adolescent whose lack of direction or ambition doomed him to a life of servitude and squalor at minimum-wage venues. Dirty blond hair hung down his forehead with the limp sorrow of forlorn tresses yearning for a meaningful encounter with shampoo. [Me again. I'd washed it the night before.] His skin didn't show signs of recent eruptions large enough to cause revulsion, though it did sport a scattering of faint scars from earlier encounters between unwanted pimples and unwashed fingernails.

[Give me a break. I wash my hands. And all pimples are unwanted, so she could have cut that word.] His nose seemed both too long and too narrow for his face, giving him the aquiline visage of a second-rate medieval scholar or perhaps a rabid possum. [Seriously—what the hell?] Of his clothing, the less said, the better, but perhaps his manner of dress could best be described as a blend of indifference, ignorance, and rumpled dishevelment, punctuated with periods of confusion and misconception, capped off with wardrobial [that's not a word!] delusions about the positive aesthetic value of anything plaid or checkered. His face, in general, offered the soft ruddiness of a carnivore fresh from a recent encounter with ethically inedible atrocities.

On second thought, you don't need to read the whole thing. The remaining seven pages really provide little additional detail, and even less in the way of an accurate description. Abbie, by the way, is an overachiever. But enough of her. Let's switch to my pal, Jimby Fasborne. Here's what he wrote:

Cliff has light brown hair. It is not too long. It is not too short. Cliff has brown eyes. He has white teeth. [Told you they were great.] He isn't skinny. He's not fat, either. If I had to pick one, I guess I'd pick skinny. But not too skinny. I like his shirt. It's plaid. Cliff looks at his watch a lot in class. Sometimes his shoelaces are green. But not today.

Okay, Jimby was sort of vague in spots, and Abbie was more interested in the style of her prose than in the substance of my appearance. Maybe I should have gazed in that mirror and described myself, or strolled past that piano. But you get the idea. By the way, his name really is Jimby. That's not a nickname. His mom named him after a slurred version of her favorite bourbon. Despite the warnings on the bottle, she drank heavily when she was pregnant. And before. And after. It sort of messed up her judgment a lot, and his brain a bit, but he's a good guy. His backyard is diagonally across from mine. We hang out sometimes. And fear not—I didn't come here to make fun of anybody's disability. I like Jimby enough that I'd take a beating to protect him. I don't care that he's not super smart. Every one of us is messed up, one way or another. And every one of us is smart in some way. The problem is, we might never find that way.

I wouldn't mind trading heads with Jimby once in a while, just to be in a place where my thoughts aren't all throwing punches at each other. Sometimes my brain gets in a shouting match with itself, or tries to wrestle itself to the ground. That's one of the main reasons I'm writing all this down. If I can get it on paper, maybe I can get it out of my head. Besides, I find myself in possession of some unexpected but much-appreciated free time.

Oh, hell. I promised to spin you an amazing story, and I got sidetracked letting a stuck-up girl and a nice guy tell you I have brown eyes and limp hair of an unmemorable color.

Sorry about that. Okay, I'm back on task.

Drawn Together

DESCRIPTIONS—whether of hair, hearts, or heartbreaks— exist outside space and time, which means we are still at the moment immediately following my response to Butch's last utterance. And I was still watching Jillian from behind. My pulse quickened when I saw her pause by the door to room 238.

Go in! Go in! Go in!

She checked a piece of paper clipped to the front of her notebook, then slipped inside the room.

Physics!

We were in the same class again. The universe, in all its wisdom, was repeatedly throwing us together, trying to achieve fusion.

I would have multiple opportunities to impress Jillian each day. Or fall on my face.

That's when I fell on my face.

Literally.

And, since there is growing confusion about that lonely word on the line above, I should emphasize that I literally mean "literally."

It.

Really.

Happened.

I went down hard, face-first. Literally. Once again.

Robert had tripped me. He'd stuck his skinny-ass excuse for a leg in front of my left foot and taken me down.

I'll spare you any creative descriptions of the pain generated by my landing. I'd rather just try to forget about it. "What was that for?" I asked as I got back to my feet.

"Revenge," he said. "You hit me."

"Dude, serve it cold," Butch said.

"What?" Robert asked.

Butch let out a heavy sigh of mock frustration. She worked with sighs the way Van Gogh worked with swirls of raw sienna and Prussian blue. "What did they teach you in Jamaica? Don't you know anything? Maybe that's why they kicked you out."

"We weren't kicked out," Robert said. "We fled. By choice."

Butch pushed up her sleeve high enough to reveal the tattoo—obviously homemade—that circled her arm halfway between her shoulder and elbow.

REVENGE IS A DISH BEST SERVED COLD.

"It's an old Chinese proverb," she said.

"Then why isn't it in Chinese?" Robert asked.

"So illegal aliens like you can read it," Butch said.

"I'm nearly legal," Robert said. "And I speak four languages. How many do you speak, gringa?"

Let me briefly step away from the dialogue to point out that

Robert and Butch will be arguing pretty much whenever they are within earshot of each other. If I try to convey all that they say whenever we're together, either I will go mad or you will go away. Neither would advance my goal of leading you to the end of the story. So, from this point on, I will resort to far more exposition and far less recitation.

Robert and Butch argued in an amusing fashion.

We headed into Physics.

I guess I should add one other side note: You might be the sort of knowledge geek who is aware that Butch was wrong. The quote about revenge probably isn't Chinese. (Feel free to look it up, but I'm not waiting.) I imagine I could mark other people's mistakes with footnotes, so you'd know the misinformation wasn't mine. But footnotes are a pain in the butt to deal with* when you're trying to read a story. So I won't do that.

Let's get back to Physics.

Jillian was seated a mere two desks away from me. Physics is all about attractions and repulsions. I decided not to think in those terms for the moment—especially not the latter one.

I will spare you the classroom lecture that was taking place at the front of the room, mostly because it has nothing to do with the story, and partly because I was slightly distracted. And attracted.

I had a free period after Physics, so I headed to the Art House. That's what we call it. When the high school got overcrowded, about five years ago, the town bought the first house up Vorhees Avenue past the school, on the other side of the teachers' parking lot. They'd replaced all the doors inside with archways, so the place had an open feel. They put the art classes on the sec-

---

*See?

ond floor, and the consumer science classes downstairs. That made sense, since there was already a kitchen down there. And it worked nicely for the art students, because nothing inspires art like the smell of chocolate-chip cookies or angel food cake.

I had Art right after my free period. That meant I could paint for two straight periods, if I wanted to. As seniors, taking Art 4, we didn't get all that much in the way of classroom lectures. Maybe once every month or so, we'd gather to look at some slides and have a discussion, or listen to a short lesson. It was mostly like an independent study.

We got to pick a medium to focus on each marking period. I'd started with clay, because I'd always liked sculpting. I wasn't great at planning ahead, so any material that didn't allow do-overs would be a bad choice. The one time I'd tried to carve a bust out of soapstone, I'd ended up making it smaller and smaller as I corrected my mistakes. Noses are a lot harder than they look. Finally, I'd given up trying to add any features and turned it into an egg.

Second marking period, I concentrated on pencil draw-ings. That's very basic, but it's also very portable. I carried a sketchbook with me the whole time. It made me feel authenti-cally artistic. Third marking period, I tried stained glass. That was fun, except the nurse got tired of having me show up for Band-Aids.

This marking period, I was trying acrylics. I've been paint-ing for most of my life. Way back when I was in second grade, my mom got me a tray of watercolors. I liked them right off, and I liked them even better when my uncle made a deal with me. I guess he wanted to encourage me to paint. He told me he'd pay me a dollar for every painting I made, up to seven dollars a week. I turned into a little art factory, until a couple weeks later when Dad shut things down. He said he was doing it for my own good because he didn't want me to get the idea that I could make a living as an artist. It didn't matter. I still painted every day for a long time after that. And I held on to the idea that artists could make money, though I kept that belief to myself.

My first acrylic painting was a dragon. I'd started as soon as the marking period began, on April 10. That was last Wednesday. I'd finished it yesterday, on the fifteenth. I thought it looked pretty slick, sweeping a blast of fire across a group of knights, one of whom had already been totally slagged by the heat. My teacher, Ms. Gickley, told me it had nice lines and powerful sense of motion, but that the details were a bit sketchy.

"Check out the impressionists," she'd said, pointing to the shelf of art books behind her desk. "You might want to explore their way of looking at the world. It could be a good fit for your strengths. And maybe you could think about taking a little more time with your next painting. This isn't a race."

"I'll do that." I already knew the impressionists, and liked them—especially Renoir—but I wasn't interested in mimicking their style. My worldview had little room for vaguely rendered misty dragons resting on hazy lily pads or attending the ballet.

Dalí, on the other hand, was a great role model. A lot of people know his painting with the melting watches, but one of my favorites of his was a crucified man. It was surreal, but with a touch of cubism. I wanted to do something like that, but give it contemporary symbolism. After thinking about it for most of the free period, and discarding a slew of not-quite-right ideas, I decided to make the crucifix the cross pad on a game controller. There were a ton of ways that this could be symbolic. And the crucifixee, or whatever he's called, could be a gamer.

As the bell for fourth period rang, Ms. Gickley walked past me, heading for the supply closet in the next room, where she grabbed a paint box and a canvas. On her way back, she nodded toward my own blank canvas and said, "Take your time."

"I will."

But the idea had seized me, and I was ready to bring it to life. It was going to be awesome. As I was sketching the controller, I realized I could add a cord, like they use for charging the battery, and wind it around the player, binding him to the cross. Oh! And then, the other end could be a crown of thorns. This was great. Everything was falling together in my mind. I loved it when an idea gelled. That was the best part about painting— coming up with an awesome idea.

"Sweet," I said to myself as I sketched in those details. "Totally sweet-ass bitchin' awesome!"

I really needed to learn to either keep my mouth shut, find some socially acceptable exclamations, or become more aware of my surroundings.

IT'S SALIVA!

AS I WAS showering myself with enthusiastic praise, I realized I'd heard, and ignored, the footsteps of someone coming
up the stairs and entering the room. Those footsteps stopped
right when my words did, and right behind me. I looked over
my shoulder at Jillian. She had a wooden paint box in one hand
and a stretched canvas in the other. I guess she was in my Art
class, too.

I froze, brush in hand, as my half-shouted cry of "sweet-ass,"
a phrase I used far too often and far too enthusiastically, ricocheted around the room like a fart at a funeral.

Jillian stared at me. Her lower lip moved slightly, as if she
were contemplating saying something in response but wasn't
sure what would be appropriate. Oh crap. Did she think I was
talking to her? Or talking about her? *Sweet ass?* What kind of
communication did that imply? In my head, I could hear

Robert, Jamaican accent and all, saying, "He talkin' 'bout your sweet booty, cutie."

What could I say to clarify things? *I was talking about my idea.* Right. That would impress her. Girls adore guys who are in love with their own ideas to the point of sweet-assdom.

She still didn't say a word. Instead, she gave me a quizzical look, as if waiting for me to explain myself. This made things even more difficult, because it was the cutest damn quizzical look anyone had ever given me. Picture a perfect nose and mouth twitched just enough to achieve adorable asymmetry, along with eyes so open and innocent, they'd make the grateful gaze of a rescue puppy seem evil by comparison, and you'll know exactly what I mean.

"I, uh . . ." Further words evaded me.

Brilliant. All I needed to complete the impression that I lacked any sort of functioning brain was to let loose with a stream of drool. As that thought hit me, I felt something warm and wet roll over my lower lip and down my bruised chin.

Holy crap, I'd just stared at Jillian, gape mouthed, and drooled. Maybe I should complete the perfect impression I'd created by screeching out chimp sounds and grabbing my crotch. Which happened to be exactly where, as confirmed by a lightning-quick downward glance, the drool had splashed to a landing.

I swallowed, then managed to speak without spraying saliva in her face. "New idea." I pointed at the canvas, which sported my scrawled sketches. It was crude enough at this stage that it could have been called *Bondage Jesus.*

"Oh." She turned away and went into the adjacent room, where there were several available easels. Had there been a door to close, I suspect that would have been her first move. She could have escaped even farther, but the end room was reserved for ceramics, and most of the seats were taken up by a ceaseless stream of freshmen who seemed enthralled by the pottery wheel and the kiln.

I turned back to my sketch and forced myself not to look in Jillian's direction even once during the rest of the period. Her room was to my right, but I was angled in such a way that I'd have to rotate ninety degrees on my stool, or look over my shoulder, to see her. By the end of the period, my eyes ached from the strain of not wandering.

I had lunch after art, which meant a trip back to the main building. I was careful to keep far from the Pit this time. I bought an assortment of the basic fried-food groups, then met up with Robert, Jimby, and Butch at our usual table.

"We should go on a road trip," Robert said.

"Where?" Butch asked.

They both looked at me, like I would have some great suggestion. I had a tough time clearing a whole day free of work, but I loved the idea of getting away from everything.

"New York?" I said.

"That would be a train trip," Robert said.

"A road trip isn't defined by the manner of travel," Butch said.

"What about New Hope?" I said. "It's less than an hour away." That was a cool town to walk around. There were a lot of shops that sold weird stuff, and a great ice cream place with bizarre flavors.

"Who says you get to say what defines anything?" Robert asked.

"Who says *you* do?" Butch said. "As a native-born American-

English speaker, I have more authority than you concerning the nuances of my mother tongue."

"Delaware Water Gap?" I said. "We could go for a hike."

"As a multilingual world traveler, I have more insight into the subtleties of language than you," Robert said.

"Deportation isn't travel," Butch said.

And that's why we never seemed to go anywhere. Following Jimby's example, I turned my attention to my food and tuned out the discussion.

As I fed myself fries, meat-of-some-kind nuggets, and breaded-fried-vegetable-of-some-kind lumps, I kept my eyes on the cafeteria entrance. Eventually, Jillian came in. I watched her scan the room, but looked away as the scan swept past me. It was like playing some sort of minimalist stealth game.

I wondered what she thought of our microcosm. To me, every person and every clique was well defined. Jillian was taking it all in for the first time. She couldn't look at Clovis Hunt and his crew of future inmates and know all the harm they'd caused. She couldn't see Christopher Lane's or Brad Weng's popularity, Dwight Fulmer's record on the football field, or Peter Decker's ability to turn anything into a joke. She'd have no idea that Amanda Carter's skill and ambition had led our cheerleaders to a state championship last year, or that Abbie was obsessed with being better than everyone at everything.

"Wave her over," Butch said. "She wants to be invited. It's tough being the new kid."

I glanced at my crotch, which contained just the faintest amoeba-like reminder of the previous drool splotch. *Sweet ass* . . . "This would not be a good time."

Robert stood up and waved like he was frantically trying to grab a cab during a cataclysmic cloudburst. "Hey! New girl!

Over here! Come visit the islands! Come feel the sunshine and the burning hot sand!"

"Hot sand?" Butch said. "Just what every girl dreams about in her erotic fantasies."

Fortunately, the noise level in the cafeteria masked Robert's shouts. Jillian, who seemed unaware she was the intended recipient of Robert's failed flailings, headed toward an empty table. As much as I would have loved for her to come over, I wanted to give her time to forget our initial encounters, and give myself time to construct a smoother conversational interaction centered around more appealing phrases and actions than "sweet-ass" and slobber.

Chi la dura la vince.

That's Italian for "He who keeps trying wins." That's also my way of letting you know my next class. After Italian, with Ms. Beatrice, I have English, with Ms. Kovanob. She wasn't as enthusiastic about literature as Mr. Piccaro. We mostly talked about whatever book we were reading at the time—currently *The Things They Carried*. But I liked talking about books, and even arguing a bit, so that was okay.

After English, once a week, I have gym. I also have library once a week. The other three days, including today, I have Jazz Band. I play trumpet. Badly. But so do most of the other trumpeters. The band room is in the basement. That's probably not deep enough.

Four out of five days, I'm happy. The fifth day sucks. My gym teacher, Mr. Dumshitz, is a sadistic lout. (As you might have guessed by now, I changed most of the teachers' names. It seemed like a good idea. I changed some of my classmates' names, too. But not all of them. It was too much work.) Happily, nothing that happens in that class has anything to do with the story. Which means, wonder of wonders, we can skip gym.

There was no sign of Jillian in Italian, English, or Jazz Band. And she definitely wouldn't be in my gym class, or the locker room, though I would have sacrificed a finger or two in exchange for making that happen.

Too much? Is my honesty about the depths of my lust making me monstrous, or more human? I suppose it depends how honest you are about your own desires. Do you admit, at least to yourself, your needs and passions? Do you accept that we are all driven by hormones and horniness? Do you dream about seeing others unclothed? Do you imagine flesh pressed against flesh? I can't worry about it. Either you're with me, or you're history.

Speaking of which, last period of the day, I had Government, which is what they switch to when they run out of history to teach. We actually had a variety of choices. Butch, Robert, and I had all picked Economics, so we'd be in class together, but I got screwed when Guidance made up the schedules.

Mr. Tippler, our teacher, was pretty much of the opinion that we, as a society, were doomed. He also liked to shout. Add to that the fact that, unlike Physics and Calculus, Government was very democratic in how it populated the republic of the classroom. Translation—there were thugs scattered throughout the room, including the brutal, stupid aforementioned Clovis Hunt, who held sway over a handful of surly, dangerous scoundrels and nurtured a disdain for anyone who was capable of high-level thought, or who exhibited obviously unacceptable traits such as an enthusiasm for reading, a desire for clean clothing, or a vocabulary that allowed him to toss off phrases such as "nurtured a disdain." Since Clovis and his crew were fond of working on cars (and had probably stolen a tire or two), I called them the Thug Nuts. I guess I could have called them the Jack Ups. It seemed prudent not to inquire directly with them as to their preference.

Needless to say, Government wasn't my favorite class. It became less of a least favorite class when I spotted Jillian. But I'd had the benefit of three periods of introspection since lunch, during which I decided that I definitely needed to take my time and wait for an opportunity to catch her attention with clever words or an act of chivalry. Preferably when my mouth was fairly dry and I wasn't half distracted by the pain of recent collisions with the floor.

As I sat in my seat, imagining a successful future effort at winning Jillian's attention and admiration, Paul Jambeau got out of his spot by the end of the aisle and slithered to the seat next to her. The empty seat. The seat I could have taken if I hadn't recently splattered myself with drool in her presence or made her think I thought she had a sweet ass.

"Hey," he said. "You like music?"

My gut rippled like I'd just chugged a gallon of battery acid. Paul was a player—in both senses of the word. He and two other guys from class, Zachary Stone and Tim Blunt, had a band. And he had a lot of moves. If Paul set his sights on Jillian, it was game over for me before the game could even begin.

HeaD Home

I WATCHED PAUL move in to steal Jillian. I guess
he couldn't steal something from me that wasn't mine. But he
could steal something before I had a chance to make it mine.

I won't defend myself against the charge that I was delusional
if I seriously thought I could "make her mine." You know exactly where my mind was. You've been there. You've sat in this
seat and gazed at your Jillian through a filter of daydreams. We
all believe our fantasies exist somewhere above the realm of the
impossible.

Paul said something. I couldn't hear his words above the pre-
class chatter of my fellow students, but I could tell from his body
language that he thought his offering was slick and awesome.

Jillian gave him a cool stare. Paul body-motioned himself
through another clever sentence, guaranteed, when combined
with a charming Cajun accent, a casual toss of hair, and a dev-
ilish smile, to make ladies swoon. Jillian's face didn't even twitch.

Inside my skull, there was an entire stadium full of me, fifty thousand Cliffs cheering in unison, stomping and clapping as Paul got up and went back to his seat. It would have been perfect if he'd slinked. Or slanked. Or slunk. But he strided. Or strid. Or strode. Some verbs suck. But not as much as some guys.

I was completely dying to catch Jillian's eye and exchange a meaningful look with her, letting her know that I knew that she had displayed great wisdom in rebuffing Paul's advance.

But I figured any attempt to do that would lead to me splattering my crotch with another drool bomb, losing an eye, or maybe accidentally blowing myself up.

When the bell rang, ending the school day, I found myself following Jillian down the hall.

Halfway to the front exit, I forced myself to stop. Isn't this how pervs are born? One day, you're wondering where someone lives. The next, you're hiding in the bushes, wearing nothing but a raincoat and sneakers, jerking off to glimpses of the beloved snatched through a gap in closed bedroom curtains.

I'd seen plenty of stories on the news about obsessed stalkers hounding celebrities. Some of the stalkers do ridiculous things. Others do scary and dangerous things. I didn't want to become ridiculous or scary. I leaned against the wall and let the escaping crowds flow past me like spawning salmon.

I'd actually been going in the wrong direction—both metaphorically and geographically—while I was following Jillian. The shortest route to my house is out through the gym and across the football field to Leary Street, which runs parallel to Vorhees on the other side of the school.

I was almost at the door at the rear of the gym when something smacked the back of my head. I could try to craft a clever literary device to convey disorientation total my but that thing of sort is half too clever by. So, it with on get let's.

After the moment of orientdisation and foncusion, I noticed a football wobbling to a stop within rebound range of my skull. Scanning farther afield, I saw a cluster of Thug Nuts tossing footballs near the middle of the gym. Football was out of season, but meanness wasn't. I guess I was lucky I hadn't been clocked by a baseball. Clovis was there, of course, wearing his usual smirk. It was obvious he'd thrown the football at my head. It was also obvious he felt damn proud of his achievement.

I thought about picking up the ball and hurling it back at him, but I could already picture my pathetic throw. No matter how hard I hurled the ball in my mind, it always rolled off my fingers at the wrong time, turning the killer bullet into a harmless flapjack. Why doesn't my mind have my back?

I pushed my way out the door, fighting against the efforts of my back muscles to pull my head down in anticipation of a second assault. I managed to escape the gym unrescathed. As I cut across the field, I scanned the perimeter, making sure none of Clovis's crew had gotten their hands on a javelin, discus, or other lethal projectile.

I live a block and a half away from the school, which is pretty convenient when it comes to things like sleeping as late as possible. This is an older part of town, but most of the houses are in good shape. Our house had two stories, with the bedrooms upstairs. There's also a small attic and a large basement. So, in essence, there are four stories, though one was subterranean and the other superficial.

Dad was in the dining room when I got home. He'd converted that space into an office. Or, as Mom called it, his war room. That's where he spent his time, searching for a new job.

The dining room was past the living room, but Dad could see the front door from his desk, if he wanted to.

He was staring at his laptop and tapping the chair arm the way he always does when the Internet is too slow. He didn't look up when I came in. I think he was still bummed about yesterday. April 15 used to be a big day for him, when he had a job. That's the day all the tax returns were due. It was a high-pressure time at the accounting company where he worked. At midnight, they had a party with champagne and lobster. Mom would meet him there. They'd stagger back around 2 or 3 A.M., talking too loudly, laughing too quietly, and banging into things. The company got taxis for everyone, so they could party hard and get smashed, but not get into a smashup.

Seven or eight years ago, the company took all the employees and their families to Bermuda. That was a great trip, except for the sunburn I got on the second day. The year I had my appendix out, back in sixth grade, they sent me a fruit basket and a handheld video game. And they gave small scholarships to employees' kids, to help pay for college.

But all of that was gone. Dad lost that job two years ago. He'd found another job about six months later, but that one hadn't lasted long. As I moved past his line of sight, I guess he finally realized I was home. "Cliff," he shouted, "did you deposit your last paycheck?"

Crap. I'd forgotten. It wasn't like it was enough money to make a fuss about.

I flinched as I heard him slam the desk. "Damn it, Cliff, you need to be more responsible!"

"I'll stop at the bank on my way to work," I said.

I didn't have my own savings account. I know that sounds crazy, but Dad had explained everything to me way back when

I was little, right after I'd gotten money from my grandparents—the ones on Mom's side—for my tenth birthday. The more money I had in my own name, the harder it would be to get a good student loan. So all my college savings were in my parents' names.

When money started to get tight and the savings dipped, Dad figured out the total cost of college, including tuition and an estimate for textbooks (adding in a recapture when the used textbooks were sold back to the bookstore) and decided that anything above that amount could be better spent on our family's current living expenses. As my college savings dwindled toward that level, Dad realized I didn't have to go to an expensive university. Not long after that, it dawned on him that I didn't even have to be a full-time student. I could split my time between working, to earn money for my expenses, and taking classes. I went from "I'm going away to college" to "I'm going to County" to "I'm probably taking a class or two." So, yeah, I'd be living at home for a while longer. But not forever.

Usually, I started doing my homework as soon as I got home, but I was beat. I went up to my room and napped until I was awakened by the clatter of dinner plates in the kitchen. It was only five thirty, but we eat early, since Mom tries to go to bed by seven or eight o'clock. It smelled like we were having meat loaf. That's one of my favorites, but I wasn't feeling very hungry.

Before I went down, I checked myself in the mirror. My face got off better than my hand, but it was red and puffy on one side of my jaw, making me wish I'd grown a beard. Okay—making me wish I *could* grow a beard. I pulled up my shirt collar a bit, and hoped nobody would notice anything.

No such luck. The instant I took a seat at the table, Mom gasped and pointed to my face. "What happened?"

"It's nothing. I fell."

"You have to watch where you're going," Dad said. "That clumsiness will get you killed. Or turn you into a perfect playmate for that drooling idiot you like to hang out with."

"He's not stupid," I said. I didn't bother to add that I was already at least halfway qualified for the "drooling idiot" label. Possibly even three quarters.

"Fell?" Mom asked. She sounded like she didn't believe me. She stared at Dad, as if wanting him to help her get to the truth. I guess she couldn't accept that I was clumsy. I doubted she'd feel better if I explained I'd been distracted by fantasy and lust. I decided to skip that detail.

"Remember the Pit?" I asked. Mom grew up here. This was actually my grandparents' house. They'd moved to South Carolina five years ago, for the weather.

"Sure," Mom said. "They added that wing during my senior year. A lot of parents felt the Pit was dangerous."

"They were right." I held up my hand, displaying my injured palm, and then rotated to show undamaged knuckles to prove I'd really fallen and not fought. She seemed satisfied.

I took a small serving of meat loaf, potatoes, and green beans and ate quickly so I'd have more time to do my homework. An hour or so after dinner, I'd head out for a stretch of real-world work. I have two part-time jobs. I work the deep fryer and cash register anywhere from two to four times a week at Moo Fish, a burger and fried-fish place in the mall. And I stock shelves three nights a week and bag groceries on the weekends at Cretaro's. It's an upscale supermarket just a half mile from here, where people go to pay too much for food and snarl at each other. But half the time, there's nothing to do, so I always take a book.

I went out to the backyard to do my homework. We have an old picnic table, painted the dull red that looks like last week's blood, flanked by benches of similar hue. The table's on a small rectangle of bricks that we think of as a patio. I like being outside. If I had some free days, I'd love to go hiking, or just sit by a lake somewhere and watch the breeze blow ripples across the surface of the water.

The kitchen window was open. My parents were still at the table. Mom would be drinking herb tea. Dad wouldn't. I could hear them talking.

"I think it would be good for Cliff if he could go away to college full-time next year," she said.

"And who's paying for that?" he asked.

"We could get a loan," she said. "Or refinance the house."

"I'm not risking our future so he can go party and play beer pong with a bunch of other aimless losers."

"Think about it," she said. "It could help him mature."

"He's a dreamer. College won't mature him. It will just make him believe he can earn a living doing what he likes, no matter how impractical or absurd it is. There's nothing to think about."

That was the end of the discussion. I felt good that Mom wanted me to go off to college. I felt bad that she'd brought it up. I'd get there someday. I tried to picture myself at a university. Butch had taken Robert and me to Princeton once, when she'd gone to see Judah. I'd slipped into a lecture hall and sat at the back. It was pretty awesome. And a little scary. Not that it mattered either way. For now, the closest I'd get to the Ivy League was doing homework at a picnic table on a patio, with broadleaf weeds growing through the cracks between the bricks.

I pulled my calculus book from my backpack, grabbed a

notebook and pencil, then sat there, staring at the clouds and thinking about Jillian.

She was so amazing. Which made it all the harder to accept that I'd have just as much chance getting a date with her as I would with Aphrodite or Lara Croft.

"Hey, Cliff."

I guess I'd dozed off, because the voice startled me. I looked up at the sound of a shuffling step. "Hey, Jimby."

He came over and sat across from me. He's a good-looking guy—always smiling, but not with a stupid smile. He's just basically content. He's got green eyes, nice reddish-brown hair, badly cut, and what most parents would call "a healthy complexion." He was wearing a Mets Windbreaker and a Jack Daniel's hat, brim forward. I don't think there was any irony intended on his part. The hat was probably a present from one of his mom's guy friends.

"How would you let a girl know you liked her?" I asked.

He shrugged and blushed at the same time. "I'd kiss her."

"You can't just kiss a girl," I said.

"Course not." He gave me a look like I was an idiot. "You have to ask permission."

"Good point," I said.

"Nobody has the right to kiss you without permission," Jimby said. "Or touch you in bad places. Or hit you. And you can't hit a girl, no matter what. Not ever."

"What if she's coming at you with an ax?" I asked.

Jimby didn't answer me right away. He appeared to be giving the question some serious thought. Finally, he said, "Okay. You could hit her then. But just hard enough to knock the ax out of her hands. Though, I guess if she had a good grip, you'd need a pretty hard hit." He swung a right hook through the air, knocking the imaginary ax clear across the yard, then shook his head. "Still doesn't seem right to hit a girl. I think I'd run."

He plucked a long splinter from the edge of the table and stared at it for a moment, then said, "Wait! Is she pretty?"

"Unbearably so," I said. I thought he'd gone back to the kissing question.

"Then I'd let her hit me with the ax," he said.

"Why?"

"So she'd feel guilty. Then we'd get to know each other and fall in love."

"Good plan," I said. "As long as you don't let her hit you too hard."

We discussed the range of severity of ax wounds. Somehow, that got us into an examination of the relative destructive powers of zombies, shotguns, and Apache helicopters. After we'd exhausted those topics, Jimby headed home.

Ask permission to kiss her.

What a wonderful world it would be if dating were that simple. Or if I were that brave.

Back to calculus. And since nothing noteworthy happened that evening, at work or at home, I will now, through the magic of being able to travel through space, time, and text at the blink of an eye, or the click of a pen, take you back to Calculus class the next day, when things took an interesting and unexpected turn.

press pass

PICTURE THIS—ADMITTEDLY, a strange request, and probably an unnecessary one, given that you've been picturing everything I've said. I guess we'll have to agree that "picture this" is a polite way of asking you to pay close attention, and not just skim these words while you're doing seven other things.

Picture, if you will, rows of desk chairs crammed a bit too closely together in a classroom because budget cuts had reduced the number of teachers last year.

If your pictorial memory is solid, you'll see that Jillian was three seats to my left and one row ahead of me. As I sat in Calculus on Wednesday morning, listening to Mr. Yuler delve into the intricacies of finding the first derivative using the chain rule, Nola, who sat immediately to my left, leaned against me.

Feeling that I was invading her space, I leaned away. Feeling, also, that I was somehow at fault for this intrusion, I got ready to offer an apology.

Nola leaned farther, reconnecting.

Was this some sort of game? Nola had sat next to me for three marking periods, without any interaction above the level of *Can I borrow a pencil?*

If I kept leaning away, I'd eventually topple over, or press against Lucas. Instead, I returned to my original upright position, which increased the pressure. I enjoyed the warmth of Nola's shoulder against mine. It was the first female contact I'd had in a long time.

I looked over at her, turning my head without moving any other part of my body. She didn't respond. Her eyes remained aimed at the board. Her pencil eraser pressed lightly against her cheek, right where a dimple would have been if she'd had a dimple. Loose strands of her blond hair were trapped between our shoulders, but the bulk of her hair was free, and lovely. It had the scent of some herb that guys can recognize but never name.

I took the liberty of a longer survey. She was wearing a sweater. I think it's the kind they call a cable knit, though that's a guess. It was off-white wool, with raised patterns on it that looked sort of like a knitted cable.

Sweaters are hot. I don't mean in a Kelvin/Celsius/Fahrenheit sort of way. I mean in a body-caressing, viewer-stimulating, testosterone-simmering way. They flow over all the interesting parts.

On the other hand, they offer no hope at all of any cleavage sightings. All the mysteries are shrouded. Crap. I really do sound like a perv. It's not like I spend all my time trying to catch a glimpse of part of a breast. But I sure don't avert my eyes in fear that the Angel of the Lord will strike me blind with a vengeful blast of lightning if my gaze moves within five centimeters of forbidden surface features.

I shifted my attention three seats over, one seat up, at an acute angle, toward a cute angel. My overdriven fantasy generator watched Jillian spin out of her seat, point at me with a rage-quivered finger, and say, "I knew it. Men are pigs! You blew it, Cliff Sparks, you horny bastard!"

So there I sat, pressed shoulder to shoulder with Nola, while wondering if I was being unfaithful to someone I had absolutely no relationship with.

Good God! What if I pretended I was in contact with Jillian? Would that be the start of a twisted journey to a place I didn't want to visit? Was I moving beyond stalker into the world of sociopath? The crazy people you see in the news—the ones being led, handcuffed and wild-eyed out of a run-down house where they've done unspeakable things to their fellow human beings—did they start out spinning some half-innocent fantasy scenario like this? There's no way I wanted to go down that path.

But I was trapped between Nola and Lucas. I was pretty sure he'd react to shoulder contact from me with a suitable, and understandable, lack of enthusiasm. Or a punch in the nose.

And the contact—which I had not initiated—did feel nice. In the end, I let things remain the way they were and spent an entire period in Calculus enjoying shoulder pressure from Nola, dreaming about what lay beneath those knitted cables, flitting into fantasies of rubbing shoulders with Jillian, then snatching my mind back like it had brushed a glowing filament.

Differentiating composite functions using the chain rule?

Beats me. I was lost in other chains of thought until the bell rang.

Nola dawdled, gathering her books. I dawdled, gathering my thoughts. Butch and Robert walked ahead, arguing amusingly.

As I trailed Nola out of the room, I decided to show her how witty and desirable I was. After making sure Jillian was well ahead of us, I moved within speaking range of Nola and gave her my best line.

"Hi," I said, managing not to drool. I cleared any sign of *You're my backup fantasy* from my face.

For a fraction of a second, during which my heart beat seventeen times, I wondered whether she'd even heard me. Just as older people can't detect high-frequency sounds, I frequently got the feeling my voice fell outside the range of human hearing. Especially human female hearing.

But this time, I guess my words—I mean, word—registered. Nola looked at me, narrowed her eyes in a sexy gaze, gave her lower lip a slow, erotic swipe with her tongue, breathed in a deep breath that made her chest rise in wonderful ways reminiscent of Maddie's landmark yawn, and said, "I don't understand my boyfriend."

NO! You're not supposed to say that. You're supposed to say, "Hi. Want to have sex?"

"Uh, what do you mean?" I asked.

"He wants to touch me all the time," she said. "Why do guys want to touch girls?"

"Because we don't have stunningly awesome breasts of our own to fondle."

Yeah. You know I didn't say that. I probably didn't even think of that reply until hours later when I was safely under my covers, and simultaneously uncovered. I can't even remember what I said. And it doesn't matter, because the conversation ended at that point, thanks to a combination of me having no idea at all how to respond and her deciding to hurry to her next class.

I had no clue what her game was. Or whether there was a game. Maybe she just wanted to touch a boy who couldn't touch back. Lucky me. I didn't even know who she was dating. It was probably a guy from another school, since I'd never seen her committing a public display of affection in the halls of Rismore High.

Robert and Butch had gotten way ahead of me, so I was walking by myself toward Physics. Just before I reached the door, I felt someone slip up behind me.

"Keep walking," he whispered.

I kept walking, going past the door.

"Don't look down," he said as he moved to my right and matched my stride.

I didn't look down.

"Take it." Another hoarse whisper.

He placed an object in my hand. It was slim and light. Not Russian, for sure. Probably not British. He turned off as we passed the corridor for the new wing.

I tore open the brown paper wrapper that had been neatly folded and taped around the package, revealing a paperback copy of *Slaughterhouse-Five*. Well worn, but in readable condition. I'd heard about it, but never read it. I liked that it was thin. There's nothing wrong, and a lot right, with hunkering down for days or weeks with one of the weightier, longer works of literature. I'd spent three weeks with the last book he'd given me, *The Name of the Rose*. It was worth every minute. But a thin volume, if it was good, was like a lightning storm.

Bam! Blah-bam! Babam!

Flash upon flash, boom upon boom, in rapid succession, and then the skies clear, leaving you flash-boom dazzled, ozone dazed, bright-light blazed, strangely changed, and eagerly evangelizing the novel to your small circle of friends.

Mr. Piccaro liked lending books to me. He also liked James

Bond. He liked George Smiley even more—whoever that was. Sounded like a weird name for a spy. Might work better for a dentist. Or a salesman. Better yet, a dental salesman. Mr. Piccaro hadn't given me a bad book yet. One or two weren't what I was in the mood for at the moment, but he had a batting average double that of the best major leaguers. I'd especially liked *Edisto* and *The Periodic Table*. He also seemed to get a kick out of wrapping the books in paper. Sometimes he'd scrawl *plain brown wrapper* on the plain brown wrapper. After I finished each book, I returned it to the "dead drop," which was actually the last locker before the boys' room on the second floor, which never got assigned to anyone, because the lock was broken.

I walked to Physics, took my seat, and skimmed the back cover of the book. I had a feeling I was going to like this one a lot. It was nice to have something to look forward to. Though I guess I was also eager to work on my painting. When I got to the Art House, I saw that Jillian had filled in her canvas with a very detailed drawing of six objects against a flat background. Damn, she had talent. If she could paint as well as she drew, she was going to create something dazzling. I turned my attention to my own painting, which I felt could also be pretty awesome, and got to work.

The rest of the week passed without any further falls, collisions, or massive drool spills. By Friday, Jillian's painting—which I swear I wasn't obsessively staring at as a surrogate for staring at her—had progressed to the point where her talent was indisputable.

The background remained a solid blue. It looked like cobalt blue, lightened with just a touch of titanium white. At least she hadn't settled for a color straight out of the tube. But there was no shading, or a suggestion that the blue was anything other than a featureless setting for the objects that floated in front of it.

She'd been working slowly. So far, she'd started to paint only one of the objects she'd drawn—a half-peeled orange. Jillian had rendered it with intricate detail. I felt if I scratched the peel, I'd see a spray of oil and smell a scent of citrus.

I stared for a while, transfixed by the skill displayed in that image. Each year, when I looked at the works in the student art show, it was obvious there were kids who were pretty good, kids who were awful, and a small handful who were great. I liked to think I was solidly in the "good" category. I didn't know if I could ever be great. But maybe I could be good enough to do some sort of art for a living. Not that I could take any art classes in college while I was still at home. Dad would hit the roof if I signed up for something that he considered a waste of money, even if it was money I'd earned. And art would definitely fall into that category.

Damn—Jillian was beautiful and talented. Doubly close to being dangerously out of my league. I wondered whether she was smart, too. She hadn't said much in class. But I had a suspicion her mind was as exceptional as her body.

My thoughts were broken as Abbie walked by on her way to the supply closet. She sniffed, as if Jillian's background had been painted with cow dung, tinged with a touch of fox urine, and said, "How mundane and plebian. Photo-realism is *so* last week."

"And calling something 'so last week' is *so* last year," I said.

She awarded me with a parting sniff of equal disapproval and slithered off.

INTER LEWD

HOLD ON.

Something else just hit me.

Whenever I start to read a novel, I assume the main character is just like me, until stuff pops up to show me I'm wrong. I
guess it works both ways. I assumed you're just like me, too. But
I realize I could be totally wrong about who you are.

And that could cause trouble.

I've been talking to you like you're one of the guys. But you
could be older, or younger. And you might not be a guy. Which
means, the whole time I've been extolling the glories of female
breasts, recounting my overwhelming desire to have sex, or revealing the wild nature of my fantasies, you might not have been
thinking *Yay! Breasts!* so much as *You pig!*

Whenever I used "he" for an unspecified subject, I might
have pushed you slightly further away from the heart of the story.
There are so many ways my lazy assumption could ruin our

relationship. Narration, it seems, contains some uncomfortable similarities to life in the real world.

As hard as it is for us to see ourselves as others see us, I have to hope that you can not only see me as I see myself, but also let me speak to you as if you are one of the guys. It's my native tongue.

parm for the
course

SATURDAY, AFTER A long morning frying Moo Fish's bacon-wrapped sausage-and-haddock breakfast biscuit and wondering how I managed to get through a shift without throwing up, followed by two hours of bagging groceries for unhappy people at Cretaro's, I had a chance to spend quality time with Billy Pilgrim, the hero, to use the word loosely, of *Slaughterhouse-Five*. It was time well spent.

Mom was at the kitchen table, reading the paper, when I wandered out of my room. She looked tired. Her day starts ridiculously early. People want to buy bread at 6 A.M., which means someone has to start the mixing, kneading, and baking process at 3 A.M. As Mom turned the page, I let out a gasp.

"What's wrong?" she asked. Her eyes widened briefly, in the typical maternal overreaction to any sort of offspring-generated rapid respiration.

I pointed to the ad on the bottom left, beneath the half-page red-white-and-blue WE BUY GOLD AND DIAMONDS announcement. "I didn't know they were playing here."

"Is this one of the groups you like?" she asked.

"Big-time." I guess headphones had gone a long way toward helping people keep their musical passions to themselves. If Mom or Dad had to name three groups I liked, or even three songs, they'd be in trouble.

"The Mack and Mary Zymosis Zone," Mom said. "That's a strange name for a group. But it can't be too expensive. They're playing at the college."

"I hope so. I'll go check." Just as "the city" meant New York to me here in North Jersey but Philadelphia to my cousins in West Chester, Pennsylvania, around here "the college" was Saint Jasper's. It was local, and a lot smaller than Rutgers, in New Brunswick. Mom was probably right about ticket prices. The concerts I'd gone to there hadn't been very expensive.

My laptop died last year, and my phone was on the cheapest voice plan, so my only real Internet option at home was the ancient desktop PC and monitor Butch had dredged up for me from her basement right before school started. I got online and checked for Mack and Mary (as hard-core fans called them) tickets. The cheap ones were sold out. I guess tickets had been on sale for a while. The few remaining seats were out of my range. It looked like I could forget about the concert.

THAT NIGHT, MY parents and I did something we hadn't done in months. Mom's boss had given her back the hours she'd lost at work, along with a bonus. I guess the people who owned the bakery had noticed how hard she worked, and saw what happened to sales when she had fewer hours. She'd decided we should go out to dinner to celebrate.

Dad didn't like the idea of splurging on a meal. But Mom convinced him it was important for families to do stuff like this once in a while, even if money was tight. "We're not buying a meal," she'd said. "We're buying a memory."

I wasn't exactly wild about going out with them, but Mom had made a reservation at Stenardo's. Their chicken parmigiana was awesome. They pound the crap out of the chicken, so it's almost as big as the plate, fry it to crispy perfection, melt mozzarella cheese on it, and serve it over thick spaghetti, with lots of tangy sauce. The garlic bread was world class, too. They didn't use garlic powder. They used chopped-up bits of garlic. Vampires beware.

An hour before it was time to head out, Mom went upstairs to get ready. I stayed where I was in the living room, reading more of the Vonnegut novel, since all I had to do was change my shirt.

Dad came in from the war room, carrying the newspaper. As usual, he'd circled a bunch of listings in the help-wanted section. "You didn't even try to talk her out of it," he said, smacking the paper down on the table. "I could have used some support." He shot me an *Aren't we on the same team?* look.

"It wouldn't make a difference. I have no influence with her," I said. "She wants to go. We should go. It'll make her happy." I was about to add *She works hard enough.* But I caught myself. That was not Dad's favorite topic.

"No appetizer," Dad said. "They really jack up the prices on them. That's where they make all their money. That and soda. If people understood the economics of the food industry, they'd never eat out. You're getting water."

"Sure. No problem."

I waited to see if there would be further instructions, such as *Don't you dare order something you'll enjoy,* or a suggestion that I should offer to wash dishes at the restaurant in exchange for my meal. At least I knew the chicken parm was relatively inexpensive, compared to some of the steaks and seafood on Stenardo's menu. And the garlic bread came with the meal, so it wasn't like I'd be asking for something extra.

Mom drove us there. I guess she didn't want to give Dad anything else to grumble about. When we got seated, Dad ordered spaghetti with sauce. No meatballs or sausage or anything. Mom had a Caesar salad with grilled salmon. I had chicken parmigiana, of course.

We were at a table in the main dining room. The cocktail lounge was off to the side, but there wasn't a real wall between that area and where we sat, just some columns. So I had no trouble hearing the angry shout from the bar, and the punctuating crash that followed it.

TENURE ITCH

SOMEONE HAD THROWN a glass at the mirror behind the bar. The encounter shattered both objects, and the ambience.

"You don't cut me off!" the guy shouted. "I ordered another drink. You bring it to me!"

People seated at barstools on either side of the guy were scrambling away like he was a bomb with a lit fuse. Well, I guess he was lit. And bombed.

The bartender, a middle-aged guy in a white shirt and black vest, had one hand out, like he was trying to say calming words. He didn't seem scared. I guess he was used to handling angry drunks.

I stood up so I could get a better look at the action. Oh, hell. The angry drunk was Mr. Tippler, my Government teacher. Apparently, he didn't restrict his yelling to the classroom. He continued to shout at the bartender, but there was enough other noise surrounding us—including increased chatter at all the occupied tables—that it was hard to extract any meaning from the slurred sounds. My brain took the shouts and warped them into lecture words. *Quorum! Legislature! Two-thirds majority! Fungible document!*

The external wail of a siren quelled some of the interior noise and drew everyone's anticipatory gaze toward the entrance.

Cops came.

It was pretty much like the way they show it on TV. Except there was no dramatic music, or gorgeous female detectives with their blouses open to the third button and a perfect overbite with which to tease their lower lips as they contemplated the crime scene. Nope. There were just the same violins that had been playing on the canned background music throughout the meal, and two cops who looked like they'd much rather be dealing with someone who hadn't replaced all his blood with alcohol.

The police marched Mr. Tippler out in cuffs, half-carrying him. He must have been heavily sloshed. As he passed by me, two tables away, his head dangling like a man preparing to try on a guillotine for size, our eyes met. No, my eyes met his. His met air. Or water. Or maybe a kid with the head of a goat and a three-foot tongue. I'm pretty sure he wasn't seeing much of anything. Not anything real.

And then he was out the door, and for a moment, the only sound was the background music and, in counterpoint, the scrape of straw against wood, and the tinkle of glass as the bartender swept the floor behind the bar, gathering the shattered fragments of Mr. Tippler's life into a long-handled dustpan.

Mom stared toward the door as the red flash against the window faded. "That poor man," she said.

Dad had already swung his attention back to his spaghetti. But he muttered, "What a loser," between slurps.

As I turned my own attention back to my chicken, I wondered whether Mr. Tippler would be out on bail and back in the classroom by Monday. I figured they might not even put him in jail.

But everything we do is public these days. It turned out some guy at Stenardo's had captured most of the shouting, and all of the arrest, with his phone and posted it online. By Sunday afternoon, as word spread, every kid in school, and I guess every parent, had seen the video. So nobody was surprised when Mr. Tippler wasn't in class on Monday.

I figured maybe they'd let us go to study hall for the rest of the year, since there was only one marking period left, and since we were seniors. Everyone who was going to college had already been accepted. Everyone who wasn't going to college had other plans, none of which required the knowledge contained in the final marking period of a high school Government class.

But Mr. Tippler also taught freshman Social Studies. Maybe that's why there was a sub in the room when I got to class on Monday, and not a disgruntled teacher who'd been snagged for unexpected study hall duty. It was an old guy. He looked like he hadn't gotten much sleep. I think they call substitutes pretty early in the morning when they need them.

As the sub was writing his name on the board, Clovis made a farting sound. I'm assuming he did it with his mouth, since no stench accompanied or followed it, other than the stench of moral decay that permeates his existence.

The mouth fart was pretty juvenile, but it had an effect. The guy whirled around and yelled, "Stop that!"

"Mr. Tippler encourages class farticipation," Peter said.

"That's not funny," the substitute said. "All of you. Shape up and act your age. No more rude noises."

His reaction was a big mistake. Others joined in with random fart sounds and burps throughout the period. As these seniors performed their sophomoric actions, the sub, Mr. Strawbroke, tried his best not to turn away again. But that's hard to do when you're fidgety, like to pace when you talk, and need to write things on the board. Halfway through the period, the assault escalated. The Thug Nuts started throwing stuff. Erasers. Pencils. Wads of paper.

I guess I could have done something brave, like tell them to stop. I glanced at Jillian as I thought about speaking out. Would she admire me if I did that? It was pointless to ask the question. I might as well have wondered whether she'd admire me if I flew out the window, sailed up toward the clouds, and blew enough smoke out of my ass to skywrite, SURRENDER YOUR HEART TO ME, JILLIAN. There was no way I was going to do anything that would make me Clovis's favorite target for the rest of the year. The random hit with a football had been bad enough. I knew I could never survive a concentrated and dedicated assault.

Mr. Strawbroke almost made it to the end of the period, which would mean he'd made it through the day. Almost. Finally, about three minutes before the bell, right after a well-aimed pink eraser plunked off the top of his head, he slammed down the book he was reading from, yelled, "It's not worth the money! I don't need this!" and stomped out.

The thugs exchanged triumphant howls and vigorous high fives. Luckily, the bell rang before they realized there were no authority figures in the room to prevent them from pinning a student to the floor and disemboweling him with their pencils. Though I guess there hadn't been an authority figure in the room all period.

On my way out, Mr. Piccaro slipped behind me and said, "I trust you enjoyed Pilgrim's progress."

"And his regress," I said. I took the package from him. I'd already put *Slaughterhouse-Five* in the dead drop. The new book, also fairly slim, was a collection of short stories by a guy named Philip K. Dick. I'll admit, I laughed at the name. But I stopped laughing when I started reading at work that evening. The stories were totally off the wall, in amazing ways. It turned out a fair number of them had been made into movies.

THERE WAS A new sub on Tuesday. She looked pretty young, like maybe she'd been out of college for no more than two or three years. She had short brown hair and the body of a long-distance runner. I wondered whether she'd beat Mr. Strawbroke's endurance record.

"I'm Ms. Ryder," she said after we'd all taken our seats. "Mr. Tippler will be out for a while."

"Busted!" Clovis said. He let out a snort and exchanged a high five with Juke Johnson, one seat over.

"Arrested for disorderly conduct, public intoxication, and several other charges," Ms. Ryder said. "Does this mean he's been convicted of a crime?"

"For sure," Clovis said.

Ms. Ryder looked past him, toward Zach's raised hand. "What do you think? Has he been convicted?"

"Nope," Zach said. "You can get arrested if they're suspicious, or if someone narcs you out, but they need evidence to convict you. And a trial."

About half the class snickered, mostly because we knew that Zach had been busted more than once. I guess the substitute picked up on that.

"Are you speaking from personal experience—" She glanced at the seating chart. "—Mr. Stone?"

"Sorta," he said. "About the arrested. Not the convicted. My dad's a lawyer."

"And you're his best client," Peter said.

"Well," Ms. Ryder said. "Hopefully, if I do my job correctly, and you all do yours, you'll learn some important things about your rights. I can't force you to be interested in government. But I can try to convince you that there are lessons ahead of us that are worth learning. Letting someone take your rights is as bad as letting them take your wallet. Maybe worse."

"I'd like to take your phone number," Juke said.

A deep silence cloaked the room.

I watched her face but saw no sign of a reaction other than a slight narrowing of her eyes, as if she were focusing on a target. She walked over to Juke's desk. He smirked at Clovis, then held out his notebook in one hand and a gnawed yellow pencil in the other, offering them to Ms. Ryder. She ignored the stationery, leaned close to him, and, in a loud whisper, said, "Children who play with fire get burned, little man."

It wasn't so much the words—it was the way she said them, and the look in her eyes. The fearless-gunslinger look she shot at him and the dead-calm tone in her voice said, *Don't fuck with me*. She held the stare until he looked away. Then, she walked back to her desk. I could see Juke's face growing red, like he'd leaned too close to a fire.

Government, I realized, was finally going to get interesting.

THE ART OF
SELF-DECEPTION

⤜———————————————⤛

THE PAINTING WAS looking good. I'd added a large eye in the sky, partially hidden behind wisps of cirrus clouds, and put a rose on the ground. The eye stood for the way everybody was watching everybody else all the time. I guess it also was inspired by one of the Philip K. Dick stories I'd read, where a guy is sure he is being watched. The rose was because I'm good at roses. We'd learned to paint them in third grade, when we were making trivets for Mother's Day. Dalí painted an amazing rose, but it's not as well known as his melting watches.

I'd worked slowly all last week, hoping Jillian would stop to take a look at my canvas as she walked past on the way to her easel. Eventually, my homage to Dalí and video games (with a nod to Magritte and a wink to P. K. Dick) was finished. And it was pretty good.

Jillian hadn't said a word about my work. But two freshmen and one sophomore told me it was awesome, and Abbie had informed me it was "painfully derivative," and "simplistic in its symbolism," which was high praise from her.

Maybe I really can be an artist, I thought as I lifted the painting off the easel. I know Ms. Gickley had told me to take my time. To her, "time" probably meant months. But I'd spent a whole week on this one, both during Art and during my free period, which was longer than I'd spent on anything else I'd ever worked on in class this year. Or any year. I know kids sometimes spend a whole marking period on a single piece. Zach had gotten permission to paint a mural on the side of the equipment shed by the football field. Abbie was doing an enormous mosaic on a third-floor wall at the rear of the old part of the school, celebrating her academic achievements, and two other students were working together on a giant welded abstract sculpture. But that sort of long-term project wasn't my style.

"You are *done*," I said. I glanced in Jillian's direction, but she was deeply involved with her painting and seemed unable to process any sounds I made. If I ever had to warn her about a fire, or a venomous snake, she was doomed. On the other hand, if I were to even whisper *sweet ass*, I'm sure I'd have her complete attention.

Well, at least I had a new work of art to feel good about. The painting would look even better in a frame. The shop teacher, Mr. Xander, had a stack of them in his supply closet. He liked to make them after school, and he'd offered art students free choice whenever they needed one. He was kind of a scary guy. He shouted even more than Mr. Tippler, and he was missing two fingers on his left hand. But I didn't take shop, so I didn't really care how mean he was.

I left the Art House, crossed the parking lot, and entered the school. As I reached the corridor that led to the shop class, I ran into Mr. Yuler, who was coming out of the teachers' lounge with a coffee mug clutched in one hand. There was a rumor that he'd sold his soul to the devil in exchange for eternal life, but part of the bargain was that he'd die if he ever went more than thirty seconds without taking a sip of coffee. The mug looked large enough to cover him for the next hour or so. As I passed him, he pointed at the canvas.

"Painting?" he asked.

"Yeah." I realized I was carrying it with the back side out.

"Let me see."

I turned it around so the painted side was facing him, eager to show him I was more than just another of the countless math students he'd taught. I'd bet he'd never seen anything this creative—especially not during a random encounter in a school hallway.

I tracked his pupils as they shifted from spot to spot. He seemed to be studying every aspect of my creation with a great deal of care. I wondered whether I should point out some of the symbolism to him. But he was really smart. I was sure he'd fig-ure out most of it himself.

Maybe he was even thinking of offering to buy it. That would be amazing. I could just see myself waving a handful of cash in Dad's face and waiting for him to ask where it came from.

"Art." That's all I'd say.

Finally, Mr. Yuler raised his eyes back to meet my own and shared his opinion of my painting. "Garbage."

It wasn't exactly like a football to the head or a slap to the face, but it definitely struck me with a numbing and unexpected impact.

"Uh . . . thanks." Great. My art was getting criticized by a guy who'd never uttered more than a half dozen words at a time.

He was a stupid math teacher. What did he know about art? They were totally separate fields.

Flashes of Leonardo da Vinci's mechanical drawings ran through my mind. Okay, maybe math and art had some connection. Escher followed on the heels of Leonardo. They ran into Mondrian at the town square, where he was having lunch with several architects.

As Mr. Yuler walked away, I switched off the math/art show in my mind, held the painting up at arm's length, and tried to look at it objectively.

Garbage?

It looked fine to me. More than fine. It looked awesome. It wasn't like something Jillian would paint. My execution wasn't perfect. My objects didn't appear so realistic that you could pluck them off the page. But the canvas totally spurted ideas. I was all about the concept. It was okay to let the viewer fill in some of the details. Picasso and Pissarro didn't need to make exact duplicates of things. An artist isn't just a flesh-and-blood camera or photocopier.

Garbage . . .

Asshole.

Of course, it was possible he just didn't realize what the objects were supposed to be. I'll admit the control pad was a bit crude. I'd done it from memory, rather than bringing in a model. I suppose it's hard to appreciate symbolism if you have to guess at the symbols. Maybe I should give it another couple days, so I could tweak the rough edges and add a few more details. That wouldn't hurt.

On Wednesday, I tried to work on my painting, but I wasn't feeling very artistic. I sat and stared at it all through my free period, trying to see it with new eyes.

At one point, Ms. Gickley walked through the room, leaned over my shoulder, pointed to the bottom of the canvas, and said, "Nice carnation."

When my regular Art period started, Jillian came in and set up her paints. I turned around on my stool and looked into the other room at her painting. Against the blue background, which remained unchanged and uninteresting, she had the half-peeled orange, a jade green Buddha, a woolen glove, a sliced onion, a glass half full or—you know it's coming—half empty, and an electric drill. The drill was new. From what I remembered, she'd originally sketched in some sort of train engine. I guess she'd erased it the other day and replaced it with the drill. Nothing was scaled. Each object was roughly the same size on the canvas. They were arranged in a two-by-three rectangle, with enough space between them that none of the objects touched.

I slid off my stool, inched closer, and watched her work. She was using a tiny brush, the smallest available in the supply closet, to put on minuscule daubs of paint. It looked like she was working from memory, too, or imagination, because she didn't have any models or photographs in front of her. I was definitely impressed. Despite Abbie's disdain for photo-realism, the ability to create a realistic image from memory, or imagination, had to be pretty rare.

Jillian glanced over her shoulder long enough to have noticed me, then turned her attention back to her painting. Maybe light rays reflecting from my body were as undetectable to her as sound waves emanating from my throat. Maybe she just didn't like people. I hadn't seen her talking with anybody since she got here. Maybe I should stop trying to guess what was in her head and just ask her.

Speak, I told myself. The automatic responder in my humor

center replied to that command with a mental yelp of *Arf!* But I dug deeper into my brain, figuring I could manage a simple conversation about something we both loved. Given how amazing a painter she was, she had to love art. We definitely had that passion in common.

Gathering my courage, and hating the fact that the seemingly trivial act of uttering a simple string of words required any sort of bravery, I drew in the breath required to speak a complete, articulate sentence to Jillian.

ADMIT TWO

"WHAT'S IT MEAN?" I asked.

"Mean?" She slowed her brushstrokes briefly, but didn't stop painting details on the lotus-folded Buddha legs or look back in my direction.

"Yeah. I think I get the symbolism. Buddhism is deep, and the onion has many layers. A drill goes deep, too. Is that what you're going for? Something about depth in religion, nature, and man-made objects?" I liked that interpretation, but knew it was incomplete. I struggled to uncover some sort of symbolic depth in a glove or a glass of water. You can shove your hand deep into a glove, but that seemed too obvious. The glass wasn't tall enough to be considered deep. Maybe the water represented the ocean. . . .

Jillian turned all the way around. "I'm not going for any kind of meaning. I like the way they look together. I like painting interesting objects. What does the *Mona Lisa* mean? What do Monet's *Water Lilies* mean?"

"Oh . . . Okay." I backed away and simultaneously struggled to find some hidden meaning in the *Mona Lisa* that would make me seem both appealingly clever and suitably datable.

I failed.

Damn you, Leonardo.

I had the feeling art meant completely different things to Jillian than it did to me. But that didn't change the fact that I was dying to get to know her better. It just showed me that art wasn't the answer.

THAT NIGHT AT dinner, Mom asked, "Did you order those concert tickets?"

"Tickets are a waste of money," Dad said. "We're spending just a little too freely around here. First, we go out for an unnecessary dinner. And wasn't that a wonderful experience? Now you're talking about entertainment. That has to stop. You're bleeding me dry."

"Don't worry," I told him. "The cheap tickets were sold out. I can't afford the other ones. I'm not going."

"That's for sure," he said.

That evening, as I was stamping absurdly high prices on absurdly small jars of marinated mushroom caps, I started to calculate how many hours I'd have to work to make enough money for two of the good concert tickets. When I saw the answer was definitely going to slip into double digits, I decided I'd be happier not knowing exactly how pathetic my earning power was.

The next day, when I got home from school, I saw an envelope on my desk. I recognized Mom's handwriting. *Cliff. For you and a friend.*

I opened the envelope and found myself face-to-font with two tickets to the Mack and Mary concert. Sweet-ass bitchin' awesome! Far too soon, the thrill got tamped down by a rush of guilt. Dad was right. We really didn't have money for stuff like that. I guess Mom knew how much I wanted to go. And I guess she didn't want to make a big deal of it. She probably also didn't want to have any complaints from Dad, which was why she'd left the tickets up here in my room. I had a feeling I shouldn't mention the concert around him. But I needed to thank Mom right away.

I found her outside, putting mulch down in the small flower bed that ran along the back of the house next to the picnic table. I checked to make sure there were no open windows that would carry my voice inside.

"Thanks," I said, kneeling next to her. "You didn't have to do that." I liked the sharp cedar tang of the mulch. It reminded me of hiking in the fall.

"You work hard," she said. "You deserve some pleasure."

"You work hard, too," I said. "You could have bought something for yourself."

She smoothed out a small mound of mulch underneath a hydrangea. "I did," she said. "I bought my son some happiness. Memories are a much better investment than things."

I realized any argument I raised would only rob her of some of the vicarious pleasure she'd purchased. So I thanked her again and joined her at the pleasantly mindless landscaping task.

Even though I felt bad about Mom spending the money, I was glad she got me two tickets. I knew I'd look like a total loser if I went to the concert by myself. People noticed things like that. I'd gone alone to the movies once, when I was ten. Three of the kids in my class mocked me about it for weeks afterwards. Yeah, Clovis was one of them. A lot of kids from school would probably be going to the Mack and Mary concert. There's no way I could pull off a solo appearance without giving ammo to the haters and mockers.

I asked Jimby about the concert that evening, when he wandered over to say hi.

"I can ask my mom, but she'll say no," he said.

"You sure?"

"Pretty sure. Yeah. I'm positive. She likes me home at night."

"I don't blame her," I said. "You're good company."

That earned me a grin. But I knew he was right. As far back as I could remember, his mom had never liked him going out at night. I think she wanted him around in case she passed out and started to choke on her own vomit. If I had a place where he could stay, and parents who would feed an extra kid, I'd kidnap him and bring him home. I think Mom would welcome him in a heartbeat. On the other hand, Dad would kick him right back out the way he came in.

The next morning, while we were waiting for the first bell, I asked Robert about going with me to the concert.

"That kind of music causes me to die inside," he said. "Even the thought of it weakens me."

I asked Butch.

"I'll be out of town with my folks. Why don't you ask a girl?" Butch suggested. "You know. Like a date."

"I could do that," I said.

"I know you could," Butch said, slapping me on the back. "But I'm afraid you won't."

"Maybe I will." I guess I'd been so used to my dateless life—and so obsessed with Jillian, who I couldn't possibly ask out—that I hadn't even considered using the tickets as a springboard to a date with someone else.

And, in truth, I had other reasons to be a bit hesitant about asking a girl out. You know about the wet snake. But that's not the end of the story. I need to expose one last piece of Maddie's tale. (That definitely didn't sound right.) It turns out there are far worse things in life than a waterlogged carnival prize.

ESCAPE WINDOW

MADDIE—WHO NEVER had the chance to admire my gift snake, or look it in the mouth—was still the center of my fantasies and the focus of my obsessions when school resumed. The transition from seventh to eighth grade had failed to help me see myself or my delusions more clearly. The snake had taught me nothing.

We went on another date. A movie, this time. That outing was as awkward and unromantic as the other excursions. We did kiss once, standing in her driveway. It was a sterile, passionless meeting of tightly closed lips, not all that dissimilar from being tapped gently in the face with a pine board by someone who doesn't really want to hurt you. She broke it off quickly. But to my testosterone-fueled brain, that kiss was evidence that Maddie and I were destined to form a lasting relationship.

I decided there was no better way to tell her, and the world, about our twined destinies than to offer her something of mine to wear. And no, I don't mean clothing. I mean a significant to-ken. I'd seen high school guys do that in old movies. It looked classy and irresistible. I had a pin I'd been given when I played on the chess team in fifth grade. It was a chess knight slapped over the letter C, enameled in the school colors of maroon and white. The C, of course, stood for "Calvin Coolidge Elemen-tary." But it could very well stand for "Cliff." Or "Clueless."

I brought the pin with me on a Friday, shoved deeply into my right front pants pocket. I clutched it often throughout the day. My plan was simple: I would offer Maddie the pin, and my heart, when I caught up with her after school.

We had different schedules that year and shared no classes, but I spotted her on her way out of the building. I followed, clos-ing the gap like a slow-motion replay of Cupid's arrow in flight.

I was about to call her name when she ducked into a classroom. Her home base.

I waited by the door. My heart sped up as the door opened. But it wasn't Maddie. Sandra Warner, another girl from our class, came out.

"Maddie's in there, right?" I asked. As if, somehow, Maddie could vanish.

"Yeah. Why?"

"Nothing," I said. My voice somehow moved five octaves north between the first and second syllables of that word.

Sandra fixed me with a penetrating gaze. "You planning to ask her something?"

"Maybe." It was alarming how much girls seemed to know about the plans of random guys, just by looking at them.

"Whatever." She took three steps away, then snapped her fin-gers, spun around, and said, "Forgot my journal."

She dashed inside. Thinking back, which I do far too often,

I believe she was empty-handed when she emerged. But I wasn't paying much attention to her. I was rehearsing my words and enjoying a mental preview of the envious looks of my loner classmates as Maddie and I strolled arm in arm along the hallways.

I'll spare you those carefully chosen words, or the broad and diverse range of fantasies they spawned. But I knew for sure the next kiss would involve tongues. And maybe hands. Maddie's first seductive yawn played through my memory, filling the IMAX of my mind.

I waited.

Three more kids came out of the room. No Maddie. No sounds from within.

She has to be there.

I went in. The room was empty. One window was wide open. The half-drawn pull-down shade twisted in the breeze like a corpse on a gallows.

I walked over to the window and leaned out. There was no sign of Maddie on the street. She was long gone. She'd probably fled the room the moment Sandra told her I was hovering in the hallway. We were on the second floor, but the school was built on a hill. The drop to the ground from here wasn't far.

But still, Maddie Murough had chosen to leap from a second-story window—okay, make that dangle and drop—rather than face whatever I was planning to ask her.

How hideous was I? How undesirable?

The next day, Maddie avoided me with the subtlety of a young lady evading an unwelcome suitor. Or a plague carrier.

After no more than two or three weeks of watching Maddie dodge my approach and avoid my eyes, I finally started to take the hint and stop thinking of her as my girlfriend. It wasn't until years later that I realized she had, at least, given me the courtesy of not sharing the story of her escape with the whole school. Nobody ever brought it up or mocked me for it. I guess that was sort of classy. There are some girls who would have relished the telling, no matter what the consequences.

Yeah, I know. That was a huge side trip through my deformative years. But I wanted you to understand I didn't just sit on the sidelines. I really tried to get a girlfriend. And I really got crushed.

The rest of eighth grade, along with my freshman and sophomore years in high school, passed without any more wooing on my part. My fingers had been singed. Or amputated. And, honestly, even had I not been gun-shy, I lacked a sign that anyone would welcome my advances, or covet an opportunity to wear my Calvin Coolidge chess pin.

I courted again in my junior year. But that story is too painful to reveal so soon after the tale of Maddie and the open window. Maybe later, if I have a burning desire to feel like crap, and prove I am pathetic beyond redemption, I'll recount my junior-year trauma.

At the moment, my burning desire was to find a date for the Mack and Mary concert.

ACTING IN CONCERT

SO, WHO TO ask?

Nola came to mind immediately. But she had a boyfriend. I sorted through the various available classmates I'd interacted with at some social level in the past, and decided it would be safe to ask Patricia Klymer. She was sort of a friend. We'd gone through elementary school together, and had worked on several group projects in middle school. Her mom and my mom knew each other. And I'd seen her wearing a Ricky and the Rickettes T-shirt last month. They played the same kind of music as Mack and Mary, though they were nowhere near as awesome.

Basically, I was pretty sure I could talk to her without her shooting me down. Or leaping out a window.

I guess, since I'm telling you about Patricia here, for the first time, I should go back and show her in a couple earlier scenes. That's how they do it in most of the novels I've read. But that seems like a lot of unnecessary effort, and I'm not sure I'll want to rewrite any of this. It's already a lot more work than I expected. Though it did feel good to get all that stuff about Maddie out of my system. Not to be crude, but if you've ever been really super constipated for two or three days, you know how wonderful it feels when you finally get that dense mass of discomfort out of your system.

Besides, if you're adaptable enough to tolerate my digressions, you're adaptable enough to accept Patricia's existence on first mention. And Nicky's. But we'll get to him later.

Sort-of-friend or not, it took me a while to build up the courage to ask Patricia to the concert. Okay, more than a while. The rest of the week slipped by, and then the weekend. I finally gave it a shot on Monday, after Calculus, and after giving myself a pep talk.

What's the worst that could happen?

She could say no.

But she's not going to whip out a sword and decapitate you. If she says no, she says no. Big deal. Then you move on and ask someone else.

All right. I'm going for it.

"Hey," I said, catching up with her in the hallway. "I got two tickets for the Mack and Mary concert at the college. It's the Saturday after next. Want to go?" Just past her, I saw Butch give me a thumbs-up and a Cheshire cat grin.

Patricia flinched like I'd offered her a bite of a raw rat sandwich. "I can't."

Man, that was fast. The speed of her reply was even more disturbing than the contents. I was too surprised to say anything in response before she walked off. I'd have at least expected some sort of hesitation on her part, or maybe an explanation to reinforce the "I can't."

I have to take my cat to the orthodontist.

I promised my parents I'd stay home and watch them argue.

I'm knitting flame-resistant pot holders for orphans in Hell.

Something. Just a scrap. *I can't,* all by itself, seemed too cold. Not unlike an unexpected decapitation.

"From a distance, that didn't appear to go very well," Butch said when I caught up with her.

"She can't go," I said.

"She's just playing hard to get," Butch said.

"I can ask her for you," Robert said. "Women find me irresistible."

"You mean *irritable*," Butch said. "Like a bowel."

I wandered ahead as they argued about semantic and digestive issues.

The next day, after Calculus, having managed to become a believer in Butch's playing-hard-to-get theory, I gave myself another pep talk and took another shot at inviting Patricia to the concert. "Seriously, it wouldn't be a date or anything. I just have an extra ticket. For a friend. Robert couldn't make it," I said, trying to emphasize to Patricia that the position of concert companion wasn't based on the sex of the applicant. Or the supplicant.

"No, thanks."

If words had temperatures, those she'd just released from between her lips wouldn't even register on any scale. Again, no explanation. No sugarcoating. Was I being arrogant when I felt I deserved one? I didn't know.

"Perhaps she's playing impossible to get," Butch said. "Maybe it's time to move on."

"That's only strike two," Robert said.

"This isn't baseball." As I spoke those words, I saw myself

hurling baseballs at miniature stuffed Patricias. I consistently missed.

THIRD TIME'S THE charm.

Sayings suck. But after talking myself in and out of it a thousand times in the intervening twenty-four hours, I gave it one last shot on Wednesday, which happened to be May 1, but might as well have been exactly one month earlier, given Patricia's lack of encouragement. I'd even put the tickets in the front pocket of my shirt, peeking out ever so slightly, like I was about to perform some sort of magic trick with them. I had the wild idea that if I showed them to Patricia, she would be unable to resist the invitation. Tickets—real tickets you hold in your hand—possess a tantalizing aura.

As I headed after Patricia, Butch put a hand on my shoulder. "What?" I asked.

She lifted her pants leg to reveal a tattoo in tiny letters just above her ankle: QUIT WHILE YOU STILL HAVE YOUR HEAD.

"Marie Antoinette," Butch said. "It seemed appropriate."

"Thanks. But I have to give it one more shot," I said.

Patricia had stopped by her locker. I took that as a sign from the universe that I was making the right decision. "You sure you don't want to go see Mack and Mary?" I clipped the top corner of the tickets between my right thumb and forefinger, and started to ease them out of my pocket.

"For Christ's sake, Cliff, stop bothering me! I don't want to go to that stupid concert with you. Leave me alone." She slammed the locker door shut so hard, it flew back open, slammed it again, then sped down the hall. Around me, heads turned toward the shout. Eyes quickly lost interest after spotting the recipient. Except for two pairs that looked on in horror from the doorway of Calculus class.

I should have dropped it. If I understood Patricia correctly, it was highly likely she did not want to go to the concert with me. Nor, with me, to the concert, did she want to go. I'd even go so far as to suspect that she, to the concert, with me to go, did not want. But my burning desire to find a companion for the evening had been replaced with a hotter, deeper burn to make some sort of sense out of this inexplicable rejection. I wasn't a troll. I wasn't hideously ugly or smelly. But I'd had one girl leap from a window to avoid me, and another reject a chance to hear an awesome concert for free.

I followed Patricia down the hall. "Bothering you?" I asked the back of her head when I got within earshot. "Come on, I have an extra ticket. They're great seats for an amazing group. We're sort of like friends. Right? I don't see what the big deal is. It's going to be an awesome concert."

She spun back to confront me, her face throwing off heat and waves of anger like a nuclear weapon in mid explosion. "Cliff, I'm already a loser. If people see me on a date with you, I'm a big loser. Please. You're not a bad guy. But you're just so far from cool in every way, I can't get sucked into anything social with you. It would never wash off."

Her eyes looked dangerously close to filling with tears. I'd rather not describe my own eyes at that moment.

So, I wasn't just a loser. I was a carrier, too. Or an oil stain. I tainted everything I touched with a patina of uncoolness. All I'd wanted was to go to a concert. I wanted to hear some live music from a great band. I didn't want to go alone, like a pathetic loser.

Was that too much to ask? Too much to hope for? Was that

really just too fucking huge a desire for someone like me to have?

What's the worst that could happen?

I sure got smacked hard in the nuts with the answer to that one.

Robert and Butch were waiting for me down the hall, but I walked right past them. I couldn't talk right now. They were good enough friends to pretend, during lunch, that nothing had happened. I pretended that, too, though I had a hard time swallowing my food.

After school, I left the pair of tickets on Ms. Ryder's desk with a note, saying, *For you and a friend. From a friend.* I disguised my handwriting. I hope she liked music. Maybe I could have sold the tickets and given the money back to Mom. But I really didn't want to have to explain all this to her. She seemed to assume I led a normal, reasonably happy social life.

I felt too wretched to go right home. I wanted to kick a wall. I knew that would be a bad idea. Dad kicked walls sometimes, and it always looked like it hurt. It sure didn't calm him down. But I had to burn off some of the anger that was surging through me. I headed for the perfect place to exorcise my rage.

WHEN YOU NEED
A LIFT

THERE WASN'T ANYBODY in the weight room. That was good. I had no idea what I was doing, and I really didn't want to share that news with an audience, or have Clovis bounce a dumbbell off my skull.

I wandered around among the free weights, workout benches, and dangerous-looking devices rigged with cables and pulleys, trying to decide where to start. I knew enough to figure out how much weight was on a barbell. I found one already loaded with one hundred pounds. That sounded like a good place to start. Round numbers are nice. I bent over and grabbed the bar with both hands, then remembered the ten million times Mom, or some other adult, had warned me, *Lift with your legs, not your back.*

So, why did so many old people I know have bad knees?

I squatted, made sure my back was relatively straight, tightened my grip, and stood.

The barbell was heavy enough to make me appreciate the power of gravity, but not bad enough to make me fear a spontaneous double amputation of my arms. I decided to do a press. Picturing how they did it in the Olympics, I started to lift the weight up to shoulder height.

Oh, hell. No way. Apparently, lifting a hundred pounds to thigh level with your whole body is a lot easier than raising the weight higher with just your arms.

I lowered the barbell back down to where it belonged and went to look at the dumbbells.

Yeah. Apt term for them and me.

I grabbed a twenty-five-pounder, came to my senses pretty much immediately, put it back down, picked up a ten-pounder in each hand, and stood there, wondering what my next step should be. On TV shows, the guys in prison were always doing curls. Of course, they already had enormous muscles, and a whole lot of free time. As I was trying to figure out what to do with the weights in my hands, I heard someone walk in. There were enough mirrors in the room that I didn't need to look over my shoulder to see who it was.

Nicky Foster.

That was a relief. He wasn't a threat. I didn't really know him. I just knew he kept to himself and had never been connected with any random acts of violence. I think he'd tossed the shot put, freshman or sophomore year. But then he'd quit the team.

Nicky went to a barbell resting chest-high on a rack. Each end of the bar held a stack of weights that was bigger than a small car.

He ducked under the bar, lifted it across his shoulders, and stepped away from the rack.

Then he squatted and stood.

I stared. He squatted nine more times, letting out a measured exhale with each lift, slowing somewhat on each new repetition, but he never looked like he was in any sort of distress. Then he set the weight back on the rack. He repeated the sequence two more times, for a total of thirty reps. If you added it all up, I think he'd just lifted a large bus, or a small airplane.

I was still standing where I was, captivated by the unexpected sideshow. Nicky caught me staring as he turned toward a rack of larger-than-necessary dumbbells.

"What are you looking at?" he asked.

I pointed at the barbell. "How much was that?"

"Two twenty. Why?"

I had no response. He pulled off his shirt, tossed it in the corner, grabbed a couple large dumbbells from the rack, and went to a bench by the front mirror.

Holy crap, he had muscles on top of his muscles. We'd never been in the same gym class, and he always wore loose shirts in school, so I had no idea he was that strong. He had the sort of long, carelessly groomed hair that screamed "slacker." Until now, I could have pictured him on a surfboard, or hanging out at the skate park. Standing here, bare chested, he struck me as more of a gladiator.

He did some sort of lifty thingees. I chose that phrase carefully to show off my technical knowledge of weight training and bodybuilding (which I suspect might not be exactly the same thing). Then he stared into the mirror, right at me staring at him. By this point, he'd worked up a thin sheen of sweat across his back that darkened the band at the top of his gray sweat shorts.

"What?" he asked. "Do you like my body? You seem a bit obsessed with it."

"I'm not gay," I said.

"You make it sound like some sort of disease," he said.

Crap. This was like boxing. Except instead of ducking and weaving, I was throwing my face at his verbal fists. "That's not what I meant. I just didn't want you to think I was staring at you for the wrong reason."

He turned around and faced me. "Maybe I'd consider it the right reason."

"I . . . I mean . . ." Oh man. I loved to argue with Robert and Butch, or my fellow food burners at Moo Fish, but this was an entirely different sort of skirmish. The best option seemed to be an unconditional surrender. I took a deep breath and gathered my thoughts. "I don't care who gets hot over what. I just want to get in better shape so I can get laid myself. Okay? There's this girl I'm trying to impress. It's not going well. Actually, it's not going at all. I tried to do some lifting, but apparently it's a lot harder than I thought it would be. And you look like you know what you're doing. Hell, you look like you've known what you were doing for most of your life. So, could you maybe stop screwing with my head and show me some basic stuff before I hurt myself?"

"Sure," he said. "As long as you aren't a hater. I don't help homophobes."

"I'm a dying-alone-and-unlaid-phobe," I said. "That really terrifies me."

"Hang in there and keep trying," he said. "You're kind of good-looking, in a nerdy, awkward way. Sometimes it takes girls longer to notice guys who aren't flashy or dangerous. But they'll catch on to you eventually. Hot girls like to chase wolves. But then they marry collies. Smart, loyal, pretty."

"Uh, thanks . . ."

"Oh, and one more thing. You might want to find better ways

to describe romantic encounters. 'Getting laid' makes it sound like you just want to use this girl as a moist substitute for your hand. She's not just an object, is she?"

"No," I said. "She's awesome. She's amazing." I'd never considered myself to be crude, like the Thug Nuts, or a jerk about girls, but I guess he had a point. I really did sound like a sexist idiot when I talked that way. Damn, another thing to watch out for. Life was like a minefield of words.

Over the next half hour, Nicky showed me everything I needed for a workout routine. He explained how to balance exercise and rest, and the difference between bodybuilding and weight lifting. He could have taught a class at an upscale gym if he wanted. That's how much he knew.

"Good job," he said as I was walking out, exhausted but strangely content. Then he smacked me on the butt.

I let out an involuntary shout, but he laughed and said, "That was a manly smack. Don't worry. You haven't been molested, infected, or indoctrinated. Unfortunately, you're still pathetically straight."

"Thanks for helping me," I said. "Hey, do you like Mack and Mary?" I figured the tickets were probably still on Ms. Ryder's desk.

"Mack's cute," he said. "But their music sucks. Why?"

"No reason." It had been worth a try.

On the way out, I found myself thinking that if I were gay, I would have been all over Nicky at the words "good-looking." I mean, he was more than good-looking, himself. He had the sort of face you'd see in a commercial for macho stuff like chain saws or Ford trucks. His body was magnificent. But not in a way that attracted me. I couldn't picture myself in a physical relationship with him. I was definitely straight.

I paused in the hall to look at myself in the mirrored back of the trophy case. Good-looking? Who knows? How could I expect to judge my own face? Especially now, when it was flushed and sweaty from exercise.

But I loved the feel of my shirt sticking to my body. It was pasted there with honest sweat. The last time I'd felt like this was back in July, when I did yard work around the neighborhood to make extra money.

After I got home and showered, even though I knew every muscle in my body was working furiously at becoming buff, I still didn't feel great about myself socially. But an idea hit me as I was staring at my right arm, wondering how long it would take for the muscle growth to become evident.

I decided to give myself a tattoo.

I checked the Internet. It seemed like it was reasonably easy to tattoo yourself. That would be an immediate change, far faster than muscle growth, and one I could hold in my mind like an amulet as I walked through the halls at school. I wasn't planning to make some sort of giant Asian carp or American eagle on my biceps, but I thought it would be cool to have something only I knew about. Maybe a quote. That's what Butch had on her arm and on her ankle. I thought about some of the ones I liked.

Don't let the bastards grind you down.

I don't do drug. I am drugs.

Please, may I have more?

And so it goes.

I liked that last one. And not just because it was the shortest. It was a line that appeared throughout *Slaughterhouse-Five.* Vonnegut. Hah. I just realized that if I put those words on my stomach, I'd have a Vonne-gut.

Where to place my statement? My forearm would be the easiest. But it wouldn't exactly be hidden there. I totally couldn't let my parents ever see it. Dad would definitely hit a wall or two if he spotted me with a tattoo.

My leg.

That would work. I'd place it right at the top of my upper thigh, below my pelvis. A place where nobody would ever see the tattoo unless I wanted them to. It would also be easy to reach.

I got out a marking pen and sketched the words. AND SO IT GOES. I kept them fairly small. Four words. Eleven letters. Three spaces. Not that I'd have to put ink in the spaces.

I pulled together everything I needed, and got started. In the interest of not contributing to anyone else's rash decisions, I won't detail the equipment or methods. It's better to let the Internet get all the blame if you decide to follow my example.

As I got ready to start, I realized that every puncture I made for the first letter of the quote would, literally, be an A-hole. I also realized I was stalling. I took three slow, deep breaths, steadied my hand, and plunged in.

The process hurt more than I expected. I almost stopped in the middle of the A. Actually, it stung more than it hurt. But I gritted my teeth, finished the first letter, and got started on the second.

This is a bad idea.

My mind hurled various unhelpful images at me. I pictured my leg getting infected. I pictured it getting amputated. I pictured the infection spreading to my groin. I pictured pustules of bubonic plague proportion erupting in my crotch like zombie testicles.

Despite those horrifying images, I kept going. After I finished the tattoo, I cleaned off my leg and regarded my handiwork. It was only at that point—as I was rereading the words I'd permanently injected into my flesh, admiring my skill in both the art of tattooing and the art of calligraphy, and contemplating these disciplines as possible career options—that I realized my mistake.

Picture this.

I was looking down at my upper leg, reading the words, AND SO IT GOES. From above, left to right. Reading with no effort. Looking down.

At upside-down words.

I could read my tattoo as easily as words on a street sign or a sentence in a book. But for the rest of the world, it was inverted. And so it went—upside down.

Damn. All that work, all that pain, and I'd screwed up.

On the bright side, there was no danger of embarrassment, since the way things were going in my social life, nobody else would ever see my mistake.

Inverted. Introverted. Everything is connected.

Maybe Kurt Vonnegut was looking down at me from heaven, reading my homage to him, and laughing his ass off.

Do people in heaven have asses?

Lumber Jerks

DESPITE THE INVERTED nature of my tattoo, I did feel like I was walking a bit taller the next day. Counterbalancing that, I was also walking a bit hunched over, thanks to the exercise-induced pain in my core muscles. But it was a good pain. I promised myself I'd lift again in a day or two, as soon as I was sure I could raise a barbell without screaming.

Third period, I showed the finished painting to Ms. Gickley. "If I work on it any longer, I think I'll start scraping off paint," I said. "Whether it's good enough or not, I think I'm done."

"Honestly, I wasn't concerned how this one came out," she said.

"Seriously?"

She nodded. I waited, knowing there was more.

"I wanted you to take your time. And you did. Right?"

"Right." *Because Mr. Yuler totally trashed me with one word.*

"So you've proved to yourself that you can put more time into a painting. And, more important, you know how it feels to go slowly. Does that make sense?"

"Yeah. It does. Thanks." I guess she was right. I'd had time to think as I worked. Until now, I'd always raced to finish each piece, eager to start the next one. It was like when I was eating dinner but thinking about dessert. Whether in the Art House or the weight room, it looked like this was my week to get taught. I liked that.

As I was about to walk away, I realized my ego still hadn't gotten the meal it had been hoping for. Or even a snack. "So, is it any good?"

"To me, it's better than your first painting. And that's good. It's also better than it was last week. You improved it. And that's great."

I thanked her again, then went back to the main building to get a frame. As I approached the shop class, I heard banging, like someone was moving wood around in the supply closet. And I heard laughter. But it wasn't the sort of laughter that made me feel good. It was the sort of laughter that carved a deep slash along my spine with a blunt chisel.

I was still ten or fifteen feet from the door, just close enough to catch the faint resin scent of sawed pine, when I heard a cluster of footsteps. I held the painting in front of my face, pretending to study it as I slowed my walk. I already knew, from their voices and their braying laughter, that it was Clovis and three or four other Thug Nuts who were about to emerge from the room. I didn't know what they'd been doing in the woodshop, but I decided I was better off remaining ignorant. As they passed me, I gripped the painting harder, expecting one of them to knock it from my hands. They generally seemed to respond to anything of worth or beauty with violence and anger.

But they zipped right by, as if they were eager to get away from the scene of a crime. I waited until they'd moved out of sight, then headed back to the Art House, frameless but intact.

I brought the painting home after school.

"What's that?" Dad asked from the living room couch, where he was watching an old movie.

I didn't feel like going through a replay of Mr. Yuler's art criticism. "Nothing."

Dad twirled his index finger like he was stirring a cocktail with it. I turned the painting around and held it up.

He squinted at it for a moment. "That's art?"

"Yeah."

"Is it any good?"

"I don't know."

"That makes two of us." He hit me with a snarky smirk, then turned back to the newspaper. It was obvious he was finished with our father–son moment.

That, at least, had been less brutal than Mr. Yuler's reaction. Though, in some ways, it had also been more painful.

I put the painting in my room and went outside to do my homework. I would have liked to go into town for a change, just to get a bit farther away from the source of the sting, but I really didn't have time.

There's a square at the center of Rismore. We call it "the Green." It's pretty large, maybe as long on each side as two city blocks, flanked across the street on all four sides by stores, some offices, the post office, and a church. There was a movie theater on the Main Street side when I was a kid, but that closed up years ago, after a Cinema Twelve and a Cinema Sixteen opened up on highways at either end of town. A large walkway cuts through the middle of the Green, running east to west.

There are also some smaller diagonal paths, dotted with benches. The rest of the area is grass, along with a scattering of oak trees and one lonely, twisted evergreen. The skaters, goths, punks, and other groups hang out in clusters in the south half, which is bordered by Jefferson Avenue. Random members bounce from group to group, like electrons in an ionic bond. The north belongs to thugs of various flavors. This arrangement bears absolutely no metaphorical connection to any other geographic north/south political divisions, either historical or contemporary.

If I had time to go to the Green, I'd be in the south. But I was rarely able to do that. It was about a fifteen-minute walk to town from my house. That's why I usually ended up in the backyard. It got me outside and didn't eat up a half hour during the round trip.

"CLIFF IS REMBRANDT," Dad said as I was setting the table for dinner.

Mom looked at me.

"I brought home a new painting," I said. "It's no big deal."

Her face lit up. "Let me see!"

Great. She'd be disappointed. But I knew there was no way I could talk her out of seeing the painting, so I got it from my room and brought it downstairs.

Mom gasped when I held it up. "Cliff! That's brilliant!" She snatched the painting from my hands and cradled it as if it were the newborn Christ Child, dropped straight into her waiting arms by the Angel Guggenheim, and not a blurry crucifixion on a blurry game controller, overseen by a blurry eye in the sky. "We need to get this framed."

"You like it?" After being smacked down repeatedly by artless critics, I wasn't ready to allow too much room for hope.

"So bold," she said. "So assertive, and yet subtle. It has the powerful impact of a work by Goya or Chagall."

"Uh, thanks," I said. That was high praise. I glanced at Dad, who seemed annoyed that Mom found any value in my efforts, then turned my attention back to her, though what I said next was for Dad's benefit. "I can get a frame from woodshop. It won't cost anything."

"Your work overflows with ideas," she said. "You obviously put a lot of thought into the symbolism."

She said more, showering me with compliments and comparing me to at least a half dozen famous artists beside Goya and Chagall. At the mention of some of the names, I heard Dad mutter, "Died broke," "Died crazy," or other inspiring biographical tidbits. All he seemed to know about artists was their failures.

Eventually, I managed to pry the canvas from Mom's grip. She wanted to hang it in the living room immediately. I convinced her that I still needed to make a couple small changes and go back for a frame.

As I was walking away, she said, "And I love the rose. It reminds me of the trivet you made in third grade. Do you remember that?"

"Sort of," I said.

After dinner, when Mom headed upstairs to go to sleep and I headed out the door for a short shift at Moo Fish, Dad stopped me with a hand on the shoulder.

"I've spent most of my working life doing taxes for people," he said.

"I know."

"Do you know how many artists I've done taxes for?"

I shook my head. There didn't seem to be any benefit in making a guess.

"None," Dad said. "Nil. Zip. Squat. Artists don't earn a living. They sponge off society. They live off food stamps or government grants funded by taxpayers. If that's your plan, if your dream is to be a parasite, keep painting. But don't plan on painting here."

LATER, AS I was mixing up a five-gallon batch of Moo Fish's secret tartar sauce (mayonnaise, hot dog relish, and paprika), I thought about those words. It seemed like a pretty big hint I might need to put "find an apartment" a lot higher up on my list of things to do next year.

Friday morning, I was even sorer from weight lifting. My initial enthusiasm had faded somewhat. I wasn't sure whether I wanted to keep up the exercise. This whole "no pain, no gain" attitude seemed to run counter to pretty much any philosophy I could imagine adopting.

No pain, no problem. That was more my style.

At least I didn't have gym class. It was a library day. I grabbed my usual spot at the computers between Butch and Robert.

"Watch this," Robert said. He typed "astounding breasts" into the search window, then clicked on one of the results on the first page, which linked to a site whose name I won't mention, because it was much closer to being sick than clever.

"That won't work," I said as the content filter's message popped up, announcing that the site was screened and unavailable. I cast a nervous glance toward the librarian, Mrs. Yalza, who was busy laminating a READ poster.

Robert held up a finger. "Patience. That's just step one." He tapped the bottom of the message, by the name of the filtering program: *Censor Senser.* Then he went to Google and typed "How do I get around Censor Senser?"

A bunch of hits popped up. I was impressed. Even more impressive, those pages didn't appear to be screened.

"I love the Internet," Robert said.

I shifted to a different computer, on the other side of Butch, who was deeply enough involved in whatever she was researching that she wasn't paying any attention to Robert. I figured my body was already 98 percent stiff. I didn't want to remain within sight of Robert's monitor and make it a perfect 100. Besides, like anyone else over the age of ten, I could find porn without any help whenever I wanted to. And even when I didn't want to.

But I realized that, for Robert, the thrill wasn't in going to some sleazy website loaded with artificially inflated breasts; it was in beating the system. And, even better, in using the system to beat itself. He was more enthralled with silicon than silicone.

Despite feeling like a ninety-year-old man with arthritis, I made it through the rest of the school day, all the way to Government. I was definitely enjoying Ms. Ryder's idea of civics a lot more than Mr. Tippler's. She didn't yell. And she wasn't boring. Odds are, she'd probably never go ballistic and take her anger out on an innocent mirror, either. I could not picture her staggering drunkenly around a bar, or anywhere else. She was smiling and humming when I came in. I guess she appreciated getting the concert tickets. I saw she'd written a message on the board: *Thank you very much! (You know who I mean.)*

"You're welcome," I whispered.

So there I sat, enjoying the bittersweet knowledge that I was a secret benefactor, when I heard the siren. It's never good when an ambulance comes racing toward the school. Especially when it cuts right across the lawn and keeps going, all the way up to the main entrance. Everyone rushed to the windows. Ms. Ryder didn't stop us. The ambulance was followed by a hook-and-ladder fire truck and two police cars, though all three of those vehicles stayed at the curb.

"Should we get out of here?" Abbie asked. "There might be a fire."

Ms. Ryder sniffed the air. "I don't smell any smoke. And they'd pull the alarm if they wanted us out of the building."

"Do you trust authority?" Zach asked.

"I work for them," she said. "Of course I trust them. But if history has taught us anything—and if it hasn't, I might as well go home right now—it has taught us that people make mistakes. Absolute trust is just as dangerous as absolute distrust. I have an idea. It's a beautiful day. Why don't we take our class outside and enjoy a bit of sunshine?"

Even sophisticated, jaded seniors will whoop and cheer at the news of an outing, reverting instantly to their inner, and outer, child.

"Recess!" Peter yelled.

"That's an appropriate vocabulary word for a Government class," Ms. Ryder said. We followed her outside, through a door by the cafeteria, about fifty yards from the front entrance.

As Ms. Ryder continued our discussion of the Tenth Amendment, I kept stealing peeks toward the ambulance. Eventually, two paramedics came out the front door, wheeling a gurney. As they turned the gurney to line up with the open back doors of the ambulance, I recognized the blue shop apron.

"It's Mr. Xander," I said. My gut churned when I spotted bloody bandages wrapped around his head.

"Shop teacher gets hammered," Peter said.

A couple of us glared at him.

"Too soon?" he asked.

Nearby, I heard Clovis snort. He wore a chilling grin. It wasn't merely the grin of someone who had seen his enemy harmed. It was the grin of someone who had engineered that harm.

Juke raised his hand for a high five. Clovis started to respond, but then grabbed Juke's arm and yanked it down with enough force that my own shoulder spasmed in sympathy. Clovis leaned close and snarled a warning. Juke responded with a dull nod. I felt a deeper chill as the meaning of all this fell into place with a cerebral clank.

Maybe I should have known that something like this would happen. Yesterday, when I'd seen Clovis, Burton, Leon, Juke, and Quin clamber out of the woodshop, they were laughing and hitting each other on the arm like a volleyball team that had just won a tournament victory against a stronger opponent. I recalled snatches of their conversation. Their words had meant nothing to me at the time, as I cowered behind my canvas.

"Upside the head . . ."

". . . crash . . ."

"Like a ton of bricks . . ."

"More like a ton of wood . . ."

". . . has it coming . . ."

"No more detention . . ."

I was so used to them talking about acts of violence, from real life, TV, movies, and games, I hadn't connected their words to their presence in the woodshop. Now I knew what they were talking about. They'd booby-trapped the supply closet. Mr. Xander lets us look through the frames he makes, but he doesn't let students select the wood for their projects. He gets it himself. Today, he got more than he'd expected. There really is a ton of wood stored there.

I flinched at the thought of a pile of lumber crashing down on someone's head. That had to hurt a lot more than a football. I hoped he was okay. As I was recovering from my own imaginary encounter with an avalanche of wood, the ambulance pulled away. They had the siren on, but they didn't seem to be racing off at full speed. I guess that was good. If Mr. Xander were dead, there'd be no siren. At least, I think that's how it works. If he were dying, or in serious trouble, they'd be tearing around corners to get him to the emergency room. So he was down, but not out. Still, what a rotten thing for those guys to do. I thought about telling someone what I'd seen and heard yesterday, but I had no proof of anything. And no desire to be the next person Clovis set out to harm.

DO IT,
YOUR SHELF

BUTCH SNAGGED ME at the end of the day. "I need your help."

"Okay. Sure. What's up?"

"A shelf," she said.

"What?"

"I'm putting up another shelf in my room. You're good with tools. It won't take long."

"What about me?" Robert asked.

"*That* would take long," Butch said. "And there've been enough industrial-arts accidents for one day."

Robert and Butch argued about Robert's lack of manual skills as we walked to the parking lot. Butch's parents had gotten her an electric car. Since she forgot to plug it in fairly often, she caught a ride to school with Robert most days. He had an ancient Volvo. His parents has insisted on him getting the safest possible car. I didn't have any sort of car, mostly because my father had insisted on controlling my money so I could get a good student loan. But I didn't want to dwell on how well that was working out at the moment.

I got in back, and we rode to Butch's house. Or mansion, I should say. Okay, that's an exaggeration, but the house was huge, and it had an elevator. Butch's grandfather had invented something that makes it easier to produce high-grade steel. He'd earned a pretty nice fortune before the American steel industry took a dive. And he'd passed it all along to his daughter and two sons, one of whom was Butch's father. He was a professor of Medieval Literature at Fairleigh Dickinson. He didn't have to work. But, as he once told me, the money he'd inherited gave him the opportunity to study whatever he wanted. And there was no point learning about all that literature if he couldn't pass the knowledge along and share the passion. He told Butch she could study whatever she wanted, as long as she put her whole heart into it. That's why she'd be able to major in theater. Butch's mother was involved in a lot of charity projects.

Since I've told you more about Butch, I guess I should give Robert equal attention. He, along with his two younger sisters and his family, had been pretty much broke when they got over here from Jamaica. I don't know the details. They hadn't been one of those unbearably poor families you see on the news in places like Haiti. But they didn't have much, and they'd spent most of what they had to get here. His mom got a job cleaning houses. His dad started out working as a hole digger for a nursery. But he was really good with plants, and the owners quickly realized that he was worth more as a landscaper than as a hole digger. Three years later, he and his wife had their own nursery, and dreams of expanding. That's why Robert was planning to get a business degree.

We reached Butch's house, and I got to work. I wasn't actually helping her. I was doing the whole job by myself. Her tool skills were on par with Robert's. She had her newest skulls and ponies piled up on her bed, awaiting their promotion to shelf-dom. The smell of freshly unwrapped molded plastic mixed with the bedroom's ever-present aromatic evidence of Butch's fondness for cinnamon toast.

Seeing the piece of pine propped against the wall, I couldn't help thinking about Mr. Xander.

"I'm pretty sure Clovis and the Thug Nuts booby-trapped the wood supply," I said as I opened the package of shelving brackets.

"Did you see them?" Butch asked.

"Just about," I said.

"Stay out of it," Robert said. "The bad outweighs the good big-time. At best, they get in trouble. At worst, you get crushed."

I looked at Butch. She was the one who cared the most about justice and stuff like that. "I can't argue with Chicken of the Islands, here," she said. "Unless you captured them on video. Otherwise, you don't have any real proof. There's probably no evidence."

"There could be fingerprints," I said.

"You watch too much television," Butch said. "It's not as easy in real life to get fingerprints or DNA."

"I guess you're right," I said. "But I'd love to see those guys get what they deserve." I dropped my concerns and picked up the humorously named but highly useful stud finder I'd plucked from Butch's parent's toolbox.

It didn't take long to put up the shelf. After I was finished, I sat on the edge of Butch's bed and watched as she arranged the newest members of her skull collection, along with a scattering of ponies and kitties. That took a while, since she ended up shifting a lot of them from shelf to shelf in search of the perfect balance. There were realistic skulls of all sizes, designed to serve various utilitarian functions: coffee mugs, pencil sharpeners, and even a music box that played "Happy Days Are Here Again." I knew enough not to offer to help. Robert, who also should have known better, tried to make suggestions. After getting rebuffed several times, he decided to drive into town to check out what was going on around the Green.

"See you tomorrow?" he asked as he headed for the door.

"Sure," Butch said. She looked over at me. "Going?"

"Maybe . . ." There was a dance at the Crab Locker. That's a club near the school. The dance started after my shift at Cretaro's ended, so I didn't have a good excuse not to go. "I might be too tired."

"You're going," she said. She turned her attention back to her skulls.

I don't really collect anything right now. I have a couple dozen wooden tops of various kinds. My uncle Steve—the same uncle who had been my first and, so far, only art patron—sends them to me when he travels. I have no idea why. They're fun to play with for a minute or two, but I can't see myself spinning them for endless hours, building a display case, or subscribing to *Top Fancier* magazine. I like tennis, but I'm not good enough to go out for the team. I like miniature golf, but I can't remember the last time I played. Maybe two summers ago. I read a lot, but I don't really think of reading as a hobby. It's just something I do. I guess art is my hobby. But it feels weird to call it that. "Hobby" makes it sound like I go out on the weekends with my paint box, meet up with the other art-club members, and sit together, painting pictures at the edge of a scenic forest.

"Thanks," Butch said after she placed the last skull on the shelf. She stretched, arching her back and letting out a contented sigh.

As Butch's T-shirt rose above her navel, I had a flashback to Maddie, and that first amazing yawn. Butch and I were alone in the house. We'd been good friends for ages, so I didn't want to have sex with her. No—that's not the right way to put it. I wanted to have sex with anyone who'd let me. Just so I was no longer a virgin. If Butch didn't have a boyfriend, maybe I would have asked her to take pity on me. But it felt weird thinking about asking a friend for sex. I wonder whether girls ever thought about boys this way. It seemed like they had it easy, as far as I could see. If a girl wanted to stop being a virgin, she'd have no trouble finding a willing volunteer among her circle of friends and classmates. The whole give-versus-take aspect of sex was almost as difficult to sort through as time travel paradoxes.

"Hey," Butch said, tapping me gently on the head with a leftover piece of pine shelving. "What are you thinking about?"

I guess she could tell my mind was drifting. I panicked briefly, as if I'd been caught with my hand down my pants, then came up with a reasonable answer. "Mortality," I said, pointing to one of the life-size skulls. "It seems inescapable. Especially within these walls."

Butch picked up a small bottle from her dresser. "Speaking of death, decay, and all that good stuff, want a tattoo?" she asked.

"What? You want to give me a tattoo? Just like that?"

"It's henna, stupid," she said, giving the bottle a shake. "You paint it on. It looks real, but it fades after a while." She pushed up her sleeve to show the faint hints of her revenge tattoo. "You could do a quote about mortality, like *memento mori*. Which would be nicely ironic, since the tattoo will be gone a lot sooner than the tattoo wearer. At least, I hope so, unless you do something really stupid."

"So that wasn't permanent?" I thought about my own now-and-forever upside-down tattoo.

"Are you kidding? I change my mind all the time. There's no way I'm going to get anything permanent written on my flesh until I'm really sure what I want. And maybe not even then." She put the bottle back on her dresser. "I mean, who'd do a crazy thing like that?"

"Yeah," I said, crossing my legs so another layer of skin and bones covered my tattoo. "Who'd be that stupid?"

Speaking of stupidity, pain, and permanent damage, while I didn't have a good excuse not to go to the dance, I definitely had a good reason. I said I wouldn't talk about this too soon after telling you about Maddie and the window, but let's rip the bandage off the wound and get it over with. You might want to grab a Coke and find a comfortable seat. I'll wait.

A Band,
End All Hope

I TOLD YOU that Paul was a player. He's also a friend of mine. Sort of. He moved up here from New Orleans three years ago. We started hanging out soon after he arrived, mostly because we both liked to go hiking. That was back when I had lots of time to trek through the woods. I'd usually take a sketch pad. Paul would take a harmonica. He'd spent his whole life around woods, rivers, and lakes. I knew all the hiking trails around here, including some you could get to by bus. I felt bad for him because his folks had lost everything in one of those floods that happened years after the big hurricane everyone always talks about. I think he'd seen people drown, and maybe even get shot, but he never talked about it, except once last year, when we'd shared a bottle of Jack. But that night's pretty much made up of fuzzy memories and vomit.

About a year after he came here, he formed a band with Tim on guitar and Zach on drums. Paul played keyboard and harmonica. Three months later, they added Megan Rox, who'd already graduated, as a singer. It turned out to be a smart move. Thanks to her stunning voice and high-energy stage presence, they got pretty popular locally. Paul didn't have much time to hang out with me once they started playing a lot of gigs.

That's not the bad part. Friends drift away all the time. But, at least for me, girlfriends are rare. I started dating Shelly during my junior year. She was a sophomore, slim, with red hair cut short and freckles dusted across her face like the all-American athletic-looking girls in the fashion ads. I'll save the description of her heart for later. She'd moved to Rismore in February. It took me two months to get up the courage to ask her on a date.

We'd gone out twice. Once to a movie, and once to the diner for lunch on a Saturday. We were still at the awkward friends-or-dating? stage. But I hoped I'd eventually make my big move from walking side by side, with nothing more than occasional accidental arm contact, to walking side against side, arm around shoulder. I needed to break the ice with a bit of socially accept-able body contact. A dance seemed perfect for that. A nice, long, slow sweaty dance. Chest to chest. Hips to hips in intimate contact. Clutching tight. Grinding. One hand slipping slowly down her back . . .

Hang on.

I hate to break the narrative flow, but I'm going to grab a quick shower. Take a break, too, if you need it.

[. . . a wet, steamy interlude ensues for at least one of us . . .]

Sorry about that. I'm back. As I was saying . . .

Paul's band, Jersey Bayou, was playing at the Crab Locker. If you head up the hill past the Art House to the traffic light where Vorhees Avenue meets Jefferson Avenue, the Crab Locker is on the right, just around the corner, past the liquor store and the good deli. (The bad deli, where the owner hates students and yells at us even if we buy something, is on the way into town.) If you stay on Jefferson and go west for another mile, heading toward Rismore Heights, you reach the state park. If you turn left at the top of Vorhees, and head east on Jefferson, the Green is two long blocks away. The Krome Kadillac Diner, where the food is far superior to the spelling, is northeast of the Green, downhill, across from the train station.

Normally, you had to be at least twenty-one to get into the Crab Locker. But every two or three weeks, they had a teens-only event with one of the local bands. Once or twice a year, usually during vacations or around graduation time, they booked a bigger act. Jersey Bayou was just what I needed to get closer to Shelly. They played a mix of fast and slow music. Better yet, Shelly would be impressed that I knew the guys. It would be a perfect way to get closer to her. I asked, and she accepted.

"They're a great band," I said as I paid our way in at the door.

"My sister heard them last year at a club in Mendham," Shelly said. "She told me they were fabulous." Shelly was wearing a brown thigh-length skirt and a dark blue sleeveless top, giving my eyes a lot of places to avoid being caught staring at.

The Crab Locker is basically just one large room with dark green walls, a low ceiling, a bar at one end, and a stage at the other. There were bathrooms off to one side, with HE CRAB and SHE CRAB written on the doors, but no other sign of crabs or lockers in the decor. Jersey Bayou was onstage when we went in, tuning up, dwarfed by towers of black amps. "Come on," I said. "I'll introduce you."

I threaded my way through the crowd. I wanted to take Shelly's hand, but I wasn't sure she'd like that.

I waved to Paul when we got near the stage. He gave me a nod and flashed a smile at Shelly. He totally looked the part of a rock star, with shaggy jet-black hair that just brushed his shoulders at spots, torn jeans, and a purple silk shirt draped unbuttoned over his lanky frame. Oh, crap—"lanky frame" sounds like the kind of overblown phrase Abbie would use in a description. But you get the picture.

When the first set began, Shelly and I stood in the back, near the refreshment stand, which is what you call a bar when you remove the kegs and stock up on soda. Shelly was swaying to the music, sort of dancing in place. I thought about starting to subtly move along with her, side by side at first, and then shifting face-to-face by means of a slick and rhythmic pivot, turning her solo motion and my solo motion magically into us dancing together. I decided it would be better if I waited until we got closer to the dance floor. Girls can dance anywhere. On the dance floor, off the dance floor, in the middle of an empty room. In a closet. At the supermarket. Probably even in their sleep. It doesn't matter where they are, or even whether there's music playing. If they feel like dancing, they dance. Most guys can dance only on the dance floor—if even there. Except for Christopher, who I spotted dancing by himself in the far corner. He was holding a cup full of soda and not spilling a drop. While I watched, two girls walked up to him and joined his dance. He and Brad seemed to have been born popular.

"Let's get closer!" I shouted to Shelly over the blaring music. She nodded.

I congratulated myself for my problem-solving abilities. *Closer* would put us on the dance floor, where I could legitimately join Shelly in a dance. We snaked through the crowd again. Up front, the music dominated everything, blasting us away even as it drew us forward.

"This looks good," I said when we'd reached a gap in the sea of flesh. But Shelly kept going. She crossed the dance floor and went all the way to the edge of the stage. I'd missed my brief chance to start dancing. I felt like I was throwing baseballs at skinny cats.

Shelly kept dancing. Finally, I got up the nerve to point toward the dance floor and shout, "Wanna dance?"

Her head bobbed in an affirmative manner, and her lips formed a syllable that might have been, "Sure."

We wedged into an open spot and danced. It was a fast dance, awesome for her, awkward for me. Her body moved like it had been strung together loosely but lovingly by a slightly horny and highly skilled marionette maker. My designer seemed more fond of Legos.

When the song ended, I was drenched. "Want a drink?" I asked. I figured, when I gave her the drink, I could put a hand on her shoulder.

She responded with a double nod.

I headed toward the refreshment stand and tried to picture the best way—or any way, for that matter—to carry out that casual act of first contact while juggling two full cups of soda in my hands and avoiding dozens of flailing arms. The line was brutal. By the time I bought the sodas, the music had stopped. The band was on break. At least I'd figured out I could give her a soda and then put my hand on her shoulder.

I made my way toward the front. Shelly was talking with

Paul, who'd climbed down off the stage to join her. I was halfway there when he put his hand on her shoulder. It was casual—not like some sort of groping. He made it seem so natural, like they'd known each other for years. I tried to imagine myself doing that, but the imaginary Shelly flinched at my touch.

Paul said something. Shelly laughed.

He turned toward the rest of the band and called Zach over to the edge of the stage. They spoke. Zach nodded and said something to the other band members.

"We're going to mix it up a little, and show you I'm not the only lead singer in the group!" Megan told the crowd. "Time for something slow and slinky. So grab whoever is close, hold them tight, and feel the music move your bones."

She nodded to Tim, who hit a chord. It rose, then tailed out. He hit a second chord, bending it. Zach moved up to the floor mike and started singing a ballad. It was an obscure Dylan song called "Wallflower," as I learned later in a totally unrelated moment of musicology. In the first line of the lyrics, the singer asks the wallflower to dance with him.

Juggling the sodas as I threaded through the crowd, I watched Paul put his arms out. Shelly, my date, my future partner in passion, fell into his embrace and merged with him. Flesh turned fluid. They gyrated, making love with their clothes on as their hands kneaded and caressed each other's bodies.

I stood, feeling the weight of the soda in its waxed cardboard cups. The sweat from the humid air condensed on the outside of the cups and rolled across the backs of my hands, as if my fists were weeping.

They danced.

I, still the wallflower, died a little. Not because a girl I'd lusted after seemed to be dropping me. Okay, yeah, because of that, too. But also because my friend didn't hesitate to snatch away my happiness. In five years, I'd asked out two girls. At this rate, I'd go on my next date in the middle of college. And then lose that girl to a professor.

When the song ended, Paul whispered in Shelly's ear. She smiled and kissed his cheek. It was just a peck, but she followed it with a tongue flick against his ear. Then they unwrapped themselves from each other and Paul returned to his keyboard. Shelly remained pressed against the stage, as if her hips were reluctant to give up all contact with Paul.

What to do?

What I always did. Take the kick in the crotch, smile, and see if I could fit in another blow to the gonads before the evening ended. Might as well make sure both testicles had been thoroughly crushed, for the sake of symmetry.

I edged over to Shelly and handed her a soda. It wasn't easy getting her attention.

"Thanks," she said. She glanced at me as if I were a distant billboard, then turned her eyes back to the stage.

"Sure." I stood next to her. Apart.

"Hey," she said a moment later, putting her hand on my arm. Her touch was electric in a submolecular way, sending my nerve endings into erratic behavior. I couldn't help imagining her tongue flicking at my ear in that same hungry, promising way.

"What?"

She stroked my arm. "If it's okay with you . . ."

I waited. Nothing truly requiring my permission, or even my

acquiescence, would be okay with me. And, fuck me, I wanted to absorb every pico-second of that touch, even though I knew it was a brush-off.

"Pat said he'd give me a ride home after the concert."

Pat? That threw me off.

"The band's going to the diner," she said. "Pat invited me."

Oh. "You mean, Paul?"

Even hearing the name as a correction made her smile. "Right. Paul. He's awesome. Thanks for introducing us. You're really sweet." She put her soda down on the stage. Her other hand grabbed my other arm. The lingering chill from the cup gave her palm and fingers a corpselike coolness. We were face-to-face, but worlds apart. "So, do you mind?"

"I guess not."

The hands unclenched; the arms withdrew. I took a step back, away from her. She didn't notice.

I walked outside, where I dropped my soda in a trash can by the curb.

A week later, when Paul and Shelly strolled past me in town, his arm draped across her shoulder, her arm locked around his waist, their hips in intimate contact, he nodded and smiled as if all were right with the universe. I guess it was, for him. Shelly acknowledged my existence with a stiff, slight nod. No smile. I thought I could detect a hint of a whisper of the remnants of a shred of a faded scent of guilt, but that might have been my imagination.

Paul dated Shelly for about two months. Then they broke up. She moved away during the summer. I still hung out with him once in a while. He didn't seem to have a clue what he'd done to me. Maybe being a rock star—even a small-town one—makes you less aware of the vulnerability of the people around you.

I guess, if I had any real self-respect, I would have told him how I felt. Or at least stopped hanging around with him. But sometimes *I'm with the band* fills a bigger need than *I have principles.*

away Game

I ENDED UP going to the dance after work, Saturday. Mostly because Robert and Butch picked me up at Cretaro's when I was leaving. Cannibal Gazpacho Clots, fronted by Diego Sanchez, who'd graduated two years ago, was playing. They're probably the best local band. Right after we went in, we ran into Nicky, who'd gone there by himself. He didn't seem to care about being a loner.

But he came over when he spotted me. "How's it going, muscles?" he asked. Or something like that. It was hard to tell for sure. The volume was somewhere between pulverize and ionize. But that's what we came for.

"Painfully slow," I said. I'd lifted a couple more times, but hadn't run into him in the weight room. I pointed at my friends and shouted, "Robert and Butch."

Nicky said hi. Butch dragged Robert onto the dance floor. They both dance a whole lot better than I do. So does my refrigerator. After Robert was worn out, Butch dragged Nicky to the floor. She left me undragged. She knew about my experience here with Shelly. I guess Butch knew most of my secrets, though I hadn't told her the depths of my obsession with Jillian.

After about an hour, I needed a break. I got my hand stamped, then stepped outside to grab a breath of quiet air. There was a bit of haze in the night sky, but the brighter stars were still visible. I leaned against the wall of the Crab Locker and felt the thump of the bass frequencies against my back, punching rhythmically at my shoulder blades through the bricks.

There were two guys and a girl outside, smoking. They went back inside soon after I got there. A short time later, I spotted someone walking toward me from far off. I wondered where he was coming from. There wasn't much in that direction except the state park. When he got closer, I saw it was Lucas, the Calculus neighbor with whom I did not rub shoulders. I noticed that his clothes looked especially rumpled, like he'd grabbed them from the depths of an overloaded hamper, or fallen asleep on the couch without changing for bed. When he reached me and the wind shifted, I revised my simile from a hamper to a sewer.

"Hey," I said, giving him the sort of nod you give someone you know only superficially. Even though he sat next to me in Calculus, we rarely talked. I realized he'd been out on Thursday and Friday. Maybe Wednesday, too. Between the pressure of Nola and the presence of Jillian, my mind never strayed toward his quadrant of the room.

He paused, as if I'd pushed a reset button on his master control unit and he was sorting out his prime directive. I guess he knew me about as well as I knew him.

"What's up?" I asked.

"Nothing." His gaze moved past my shoulder, toward the door. He looked kind of lost.

"Cannibal Gazpacho Clots," I said. "Diego Sanchez's group."

"Oh . . . They're playing tonight?"

"Yeah. They started a while ago, but they'll probably go for at least another hour or two."

He stuck a hand in his right front pocket. "Cover charge?"

"Yup." I could tell by the way his hand lingered that Lucas was probing an empty well. I thought about offering to pay his way inside. It wasn't a lot of money, but I worked hard for everything I made, and didn't even get to keep control of most of it.

He pulled his hand out. "I'm really not in the mood for music."

I shrugged. "No loss. They aren't playing all that great tonight." That wasn't true—they were rocking—but I didn't want him to feel bad about missing them.

He stared toward the door for a moment, and then back at me. It looked like he was about to say good-bye and head off. But before he could say anything, or I could have further thoughts about offering to pay his way inside, we both turned toward the street as a Beamer heading uptown squealed through a tight U-turn and pulled to a hard stop against the curb. For a crotch-clenching moment, as sidewall met concrete, I thought the car was going to hop the curb and crush us against the wall of the Crab Locker. But it didn't.

"Oh, fuck." Lucas said. He deflated in front of me. Rumpled and deflated isn't a good combination.

A guy got out of the driver's seat. He was big. Maybe six-two or -three. He didn't even bother to close the car door. He locked his eyes on to Lucas with laser targeting. I seemed to be invisible. For once, I was not unhappy about my apparent transparency.

I figured he'd start shouting. That's what angry adults like to do. Wrong. When he reached us, he didn't say a word. Instead, he punched Lucas right in the face. It wasn't a long, hard swing. It was a short jab. But it was backed by a lot of weight, and it was effective. Lucas staggered into the wall behind him. The punch was so violent, and so unexpected, I staggered back, too.

The guy grabbed Lucas by the collar and dragged him toward the car. If this had been an abduction, I'd like to think I would have done something the instant I recovered from my initial shock. But the guy and Lucas had enough of the same face that it was obvious they were family.

Give him thirty years of angry living and bad nutrition choices, and Lucas would morph into the image of his captor.

Lucas got shoved in the passenger side of the car. He didn't show any signs of resistance.

The guy spun back to me. I wasn't expecting that. I thought the show was over. But it looked like I'd somehow been upgraded from spectator to participant.

"What's your name?"

"Huh?" Why did he care about that?

"Your name!" I saw his fists clench. Memories of that violent punch lubricated my jaw. I had no doubt he still had rage to spend, and would be happy to spend it by placing his fist in contact with my face. Like anyone who's survived middle school and most of high school, I knew what it looked like when someone was willing to take a swing at you, and unafraid of any consequences.

I told him my name. It didn't even occur to me, at the time, to toss out a lie. Good thing. I probably would have tried to be too clever and given away my attempt at deception with an obvious fake. *My name? Norm de Plume. No, I'm Sue Donim. Just kidding. I'm Juan O'Deguys.* That would definitely have earned me a smack.

He extracted a single finger from his clenched fist and pointed it at me. "Don't think I don't know he had help running away." He walked back to the car and got inside. As he did, his shouts rolled out, crashing against the brick-filtered music that held me up from behind.

"A week! That's how long I've been looking for you!" he screamed. "You think it's better out there? Look at you. You stink. Probably been eating out of garbage cans and shitting in alleys. We'll have to burn your clothes."

The car peeled down the street, sparing me from hearing any more parental wisdom or tough love.

I didn't even know Lucas had run away. I guess he didn't run far enough. I felt stunningly stupid. Between his rumpled clothes, that sewer-tinged smell, his absence from school last week, the fact that he was probably walking from the state park, and the way he'd acted when I saw him just now, I should have figured out immediately what was going on.

Sometimes I think I see the world on a five-minute delay. No, that's not right. I see it in real time, but I understand it on a delay of five minutes, five weeks, or five years. Maybe that's why I feel so out of synch with most of the girls in school. Whatever clues or cues they're sending, I fail to receive the message. I'm freakin' cue-blind.

Poor Lucas. I could call someone. Report it. I guess that was the right thing to do. He'd definitely been abused directly in front of me. But alerting the authorities was a pretty serious step. It could set a whole chain of events into unstoppable motion.

I pictured myself testifying in court. I even imagined Lucas cursing me out for getting his father in trouble. I'd read enough teen novels to know there's some strange psychology going on when family violence is involved. I needed to think it through. I went back inside and let the noise of hyperamped music wash over me and rinse away some of the shock.

"You okay?" Butch asked. "You look weird."

I tried to tell her what had happened, but the music was too loud for any real conversation. I saved the story for the ride to Robert's house, where his mom was rumored to be awaiting us with mouthwatering treats.

When I got to the point where Lucas's father punched him, Butch flinched. Robert barely blinked. I think girls, and women, feel the impact of things that they hear more viscerally than guys. I can see that when my parents watch the news. Mom is always making sympathetic sounds. Dad doesn't react at all to stories of tragedy or disaster, except to show approval when the injured person was a criminal or a member of a football team he doesn't like—or both. I don't really react much at all unless the story involves a kick to the groin.

But I sure flinched when I *saw* Lucas get hit. And, empathetic or not, Robert, Butch, and I all agreed that it sucked.

"Did you know he ran away?" I asked.

Robert shrugged. "I didn't really know him."

"I noticed his empty seat, but I didn't have a clue it meant anything more than strep throat or an out-of-state funeral," Butch said. "Wish I'd known. I guess we could have helped him, somehow."

"Yeah," I said. "We could have."

"It's over," Robert said. "Until he runs off again."

"You think he will?" I asked.

"Would you stay with a dad like that?" he asked as we pulled up in front of his house.

"Good point," I said. I couldn't help picturing a fist crunching into my face. Poor Lucas. "I wonder why his father is such a bastard?"

"Does it matter?" Butch asked.

"Of course," I said. "There has to be an explanation."

"When my dad gets angry, there's a reason," Robert said.

"I've never seen your dad get angry," I said. Robert's dad was a cool guy. He played guitar. He and his wife sang songs together.

"That's because I'm the perfect son," Robert said. "But *if* he ever got angry, I'm sure he'd have a reason."

"We waste too much time looking for neat, clean explanations," Butch said. "If we find out that the guy's mother decapitated his teddy bear when he was a child, does that make it okay that Lucas's father is a piece of shit?"

"Not okay. But at least it makes more sense," I said.

"It *can't* make sense. That's my point," Butch said. "The bottom line is that Lucas got punched in the face. There's no excuse. There's no explanation that makes it acceptable. Don't drive yourself crazy looking for one."

Maybe she was right. But that didn't keep me from thinking about it all evening, and trying to find a way to make some sense of the violence.

DeaD wronG

SOMETIMES BAD STUFF unfolds right before your eyes.

When I was twelve, I saw one of my classmates get hit by a car.

Sometimes the bad news gets broadcast soon after it happens.

Last year, around the end of October, I heard my mother gasp while she was watching the news. It sounded a lot more personal than her usual sympathy cries. I was in the kitchen, hunting down an elusive slice of pie in the fridge. A second later, Mom called me with the panicked scream of someone who'd just had a bad encounter with the wrong end of a large kitchen knife.

"Cliff!"

I raced into the living room. She was pointing at the TV, her face half ghostly. I picked up the remote and rewound the news to the start of the story, which opened with a scene of wrecked cars and blanket-draped bodies on the westbound side of Route 46. One car had a clearly recognizable PROUD RISMORE

MARCHING BAND PARENTS bumper sticker. It turned out a freshman from our school, along with his whole family, died in a car accident on the way back from a trip to Connecticut. I didn't really know any of them, but they lived in our neighborhood.

Sometimes the bad news starts circulating the day after it happens.

When this one kid who'd been real sick—and I feel like a piece of crap for not remembering his name, but it would be cheating for me to Google it or make one up—anyhow, when he stopped coming to school, nobody thought much about it. He was out a lot. Often for weeks at a time. But a couple kids were talking one morning, maybe two weeks later, about how they'd heard he'd died the night before. They didn't have all the details, but they had the essential fact. He'd died.

Sometimes, the bad news takes its time showing up.

When Nola wasn't in class on Monday, pretty much nobody noticed except for me, and I mostly missed her for the warmth of her contact and the fuel she supplied for my daydreams.

She was out Tuesday and Wednesday, too. This was especially weird, given how Lucas had been out the week before. He was back now, with a large bruise under his left eye, and an obvious depression in his heart. We exchanged glances and nods, like weary soldiers who were veterans of the same war, and survivors of a terrible battle, but we never talked about what had happened that weekend.

Lucas reappears; Nola vanishes. Life is full of coincidences that mean nothing until we force them to fit the theories that make us feel good about the secret order and patterns of the universe, or make some sense of the senseless. I guess it's human nature to try to create fear-free symmetries. Of course, in this case, the simplest theory was that I caused people seated near me to miss school. Sometimes, simple equals stupid.

So, Nola wasn't in school on Monday, Tuesday, or Wednesday. As if in testimony to her level of invisibility, the first rumors appeared on Thursday. Sifting away the variations and discarding the wildest fragments of misinformation and absurd speculation circulating the hallways, the basic story going around was this: She'd taken a whole lot of pills from her parents' medicine cabinet last Sunday. There'd been a note. She was in a coma. She was pregnant. One of our teachers was the father of her child. She was going to die.

Confirmations and refutations trickled in, validating or eliminating the various components of the rumor. The pill part was true. So was the note part. I didn't learn the contents until later. *I'm fat and ugly. Nobody likes me. I'm sorry. I can't stand myself. Please forgive me.*

When I heard about those last written words of hers, I felt like I'd been kicked in the gut. *I liked you, Nola.* I would have been thrilled to go out with her. Even if she didn't want me to touch her.

And here is where I will rip my chest open right in front of you and reveal the darkness of my heart. Or drop my soiled shorts to the ground and show you the depth of my shittiness. Upon hearing Nola might be pregnant, I experienced the following stream, or sewer, of consciousness: *She was pregnant. That means she had sex. So maybe, if we'd gone out, she would have had sex with me.*

So there it is, laid bare. I can take even the most tragic news and find a way to use it to fantasize about my needs. About getting *laid*. I have a feeling most guys function that way, but that doesn't make me feel any better about my own twisted, selfish, lust-grubbing thoughts in the midst of this tragedy.

I tried to understand how Nola could feel so unliked, and so unlikable. She was really cute. She said she had a boyfriend. Maybe they broke up. Maybe he was one of those guys who liked to put girls down. I hoped not. She deserved to be adored.

I should have wrapped my arms around her. I should have pulled her close and told her how sexy she was, how hot and desirable. I should have ripped my attention away from the unattainable Jillian and tried to pursue the near-at-hand and right-against-my-shoulder Nola.

I tried to find any sign of her tortured self-image in our brief conversations. There was nothing. No clue how I could have gotten her to go out with me. No clue how she felt about herself.

. . . to see ourselves as others see us . . .

The coma part was true, too. Sadly, she didn't die. I say *sadly*, because she didn't really live, either. She existed. Her heart beat, unaided. Her lungs worked, with help. Her brain, her mind, her self, had moved on. For what it's worth, the pregnant part was bullshit. As, obviously, was the pregnant-by-teacher part.

I hit the weight room after school. Nicky was there.

"Did you know her?" he asked.

"Sort of," I said. "She sat next to me in Calculus. She was pretty quiet."

"You never know what someone is thinking," he said.

I searched my memories again, to see what clues Nola had scattered in my path. "You're right. I guess we all have stuff going on in our heads that nobody has a clue about. So what do you do? How do you find out what's on people's minds?"

"Ask them," he said.

"And if I asked you what you were thinking, would you tell the truth?"

"Probably not."

"Me either."

I grabbed a barbell and started doing curls. We didn't talk much more, but I was glad Nicky was there. And I think he was glad I was there. But I didn't ask him.

I never heard anything more about what happened to Nola.

As I said, I didn't find out about Nola until Thursday. I was hit with another interlocking, meaningless coincidence on Friday.

We were outside the front entrance, waiting for the morning bell, and talking about how glad we were that we didn't take shop class. Mr. Xander had returned earlier in the week and had been pretty much shouting at everyone nonstop since then. There was a patina of somberness cast across our moods, with the news about Nola so fresh in our minds. None of us wanted to talk about death, so we settled for talking about someone who'd escaped it.

"Ever think the cops will figure out who messed around with the wood supply?" Robert asked.

"I'll bet it was Clovis," Jimby said. "He's mean enough."

Robert and Butch looked at me. "Could be," I said. "But we'll never know for sure." I didn't want Jimby to have information that could get him hurt.

We drifted back into silence for a bit, until Robert said, "I can't believe he came to school today." He tilted his head toward the left.

I looked that way, wondering who in the crowd he was talking about. But then, scanning past the crowd, I realized who he meant. Lucas was walking toward the school, like he would on any other day, his backpack slung over one shoulder. But it was as if he had some sort of dark cloud about him. As he approached people, they reacted in a variety of ways. Some stiffened, like a heartless person does when passing a homeless panhandler on the street. Others seemed to grow limp, like they'd been doused with a bucket of sadness. But nearly all of them reacted to Lucas in some manner, except for Clovis and his crew, who were too busy punching each other and emulating hyenas.

"What happened to him?" I asked.

"You didn't hear?" Robert said.

"Nope. I spent all evening in the stockroom. We were doing inventory." That was the one time I had more work than I could handle. I ran a short list of possible bad news through my head. I hoped he hadn't gotten into trouble with the cops while attempting a better escape from home.

As I was reviewing my mental list of downfalls, Robert confirmed my first, worst, and saddest choice. "His dad died. Dropped dead last night. Bang. Heart attack. Dead before he hit the floor. At least, that's what I heard."

"Ouch," I said. I pictured the ruddy anger-spewing face of Lucas's father and imagined clogged arteries bulging to bursting from the pressure of rage. His sudden death was not surprising. Though it was still shocking, in a distant sort of way. We'd met only that one time—and it had been less than pleasant. But there'd been enough of an interaction to make the news of his death more personal to me, and more real.

No man is an island.

But some are volcanoes.

I pulled my mind away from my tenuous connection with

the man and returned it to the impact this had on Lucas. "That sucks."

"Does it?" Robert asked.

Good point. I thought back to the day less than a week ago when I'd seen Lucas get punched in the face and dragged off by his dad. Lucas was probably better off now. But having your dad drop dead like that—it had to suck in some ways. Even if, in Lucas's case, it was also a relief. And, not to get too deep into spirals of analysis, but I'd have to think that if Lucas felt relief at his dad's death, that would make him feel guilty. Toss in the guilt he probably felt for being a source of stress in his dad's life, and you've got a hornet's nest of bad feelings stinging you.

Shit. Sometimes a guy just couldn't win.

"I hope he had a ton of life insurance," Butch said.

As Lucas continued his walk, I realized he'd pass right by me. I couldn't pretend I didn't see him, or skitter off before he got here. I had to acknowledge his existence, if not his pain. What can you possibly say to a guy whose abusive father just dropped dead? *Hey, what's up?* A dozen fragments of conversation rolled through my brain. All of them sucked. It was better to just nod and keep my mouth shut.

Lucas moved closer. His head was down. That would make it easier. But right before he reached me, he looked up. Our eyes met.

"Hey, what's up?" I said.

He shrugged. "Nothing."

And then he walked on.

courage in profiles

ROBERT AND I headed into town after school. I needed to get my mom a present for Mother's Day. Robert had done his shopping already, but he was happy to help me spend my money. Butch was going to meet us after she finished a makeup test. That was good, because Robert's taste in gifts was even worse than mine.

Parking was scarce around the Green, so he left his car in the student lot, and we walked. When we swung left onto Jefferson at the top of Vorhees, Robert said, "I can tell right where I am with my eyes closed."

"For sure." The first block had some of Rismore's older stores. Most had been there from way before I was born. I closed my eyes as I passed Drago's Shoe Repair. The mix of leather and shoe polish was unmistakable. Two shops over, Alexander's Modern Barber Shop, which had been in the same spot for at least fifty years, wafted the scent of talcum powder and hair tonic out the door. After a scentless stretch of shops, mid-block, we passed Jim's Deli. Right before the end of the block, the mouthwatering air of Alfredo's Pizza wafted over us.

There was a large department store across from the Green, on the southwest corner, and two small gift shops on that same block. We went into one of them, the Plucked Ptarmigan. The place had a lot of high-priced small stuff I would normally never look at, like napkin rings and candleholders. But I was really just killing time until Butch showed up.

As Robert and I cruised an aisle with silk scarves and knitted hats, I noticed the store owner was following us. She'd been behind us in the previous aisle, too. That was strange. Clerks usually ignored me, even when I stood there and stared at them, waiting to be offered help. When I looked at our stalker, she turned away and made a show of adjusting one of the scarves.

"Hey," I whispered to Robert when we reached the end of the aisle. "You go down that way. I'll meet you at the other end."

I pointed to the left. He gave me a quizzical look. But then he glanced toward the owner, nodded, and went to the left. I went down an aisle to the right. Sure enough, the owner followed Robert. As you may have deduced by now, though I'm personally too immersed in my own racial identity to be aware of what might or might not telegraph it, I'm white. Robert is black, with just enough stray Dutch genes scattered through his background, thanks to distant ancestors on his father's side from Saint Martin, to allow him to make the occasional hilarious cocoa or chocolate joke. The funny thing is, at some point each summer, if I'm doing a lot of yard work, my skin gets just as dark as his.

I rejoined Robert at the end of the aisle. "Let's get out of here."

I tilted my head in the direction of the owner, caught her eye, raised my voice, and said, "She's totally profiling you."

Robert flashed me a grin. "Of course she is. I have a handsome profile." He cocked his head at a stylish angle.

I was going to correct him, but I saw in the expression that remained after the grin faded that he knew far too well what I meant. As for the owner, she'd given up all pretense and stared right at the two of us. I had a feeling she was seconds away from screaming for help.

I raised my voice. "There's nothing but crap in here. Let's go." Then, at a volume meant just for Robert, I added, "That sucks."

"It does," he said. "But when something happens all the time, you get used to it."

"That doesn't make it right," I said. "You should steal something, just to teach her a lesson."

"But then she would be right about me," he said.

"It would still be wrong of her." I pushed open the door. "Let's wait for Butch on the Green." I didn't feel like doing more shopping right now. If another merchant followed Robert. I was pretty sure I'd start shouting even louder.

As we stepped outside, Amanda, the captain of the cheerleading squad, squeezed past us, along with her friend Kimberly.

"I'll bet they never get profiled," I said.

"They have nice profiles, too." Robert had locked his eyes on them, through the glass door. "I like their rearfiles even better."

I followed his gaze. The two were definitely attractive. Kimberly went up to the manager, who smiled at her. They talked for a moment. Then the manager nodded and led her down an aisle at the far right of the store.

"Whoa," Robert said. "Check this out." He pointed to the left.

"Been there. Done that," I said. "I am not as endlessly obsessed with every female who walks by as you seem to be."

"No, you're just obsessed with one. But that's not what I'm talking about." Robert clamped his hand on top of my head and turned it so I was looking toward the left side of the store.

"Am I that obvious?" I asked as I watched Amanda, who had split off from Kimberly, take several scarves from a display and slip them inside her shirt.

"It's like you're wearing a sign with a big scarlet *J* on it," he said.

Wonderful. "Do you think it's obvious to her?"

"No. I think you're safely invisible," he said.

Even more wonderful. I turned my attention back to the thievery unfolding on the other side of the window. "She'll probably blame you when she discovers the scarves are missing," I said.

I was sort of joking, but I could see Robert's jaw clench. A whole scenario flashed through my mind. The owner called the cops. She described Robert. Maybe even mentioned his accent. Luckily, my imagination also offered a way to derail that particular train of thought.

I pushed the door back open, pointed to the left, and called, "Amanda, those are beautiful scarves you picked. You should buy both of them." I didn't wait to see what happened, but I was pretty sure Amanda was reaching down her shirt to retrieve the scarves. And, yeah, I savored that image in my mind in slow motion.

We crossed the street and grabbed a bench.

"Thanks," Robert said.

"Anytime."

When Butch showed up, she vetoed the department store and

dragged us down a side street to a placed called Déjà Too Cool that made everything out of recycled material. To my relief, the owner greeted us pleasantly and then turned her attention back to the customer at the register. I didn't sense even a hint of distrust.

"It's all from local crafters," Butch said. "Hey, this one is perfect for your mom." She held up a bracelet made of tiny silvery frying pans and plucked chickens. "It's recycled aluminum. Maybe some of it started out as foil that was used to cook chicken. Wouldn't that be a perfect cycle of life?"

As I stared at it, she laughed and put it back. "Kidding."

"I knew that." I stood aside and let her hunt.

Several minutes later, she zeroed in on a small, pretty bracelet made of copper wire that had once carried cable TV signals but was now woven in an intricate lacelike pattern, threaded through tiny polished semiprecious gems. "This," she said.

"That?" I asked.

"Yes," she said. "It complements the color of her favorite blouse."

"My mom has a favorite blouse?" I asked.

Butch responded with a prolonged sigh. But she was right—the bracelet was a good choice for my mom. And it was in my price range.

As we were leaving the store, Robert put his hand on my shoulder. "Let it go," he said.

"Let what go?" I asked.

"You know," he said.

He was right. I knew what he meant. I was still angry about the woman at that other store. I thought about ways to get even with her, or to do damage.

"I'm not sure I know how," I said.

"Picture an angry person," he said. "Someone who is mad about everything. Someone who is never happy. Someone who takes every insult to heart, and hates the world. Someone who enjoys being a victim. Is that who you want to be?"

"No," I said. "Definitely not."

"Then let it go."

I tried.

OUT OF CONCERT

THE MACK AND Mary concert was on Saturday, the weekend after Lucas's father died. Mom and Dad went out that evening, to some kind of seminar on investing in stocks for retirement, so I didn't even have to leave the house and pretend to go to the concert. They weren't really interested in investing, and right now we really didn't have anything to invest, but the evening included a free meal. Around the time the music would be starting at the college, I headed out back to sit at the table and feel sorry for myself. I hoped, at least, that Ms. Ryder was enjoying the show.

Right after I got settled, but before I could release more than two or three deep, meaningful sighs, or relive the moment when Patricia decapitated me with the sharp blade of harsh truths, I heard Jimby walking over. There was no sign of his usual grin, and he didn't sit down across from me like he normally would.

He looked like someone whose dog had just been shot. Good thing he didn't have one.

"What's up?" I asked. "Are you okay?"

"People call me stupid all the time," he said.

"Hey, sticks and stones," I said, which was sort of hypocritical, given that I was currently brooding about hurtful words.

Jimby frowned. "What do you mean?"

"You know." I told him the whole saying.

He nodded in recognition. "I've heard that. But it's not really true."

"You're right. It's not true. But it's supposed to make people feel better, or help us cope, or something like that." I glanced toward his house. I hadn't heard any of the lively voices or loud music that would indicate his mom had made a new friend who liked to party. The guys she attracted didn't always treat Jimby very nicely. On top of that, I'm pretty sure he was a lot smarter than most of them. "You don't usually care what people say. Did something bad happen?"

"We have to write a story for English," he said. "I like stories. I figured I could write a really good one. And get a good grade. If you get a good grade, people can't call you stupid. Right?"

"That's for sure," I said.

"But I tried. I tried hard." He kicked the bench. "I don't know how to write a story!"

"Chill, man. It's not that hard."

Jimby shot me a fierce look.

Damn it. I'd just done something I totally hate when I see other people do it. I see it in school, and I see it online all the time. As soon as you say something is hard, or ask for help, whether you're trying to prove a trigonometric theorem or beat the final boss in a video game, some anonymous bully basically says, "That was easy. I did it on my first try. You must be stupid."

It's not that hard.

"Hey, I'm sorry, Jimby. I wasn't thinking. I forgot how hard it was the first time I wrote a story. You're right—it's not easy. I had to write a whole bunch of stuff before I got used to making up stories and it started to feel easy." I pointed to the bench. "Grab a seat. All you need is one good idea. We'll brainstorm."

"Is that cheating?" he asked. "We're supposed to do our own work. I don't cheat."

"No. It's okay to talk about ideas. As long as you write the story on your own, it's fine. You're not cheating. Even Shakespeare got his ideas from all over the place. Hang on. I'll be right back."

I ran inside for a notepad and a pen. I figured it would be a good idea for Jimby to write down any ideas we came up with. That way, he'd put them in his own words.

When I got back to the table, I asked him, "What kind of story do you want to write?"

"A good one," he said.

"Maybe you can think of something amazing," I said. "Amazing stories are always good."

He chewed at that thought for a minute, then shook his head. "I don't even know how to start. I told you I can't do this."

"Sure you can. Stop thinking about stories. Think about adventures. What would be something amazing for *you* to do?"

That brought an instant answer, and the return of his grin. "Fly," he said.

"Good. Real good. Write that down. What else?"

"Fight zombies." That got a bigger grin.

"For sure. Maybe you can even put a couple ideas together. What if you could fly and fight zombies?" I asked.

"Yeah! I could fly real fast with a pair of samurai swords." He jumped up on the table, leaned over at the waist, and stuck his hands wide out to the sides. "I'd just hold the swords like this and slice their heads off."

"That would be double awesome. Write that down. But let's keep going. I want to see if you can come up with five or ten good ideas."

It turned out that brainstorming with Jimby was a lot of fun. He didn't always think in straight lines, but his thoughts definitely weren't random. Even the most puzzling topical leaps he hurled at me made sense when I gave them some thought. The universe inside his head operated by a set of consistent rules. They just weren't the standard set accepted by society, which made the journey pretty interesting and enjoyable. It was sort of like being on a roller coaster that didn't need tracks and sometimes refused to believe in gravity.

A half hour later, Jimby had a page full of ideas written down on the pad, ranging from our initial flying zombie fighter to vampire mobsters and a private, steerable one-man air balloon. He had more than enough for a story. And I had the satisfied feeling that comes with doing something creative. The story wasn't due for three weeks, so he'd have plenty of time to work on it.

As he got up to head back home, I said, "Hey, good job. You're pretty creative."

"Thanks, Cliff. So are you."

His grin stayed with me after he left, softening my sadness as my thoughts returned to the concert I was missing.

SUNDAY, I WAS eager to give Mom her present, but I'd have to wait a bit. She was scheduled to work until midafternoon. Since I knew she'd be away, I picked up a morning shift at Moo Fish. There were plenty of kids who wanted to have the whole day off.

"I got Mom something," I told Dad as I was grabbing some cereal before heading out.

Dad shot me a glare. "Will you ever learn to stop wasting money?"

"It's *Mother's Day*," I said. "I had to get her something."

"You could have made something. She loves your art crap."

I opened my mouth to defend my purchase, but the words didn't come. Shit. For once, he was right. I could have made her something. But he wasn't totally right. Store-bought presents are nice.

Even with my shift at work, I got home before Mom. The instant she came in, I met her at the door and handed her the present.

"Happy Mother's Day." I watched as she unwrapped the box and lifted out the glittery copper bauble.

"It's lovely," she said, slipping it over her hand. "Just perfect. It matches my favorite blouse. You have great taste."

"Thanks." I figured it was okay not to confess that what I really had was great taste in friends, not jewelry.

I made dinner for the three of us that night. Luckily, the weather was nice, so I was able to grill hot dogs. That's about the only thing I know how to make, not counting cereal, or mac and cheese from a box.

After dinner, when Dad was taking out the garbage, Mom asked me, "So, how was the concert?"

My brain tested a variety of answers that wouldn't be outright lies, and quickly settled for, "It was an amazing night."

My gift for Mom has no further significance. On the other hand, Mom's gift to me, which I regifted, set unpredictable and significant events into motion.

impermanent
Records

WEDNESDAY, MS. RYDER plopped a cardboard box on her desk, opened the flaps, and lifted out a turntable, followed by a small amplifier and speakers.

"You all know what this is?" she said.

"First generation iPod," Peter said.

The rest of us nodded.

"I was at a concert this weekend," Ms. Ryder said. "And it got me thinking. A decade is defined as much by its music as anything else. And part of the musical experience is in the delivery."

She moved down the aisle to where Zach was sitting, reached under the hair that draped over his ears, and plucked out his earbuds.

"We walk around plugged in. In their youth, your parents might have listened to a Walkman or a Discman. Their parents had phonographs. Their grandparents had the radio. Go back a bit further, and the only option was live music. Your own children might listen to music that's streamed directly into their brains. Their children—who knows? How many of you have phonograph records in the attic?"

I raised my hand. I knew there were three or four of those plastic milk crates filled with record albums in our basement. A few of the records belonged to my parents. The rest had belonged to my grandfather. I'd glanced through them once or twice, but anything I wanted to listen to was available a lot more easily in digital form.

"Bring in an album that interests you," Ms. Ryder said. "Or that helps define something significant about its decade. We can start listening to them tomorrow, and continue on Friday."

"Will we be graded on this?" Abbie asked.

"I hadn't planned on it," Ms. Ryder said. "But I don't mind using it as extra credit for anyone who needs a boost. Especially if your choice reveals something about the reactions of the people to the actions of their government."

Creature of habit that I am, I glanced at Jillian as I imagined myself bringing in the most amazing album of anyone in the class. Of course, I had no idea what sort of music she would find amazing.

Mr. Piccaro caught up with me on the way out of school. I'd dawdled with the short stories, nibbling them as if they were exotic chocolates given to me as a onetime gift. A more crass person might say I'd stretched out my Dick, but I wasn't the sort to make such a crude joke. When I tore off the wrapper, I found a Post-it stuck over the title, with the words *I didn't give you this* written on it. That piqued my interest, because he'd put similar disclaimers on several other books—most memorably, *Fear and Loathing in Las Vegas*. I lifted the note and read the title:

Geek Love. I liked it already. And I knew, despite the note, that while Mr. Piccaro might give me books that were shocking, disturbing, or, to use a word he taught us last year, iconoclastic, he'd never give me something truly inappropriate. Though, at my age, I don't think there's much I can't, or shouldn't, handle. If something were deeply disturbing and wrong for me, I'd stop reading on my own.

When I got home, I headed straight for the basement, where the records, and a record player, awaited me. Most of the albums were rock and roll, with a mix of groups I knew and groups who were total mysteries. There were too many to listen to all the way through, but I figured I'd pull out the ones I wasn't familiar with and check out a track or two on each of them.

Most of the rock was pretty much what I expected. I liked Santana and the Doors. I wasn't crazy about Blood, Sweat & Tears. There were a couple folksingers from the 1960s mixed in. I guess that music would have told a lot about the decade. They sang songs protesting pretty much everything. One guy, David Bromberg, played good guitar, including a lot of blues. But that's not what got my attention. As I was scanning the back of the album cover, which had a stupid picture on front of him on the Empire State Building swatting at airplanes like King Kong, my eyes met a title that nearly killed my enthusiasm for the musical hunt. "Wallflower." That was the song Paul and Shelly had danced to.

I felt my mind tipping in the direction of self-pity. "Screw it," I said, tossing that album aside. I wasn't in the mood to wallow. I continued the hunt.

When I reached *Southbound*, with its bland green cover, I almost skipped over it. The guy on front had his eyes half closed. That struck me as kind of pretentious. I felt bad later, when I learned he was blind and really didn't have much choice about how he looked. He was leaning his chin on his hand, which rested on the head of his guitar. The album cover looked pretty worn. Maybe someone in the family really liked this one.

I put the record on the turntable, then flipped the cover over to see what song was first. "Walk On Boy." I'd never heard of it, but those three words sounded like good advice. Maybe I should do that. Walk away from the assignment. Walk away from my obsession with Jillian. If Robert was already aware of it, other people would figure it out, sooner or later. The last thing I wanted was to have the whole school laughing at me.

But I'd already invested a lot of time in listening to the records. I wasn't going to quit just yet. Besides, I'd enjoyed much of what I heard. I even got a kick out of sampling the music I didn't like, just for what it revealed about past decades. I guess Ms. Ryder really knew what she was doing.

I lowered the tonearm onto the first track. The guy, Doc Watson, had a good voice. But the song didn't do much for me. I was about to go to the next album, when I noticed the third cut. "Sweet Georgia Brown" was the song the Harlem Globetrotters played when they did their trick basketball stuff. And it had been the opening number of our jazz band concert sophomore year. I'd always thought of it as a band piece. I couldn't imagine it being played by one guy on a guitar, backed up with nothing but an acoustic bass.

I moved the needle past the intervening song and lowered it in place at the start of track three. After a bit of crackly emptiness, the guitar kicked in.

And the guitar kicked ass.

Wow.

When the song ended, I played it again.

Yeah, wow.

This guy had some serious guitar-picking skills. He'd played a couple nice licks in "Walk On Boy," but that was a slow song and he hadn't cut loose. Here, he'd floored the pedal and punched the turbo. I halfway remember asking if I could take guitar lessons, way back in third or fourth grade, after Mom took me to a kiddie folk-rock concert, but I think Dad had shot that idea down. I'd fooled around on the guitar a little in middle school, and played with Tim's guitar a couple of times when I was hanging out at one of Jersey Bayou's practices. I stunk at it. But I could recognize brilliance when I heard it. Most guitarists I knew, except for Robert's dad, played electric. This was acoustic. Un-amped, unfuzzed, un-anythinged. Pure steel strings, ringing out.

Plucking amazing.

I went upstairs, made a peanut butter sandwich, brought it back down, and listened to the whole album. That was not a Herculean task. Records, back then, weren't very long. But they could be very good. *Southbound* has seven songs on each side. The longest was just over three and a half minutes; the shortest, just under two.

Some of the songs were sappy. Some of the lyrics would make a college English major puke. But the guitar playing on nearly every cut blew me away. I had a feeling all the musicians in class would react that way, too. Especially any of them who'd ever picked up a guitar. They'd probably never even heard of Doc Watson—I sure hadn't—so it was like I'd be showing them music they knew nothing about. Several of the kids in class were into country music. But this wasn't country. It was something much more traditional, without the twang. I was pretty sure

Zach and Tim would like it. And Paul. I hated to admit it, but I guess I still wanted to impress him.

As I slid *Southbound* back in its sleeve, I pictured Tim coming up to me after class and begging to borrow the album. I imagined Zach saying, *Dude, where'd you find that? It's awesome.*

I looked at the stack of records on the floor. I'd sampled about twenty albums. There was no need to listen to the rest right now. I had what I needed. Though I might do that someday, just to see what else I could discover.

When I put the records back, I noticed an old manila envelope in one of the crates. There were some faded photos inside. As I looked at the first one, I think I came within a hundredth of a second of sending myself into a lifetime of psychotherapy or guilt-driven alcoholic binge drinking. It was a picture of three men and two women, standing in some kind of park, near a huge willow tree at the edge of a stream. The guys, two with guitars, one with an acoustic bass, had long hair and drooping mustaches. They all wore work shirts, untucked, over jeans. One woman, who held a flute and wore a skirt and loose white blouse, was pretty. The other, in a flowing dress, was—and here is where I had my close call—much more than just pretty. I think my brain was about a nanosecond away from offering up the observation, *She's hot,* when a deeper, reptilian beast near my spine made a desperate adrenaline-fueled sprint and blind-side tackled that thought out of bounds at the two-yard line by screaming IT'S YOUR MOTHER!

So, yeah, I was within a fraction of a second of drooling over a photo of my mom and having my mind run wild with the usual guy fantasies that burst loose whenever I saw a picture of an attractive female.

A shudder of relief, twined with instinctual tabooistic revulsion, shook my mind and body like a hard-plucked bass string.

That was close.

As I mulled over my narrow escape, I took a closer, much-more-clinical look at the photo. Obviously, they were some sort of musical group. My mom was holding a violin. Or, I guess, in a group like that, it would be thought of as a fiddle.

There were several more photos of the group, along with a newspaper clipping. Zephyrs and Dreams, all sophomores at the time, had played a concert at the Rutgers student center as part of the entertainment during freshman orientation.

Cool. I never knew my mom had been in a folk group. She and Dad had met during her senior year, when he was taking graduate classes. He'd gotten his undergrad degree in some sort of finance at Bucknell. It's funny she'd never mentioned the band, or that she'd played the fiddle. I guess she didn't keep it. I'd never seen one around.

"SO, WHO BROUGHT an album?" Ms. Ryder asked.

More than a dozen hands went up. I spotted the obvious choices arranged on desks around me: the Beatles, Grateful Dead, Nirvana. Abbie had a half dozen albums spread out in front of her, along with a stack of file cards. It looked like she was prepared to give a period-long lecture on the significance of her selections. I'd done some research, just in case I had to justify my choice as reflecting something about an era, and found that Doc Watson had risen from obscurity as part of the huge folk revival of the 1960s. And the folk revival was a reflection of the restlessness of the youth of that era, generated in large part as a reaction to government military and social policies.

CHARACTER, DRIVEN | 163

We listened to a Dylan song first, chosen by Zach. Another meaningless coincidence. If the song had been "Wallflower," I'd begin to question the benevolence of the author of my existence. But, being spared that level of synchronicity, I could continue to question, instead, the existence of my author. Wait—considering what you hold in your hands, I'm my author. And my authority. No questions asked.

Let's get back to class.

The song was "Mr. Tambourine Man." I actually kind of like Dylan, even though he sounds like he's being squeezed by a medium-sized monster when he sings. After that, we heard a couple rock songs and one of Abbie's selections, which was an antiwar protest song from the Vietnam Era called "I Ain't Marching Anymore." Abbie, of course, first had to talk for five minutes about the incorrectness of "ain't."

Then, totally off the wall, Peter pulled out an album by a guy who called himself Napoleon XIV. He passed the cover around so everyone could admire it. There were some wild titles. I was bummed Peter didn't offer us "The Place Where the Nuts Hunt the Squirrels." The song he picked was "They're Coming to Take Me Away, Ha-Haaa." I have to admit, it was nicely twisted.

"Not politically correct," Ms. Ryder said. "It's obviously from a time when less sympathy and understanding was offered to those suffering from mental illness. But humor is one way society tackles important issues, often by crossing the boundary of good taste."

Someone in the back let out a fart sound.

"Point proved," Ms. Ryder said, giving Marty Brownstain a stare. "I'm pleased you understand the importance of classroom participation."

"Or farticipation," Peter said, recycling his classic joke.

Ms. Ryder ignored him. I couldn't help comparing her calm manner with the frantic, overstressed reactions of Mr. Strawbroke, or the incessant shouting of Mr. Tippler.

"Seriously," she said, "we should take a look at humor before the year ends. Some of the most memorable political moments in history generated displays of sharp wit in a variety of media—film, editorial cartoons, songs, and stage plays. Satirical humor often displeases the people in power. If you look back at some of the things our government has attempted to censor, you'd be surprised. Try Googling 'Lenny Bruce' or 'the Smothers Brothers.' The acceptable and forbidden targets of humor at any point in history reveal a lot about a society. But let's get back to the music. Who's next?"

I checked the clock. There was time for only one or two more songs before the period ended. I hated the idea of waiting until the next class. And I had this crazy fear that someone else would offer up Doc Watson before I had my chance. Luckily, Ms. Ryder picked me from among the remaining candidates. I'd narrowed my selection to one of three tracks, all instrumentals. "Nashville Pickin'" and "Nothing to It" were killer flat-picked numbers and the two strongest candidates. "Windy and Warm" was finger-picked, and wonderful in a fluid, melodic way, but not so much of a showpiece. I figured "Sweet Georgia Brown," as brilliantly as Doc Watson played it, wouldn't be appreciated, since it was used so much commercially.

I pulled the album from the sleeve, spreading my grip wide so I touched only the center hole and the edge of the record.

"Can I see that jacket?" Ms. Ryder asked.

"Sure." I handed the sleeve to her and put the album on the turntable. After a bit more contemplation, I decided to go with "Nothing to It." As I lifted up the arm and imagined the awestruck faces of my classmates when the dazzling guitar work reached their ears, I heard Ms. Ryder let out a small squeal, like she'd spotted a cluster of kittens.

She scurried over to me. "Oh, Cliff, I love this song. Play this one!" she said, tapping the back of the cover.

I saw where her finger rested, and felt a wave of doom and despair erase all my fantasies of triumph and glory. My life was about to come to a tragic end.

CHERRY BOMB

"THE RIDDLE SONG."

Oh, for the love of God, no. Please, no. Not that one. That was the totally sappy song about giving your love a cherry. That was the song that made John Belushi go apeshit in that old movie, *Animal House,* and turn a guitar into a shower of splinters with a series of marvelous aim-for-the-fences power swings. That was the song I would have immediately deleted from a digital version of *Southbound* right after I purchased the album. That was the song that would mark me as existing farther beyond the outermost boundaries of pathetic-loser land than anyone should ever have to venture. On top of all that, it was the song with the least guitar work. No hot licks. No lightning-speed breaks. Just treacle and rose water.

I gave Ms. Ryder a silent pleading look.

My silent pleading look sucks. Her silent ooohhh-I-love-that-song look beat me down like paper beats rock. Or stone beats cherry.

I considered dropping the tonearm too hard, breaking the needle. Nice fantasy, but I was gutless when it came to intentionally ruining things.

I placed the tonearm where it belonged and watched as the needle followed the widely spaced spiral path that separated songs in the ancient, dusty days of analog recordings.

After a pleasant but undazzling fingerpicked guitar intro, the first words rose from the speakers in Doc Watson's melodic voice.

I gave my love a cherry that had no stone.
I gave my love a chicken that had no bone.

By the time the lyrics reached *stone*, half the guys in the class were exchanging amused glances. By *bone*, there was unrestrained laughter. I saw Peter make a jerk-off gesture with his curled right hand while mouthing the word "bone." I knew, given the lyrics that were coming, that this could only get worse.

I gave my love a baby with no crying.
And told my love a story that had no end.

It went on. Hilarity ensued. Clovis Hunt, an incurable brute to his very core, crossed his eyes, turned the rest of his face even stupider looking than usual, and played air guitar. Not electric air guitar, of course, with forward-thrashing head bangs. It was twangy, loose-wristed country acoustic air guitar, with sideways head sways and a mocking leer. I wanted to point at Clovis and shout, *He tried to kill Mr. Xander!* As tempting as that was, I realized it wouldn't rescue me from my current torture.

Peter was laughing so hard, he fell off his chair. Sadly, he didn't break his neck. Or his bone. Marty was playing along with a hand cupped under his armpit.

All that prevented me from dropping to my knees right there and piercing my heart with the sharp end of the stick that held the flag of Ethiopia suspended over the THIS IS WHERE WE ARE TODAY sign Ms. Ryder used with her freshman geography class, was the brevity of the song. Three verses. That's all she wrote. Or he. Or them. No. Not them. No way it took more than one lyricist to create this vat of vapid syrup. Thank goodness it wasn't a ballad. Some of those had ten or fifteen verses.

When the song ended, and the last cherry had been left unstoned, I thought about asking Ms. Ryder if I could play another track. Doc Watson could pick the hell out of a guitar. Even a hard-core rock fan would appreciate his skill. But I knew nothing could redeem this moment. Anything I tried would somehow turn tragic in a half-comic and thoroughly humiliating way. Right now, I was standing in front of the class in my underwear. The next step would leave me buck naked with an erection.

Abbie, ever eager to use the backs of even the lowest of the fallen as stepping stones, raised her hand and pointed out that my song lacked political relevance. That was pretty far down on my list of troubles at the moment. Feeling hellbound, I retrieved *Southbound*. The record, at least, had the luxury of napping within the comforting confines of a dark sleeve. Not me. I had to pass through the gauntlet of classmates.

Amused eyes followed me as I oozed down the aisle to my

seat. Comments pitched just low enough to avoid being thwarted by our teacher pelted me from all sides.

"Cherry boy."

"Ohhhh, lovely song."

"Rock on!"

Ms. Ryder, in a rare moment of less than stellar pedagogy, seemed so enthralled by the magic spell the song had weaved in the air that she appeared unaware my classmates were irreparably damaging my self-esteem.

I was even awarded with a spontaneously composed song parody, courtesy of Peter.

> *I gave my love a penis that had no sperm.*
> *I gave my love a dumb song that made her squirm.*
> *I gave my love a baby that crapped its pants.*
> *And told my love a story about eggplants.*

Afterwards, I consoled myself by realizing that, as a song parodist, Peter totally petered out at the end. But that was far, far afterwards, when the universe once again allowed for the existence of elements other than angst, self-pity, and mortification. This was now. And I was eager for now to be over and forgotten.

One set of eyes in this troubled sea of mockery followed my path but didn't seem to mock.

Jillian.

I looked away when I realized I was staring at her. My face burned even hotter as I entertained the delusion that the song had somehow touched her. *Don't kid yourself.* I knew that in reality, one song, a song I hadn't even wanted to play for the class, would never be enough to get Jillian to glance at me for longer than the fifteen seconds of shame I'd been awarded, or to think of me as anything other than a slobbering spouter of monosyllabic gibberish.

A moment later, Tim was standing at the turntable, and John Fogerty, lead singer of Credence Clearwater Revival, was howling in his magical semi-indecipherable way about getting stuck in Lodi. Lucky him. I would have killed for that sort of easy-to-solve problem. One way or another, no matter how badly stuck you might be, you can get out of Lodi. Or decide it isn't so bad after all. Wherever it is.

At least I wasn't still in the spotlight. I'd live. But I'd have nightmares. With music in the background. But no hot licks. I'd suffer in a purgatory of slow-strummed chords and nauseating lyrics.

I didn't even bother going home after school. I headed out of town, past the bridge over Kilmer's Creek, and then up the gravel road that cut through the heart of Clark Rismore State Park. There are fields of tall grass on both sides of the road. On one side, the fields border dense woods. The other side leads to an overlook. It's an impressive view of the valley, filled with rolling hills and vast stretches of forest.

I saw two people to my left, sitting under one of the trees that were scattered across the field. It was Brad and Christopher. I turned off the road and cut to the right. The woods seemed like the best place to nurse my wounds.

"Cliff! Hey, Cliff!"

I looked over my shoulder. Christopher was waving at me. I was surprised he even knew my name. I gave him a halfhearted wave in response. He motioned for me to join them.

Trick?

As I approached, I expected them to leap to their feet, shout, *Loser!* and start laughing.

But when I got closer, Christopher just said, "Hey, what's up?"

"Nothing. Walking," I said.

"I love this place," Brad said. "It's so full of . . . nature."

"Yeah." I searched their faces. I didn't want to assume they would keep talking to me. But they didn't have that *Piss off, pissant!* scowl so many of the popular kids had mastered. They were among the minuscule subsection of popular kids who didn't seem to need to enhance their status by trashing others. "Kind of makes you think," I said, turning toward the overlook. I inhaled a lungful of scenery.

"For sure," Christopher said. "It's like we're in this enormous, endless universe. We're just ants. Or bacteria. But we're important bacteria."

"I know," I said. "I think about that stuff, too." Though I also knew that if the universe was endless, it wasn't necessary to also call it "enormous." But that was not the sort of observation that encouraged further conversation. I squatted, easing my way toward getting seated on common ground, but still allowed myself room to rise and exit without awkward acrobatics if it became obvious they didn't want my company.

"Cosmic," Brad said. "It just hit me—if you think something and I think something, how do we know we aren't having the same thought?"

"We *are* having the same thought," I said.

"No," Brad said, shaking his head violently. "I mean the *same* thought. Two minds—one thought."

"Like if we see the same piece of pie?" I asked.

"I love pie," Christopher said.

"Yeah!" Brad shouted. "That's what I mean. It's like if two

people have the same idea, or even the same headache. Maybe it's one thing. Like they're sharing it."

I wasn't sure I agreed with that, or even totally followed his argument, but it felt good to have a real, genuine conversation with socially desirable members of our schoolciety. Maybe, if being seen at a concert with me could suck Patricia down among the dregs and sully her image beyond repair, hanging out with Brad and Christopher could lift me up a bit. Or a lot. Even though I sort of resented their inexplicable, intangible luck-of-the-draw popularity, it was impossible not to like them.

"I'd share my pie," Christopher said. "Unless it was a small piece. Then there wouldn't be much point. You need to eat a certain amount of pie for it to really count. A sliver just isn't satisfying. You need a critical mess."

Brad stared at him. I thought he was going to tell Christopher to stop talking. Instead, he said, "Let's get some pie!"

"Yeah." Christopher shoved his hand in his pocket and pulled out some singles and a ten. "We can totally do that."

So we went to the diner and had pie. And continued our discussion about our place as ants or bacteria in the cosmic enormousness of a universe where ideas and headaches might be independently existing entities that could be shared, and where the slices of strawberry pie at the Krome Kadillac Diner were big enough that you could share one if necessary, but all the more wonderful when there was no need for subdivision. I noticed that Molly, our waitress, had given me the biggest slice. I liked her. And I always left a good tip. I knew how hard people worked in restaurants, and I knew how much tips helped when you don't get paid very much. I didn't get tips at Moo Fish, but I got them when I bagged groceries.

After the last jellied smears of the pie on my plate had been finger-swiped and licked out of existence, I tossed some money on the table to cover my share of the bill. "Thanks," I said as I slipped out of the booth. I wanted to stay longer, but I needed to get some of my homework done before dinner.

"Thanks for what?" Christopher said.

I opened my mouth. As usual, the words I'd planned to say seemed stupid on close examination.

Thanks for . . .

. . . talking to me.

. . . talking with me.

. . . letting me sit in a public place with you.

. . . inviting me for pie.

. . . sharing your feelings about the universe.

. . . treating me like I matter.

. . . listening to my ideas.

"Just thanks," I said.

As I left the diner, Maddie and Patricia walked in. Damn. If I'd dawdled for sixty more seconds, they would have seen me hanging out in a booth with Christopher and Brad. Instead, they saw me leaving by myself, as an apparent loner. Patricia looked away. Maddie, at least, nodded at me. We'd long ago reached the point where we could comfortably breathe the same air for a brief period without causing each other undue stress. I no longer lusted after her. She no longer fled and hid. As much as I regretted the missed opportunity to show the two of them what they'd lost when they'd fled from me, I knew I'd have lots more opportunities to shine with reflected glory, now that I'd been invited into the world of the popular guys.

I headed home, feeling a bit less destroyed by the fierce mocking I'd experienced in Government class. I smiled as the word *paisano* flitted through my mind. In Italian, it meant "pal" or "good friend." But I guess it could also, in my universe, mean one with whom you can share pie.

Was it this easy to make new friends? I mean, I had friends. I was glad I knew Robert, Butch, and Jimby, and that I'd gotten to know Nicky. But we all were on the fringe, whether by fate or choice. As much as misery loves company, misery adores acceptance. Maybe I was finally learning how to interact with the popular kids. Maybe I could become one of them.

WHEN I GOT home, Mom was in the kitchen, making a cup of tea. "Your Dad went out for a job interview in East Rutherford," she said. "Keep your fingers crossed."

"I will." That would be a wish come true. I tried to remember what it felt like to walk into an empty house after school.

"How was your day?" she asked.

There were no words for the highs and lows I'd experienced this afternoon, so I offered a shrug and a grunt.

Apparently, the shrug, the grunt, or the two of them in combination communicated more than I'd wanted.

"What's wrong?" Mom asked.

I couldn't take her where I'd been. So I gave her an answer that was equally valid when it came to recounting my problems. "I don't know. It's just—I have no idea what I want to do with my life."

She looked down at the flour-dappled light brown Maple Lane Bakery apron that she'd worn home from work. Then she flicked her hand across her stomach, sending up a puff of dust. As the cloud dissipated, she laughed.

"I guess I shouldn't complain," I said. I realized Mom had

never planned a life where she'd be at work at 3 A.M., making rolls and bagels for people's breakfast. Or trying to support three people on one modest salary.

"It's not bad," she said. "I sort of enjoy making bread. I like working with my hands. There's something very therapeutic about bread dough. My coworkers are great. I'm happy I have a job. Especially now, when your father is . . ." She let it dangle.

"If you could do anything," I asked, "what would it be?"

"Music, I guess," she said. "But I know that's not a reality." She stepped closer and put her hands on my shoulders. "What would your dream job be?"

"Artist," I said, surprising myself. My art dreams had taken a couple bad beatings recently. I guess they hadn't been beaten totally out of me.

"That's a rough road," she said.

"I know."

"Which doesn't mean you shouldn't explore the possibilities. You just need to be prepared. Every artist needs a backup plan. What else can you see yourself doing?"

"No idea," I said. *Tattoo artist* didn't seem like the right sort of response at the moment.

"You're still young. Very young. The universe will send you some suggestions when it's ready," Mom said. "For now, how about a cup of tea?"

"Sounds good."

THE NEXT DAY, out front before first bell, I went right over to Christopher and Brad as soon as I got to school. Robert and Butch were waiting for me at our usual spot. I wasn't planning to abandon them. I just wanted to spend a minute or two with my new friends before joining my old ones. Later on, I could figure out how to bring the groups together.

"That was deep stuff," I said. I'd given yesterday's conversation a lot of thought. I had some new insights about our place in the universe, and I was eager to unveil them. I was also working up a killer theory about the existence and implications of shared thoughts.

Brad squinted at me like he wasn't sure who I was. "What was deep?"

"Yesterday," I said. My gut twitched, and I couldn't help thinking about various Philip K. Dick stories where people discover they aren't anywhere near the place they think they are, either in space, in time, or in degree of strangeness.

Brad and Christopher both stared at me, then exchanged glances with each other, as if looking for clues.

"At the park," I said.

"Ohhhh." Christopher flashed me a goofy grin. "Yesterday?"

"Yeah, yesterday. After school." I backed off a step, wondering whether my initial fear of being the victim of a practical joke wasn't all that paranoid, after all.

"My brother got me some killer weed from his pal in Colorado," Christopher said. "Brad and I hit it pretty hard right after school. I think it might have been dusted with something. We were like so stoned, I felt like I was tripping."

"Totally awesome. I was really spaced," Brad said. "I had ants marching across everything I saw. But they were cute ants. They had big heads with nice smiles. They were wearing top hats. And they smelled like strawberries."

"Mmmmm . . . Pie . . ." Christopher said.

"Yeah, pie . . ." Brad said.

They lost interest in me. I slipped away as my fantasy of deep conversations, loyal friendships, and late-night pie at the diner drifted into dying wisps of killer bong smoke. It looked like we'd done the opposite of having the same idea. We hadn't even had the same conversation or experience.

I joined Robert and Butch.

"What were you talking to them about?" Butch asked.

"Nothing."

I guess something in my voice said *end of discussion*, because they let it go.

The bell rang. I headed in for class, as numb as a guy who'd toked some killer weed. I drifted through the school day like I was watching it on the small, blurry display of a cheap phone.

MIDTerminaL

THAT NIGHT, AS I lay awake in bed, a dangerous notion seeped up from the darkness of my thoughts: *Maybe Nola had the right idea.* She'd just gone about it wrong. It must have been hell for her parents to sit in the hospital, knowing her body was alive but her brain was dead.

I'd never do that to my mom. The thought of her keeping vigil over my shell, waiting for the miracle of reanimated brain functions, tore me up. So pills were out. We didn't have a gun. I could get my hands on one, I guess. That seemed pretty easy. I'm not sure I could pull a trigger when the muzzle was pressed against my temple or jammed in my mouth. I'd probably flinch at the last instant and end up blasting a hole in my cheek or blowing off an ear. Then I'd get stuck with a bandaged head and a nickname like Bang Bang van Gogh. Forget guns.

I think people screwed up when they tried to hang themselves, too. And it didn't look like it was a quick or painless way to go.

Back up.

Was I really seriously considering killing myself?

I guess. Sure. Why not? We all die sooner or later. There was some appeal to sooner.

Back up again.

Was my life that awful? I looked into the past, at a road filled with bad memories. It was abundantly paved with unpleasant, painful, demoralizing moments, long stretches of loneliness, and no sense of really belonging anywhere.

What about the good moments?

I searched through different avenues, followed different branches. Yeah. Happy stuff. It was there. More often, I wasn't so much happy as what I could best describe as merely not unhappy. I guess, when you sifted through the past, you found what you wanted to find. I could fill a sack of happiness or a box of sorrow. Talk about cherry-picking.

The road that brought me here, once traveled, was fixed in stone. Or asphalt. Or nobody's fault. What about the road ahead? They were big on motivational posters in school. HANG IN THERE. IT GETS BETTER.

Was that really true? Did thirty-year-old guys who'd been miserable in high school feel life had gotten better since then? Probably. At the very least, most of them would own a car. Did forty-year-old women see the traumas of adolescence as a learning experience? Maybe. But there was no promise things would ever get better for me. They sure hadn't gotten better for my father recently. The world was full of unhappy adults. A slogan isn't a promise. An affirmation isn't an assurance. At best, it's a hypothetical. As was my current line of thought about ending my life. Unless I made a decision to go ahead and die.

Hypothetically, how would I do it?

Jump from somewhere? The door at the bottom of the bell tower in Saint Simon's Church, just two blocks east off the Green, by the library, wasn't locked. At least, that's what I'd heard.

I tried to picture that leap. I'd jumped off a ten- or fifteen-foot cliff once, at a swimming quarry my uncle Steve took me to. I didn't like how weightlessness tugged at my gut. The bell tower was a lot higher than that. The gut tugging would last much longer. I actually knew enough physics to figure out roughly how long the free fall would take, and to calculate the force of impact. I didn't know enough anatomy or physiology, on the other hand, to predict the exact effects of that force on a human body, but it would obviously be catastrophic.

I wondered whether you just bang-splat died when you hit, or if life lingered long enough for you to feel agony and regret. I thought about how I'd felt when I smacked into the floor of the Pit, and tried to multiply that feeling by a thousand. I imagined myself lying on the ground, crushed, shattered, and seeping viscous fluids like a stomped-on grasshopper.

Ew. I shuddered and considered other means. Poison? That was a gamble. I really didn't know enough to make the right choice, and I sure didn't trust the Internet. Carbon monoxide? Could work. Could end with brain damage. Coma. Life support.

If only we ran on batteries. That would make things simpler.

Maybe I wasn't serious. But you probably already figured out what I'd decided, given that this isn't a ghost story (wouldn't that suck, after all these pages?) and that we aren't near the end of the last chapter.

I accepted the fact that the slow, low-level pain of my quotidian (vocabulary!) existence wasn't enough to justify, or mandate, a permanent escape at this point in my life. I found it interesting, and somewhat disconcerting, that I could think about all this in such a cold and analytical way. Maybe this was another example, like watching tragedies on the news, where guys were more detached. I wondered what Nola's last thoughts were as she poured the pills into her hand. What was her mood? Cold? Emotional? Sad? Relieved? Did her hand tremble? Did she cry? Did she swallow the pills one by one, in a methodical march toward oblivion, or choke down a fistful in a desperate plunge from on high? Nobody will ever know.

Maybe there was something good ahead of me. Maybe even something great. I guess that was the best argument I could think of for staying alive—a mix of anticipation and curiosity, coated with a thin layer of unjustified optimism, a fairly strong dose of cowardice, a reluctance to force someone to stumble upon my corpse, and a seemingly endless talent for imagining ways that I could screw up a suicide attempt and make my life even worse. Not to mention the haunting fear that Dad's reaction to my death would be to shrug and mutter, *I always knew he was a loser.* Those reasons would have to do for now.

conversation
BLOSSOMS

I'D TRAINED MYSELF not to pause when I walked past Jillian in the Art House. In a way, it was a variation of that trick they teach ice skaters, ballet dancers, and other people who, unlike me, have to spin rapidly for the enjoyment of others. You turn your head, and then the body catches up. If you've never noticed this before, it's pretty cool to watch, once you're aware of it.

So, I was walking past Jillian after raiding the supply closet for a fresh canvas. The closet is on the side wall of the room where she sat. I seemed to go through a lot of paint. I'd also developed a habit of misplacing my brushes. As contrived as my crossings were, I never faltered in my steps or paused as I passed the point nearest to the gravitational well of her attraction, where apogee intersected apathy. She'd started a new painting. The background was solid green. The shade she'd picked looked familiar. I was sure I'd seen it in another painting, but I couldn't quite place it. She was crafting some sort of flower in the upper left. There didn't seem to be any sketches to guide her. And that was as much as I could see in my brief round-trip passage. I guess this was going to be another arrangement of masterfully wrought, insignificant, unconnected objects.

I returned to my easel and put up the new canvas. *What to paint?* I tried to figure out what I wanted to say. *People suck? Nothing is what it seems to be? We're all lonely until we die? Strawberry pie isn't enough?*

I had a feeling there'd already been ten million paintings expressing those thoughts, along with one hundred million poems. I wanted to create something different and amazing. I walked over to the front window and looked out at the street, hoping to find inspiration. Instead, I found the target of my admiration.

Reflected in the top center pane of this particular Art House window, Jillian's translucent profile hovered before my eyes. My breath caught as she touched the unbristled end of her paint-brush against her lips in thought. She cocked her head slightly, nodded as if she'd made a crucial artistic decision, then painted another stroke.

I studied her bare right shoulder where it emerged from her smock. Did this make me some kind of perv? It's not like I was peeking through her window, seeing something she didn't want me to see. I was just admiring the most amazing work of art, and biology, in the room. It was exactly what I would see, unre-flected, if I turned around.

Past her shoulder, I could see her painting. She'd roughed in some petals on her flower. My hands gripped the windowsill as I recognized her subject. Even from this distance, dimly mirrored, the pink and white petals were unmistakable. Jillian wasn't painting a flower. She was painting cherry blossoms.

The horror of my musical moment in Government class crashed back over me.

I gave my love a cherry. . . .

Was she intentionally mocking me? Or was it subconscious? Either way, it felt like the hit-and-run driver who'd knocked me down and broken my legs was circling the block for the fun of crushing my heart.

I watched Jillian for the rest of the period as she painstakingly applied the tiniest wisps of pigment onto the canvas. By the time the bell rang, my back ached from standing immobile, aligned with her reflection, and my fingers ached from clutching the windowsill. I couldn't tell for sure, but the thing she'd just started painting below the cherries looked a hell of a lot like a chick hatching from an egg. I went over for a closer look after she left. Yeah, it was cherry blossoms, and the outline of a chick.

I was almost beyond further injury at this point. I imagine that if you get kicked in the crotch after being castrated, it probably doesn't hurt all that much. It's hard to get your balls busted when your balls are already in a jar.

I decided to skip lunch and get started on my painting. I needed to make up for the time I'd lost staring at Jillian. It turned out to be a wasted effort, leaving me empty of ideas and food. There are few things so full of potential and, at the same time, so potentially threatening as a blank canvas. Ten minutes before lunch ended, I bowed to the reality of my own blankness, and went to the cafeteria.

All they had left was chicken cutlets. Even fresh, they were pretty sketchy. By now, the bottom-of-the-pan survivors were close enough to their nickname of "elephant scabs" that I felt like I'd be violating the Endangered Species Act when I ate one.

"You're late," Jimby said when I got to our table.

"Mmffff." I'd already crammed a large bite of cutlet into my mouth on my way there. I chewed, swallowed, then added, "Art."

"Safer than music," Robert said. "Especially when mixed with Government."

I glared at him.

"Sorry," he said. "But from the video, it looks like you died a thousand deaths in a hundred seconds."

"There's a video?" I asked.

"There's a video of everything," Butch said.

"I got one of us wrestling," Jimby said. "Remember?"

"Yeah. I remember that." Jimby loved wrestling. But I'd been a willing participant in that video. I didn't like knowing that my moment of humiliation had become eternal.

"Don't sweat it," Robert said. "It's not interesting enough to go viral. Maybe if you'd been hit in the crotch . . ."

"I agree," Butch said. "After I watched it five or six times, I totally lost interest." She flashed me a *just kidding* smile. I went back to consuming my elephant scabs and letting my own freshest wound start to scab over. Having real friends—even ones who kidded me—helped a lot.

DINNER WAS TENSE. Dad hadn't gotten the job. After we ate, he went out for a walk to the corner store. And probably to sneak a cigarette. Supposedly, he quit four or five years ago, but you can't hide that smell. I'm sure Mom wasn't fooled, either, but she pretended not to know.

I asked her something I'd wondered about ever since I stumbled across that old photo. "Why'd you quit the group?"

"What group?" Mom asked.

"The one where you played fiddle," I said. "I saw some old photos, and a newspaper clipping."

"Oh, *that* group. I didn't quit. We just sort of drifted apart after college."

"You didn't want to play anymore?" I asked.

"I always want to play," she said. "Life doesn't often allow you to indulge yourself."

"Maybe someday," I said.

"Maybe," she said.

There was one other question I needed to ask. "Did Dad make you quit the band?" I thought about how much he hated my art. Part of me would derive a twisted sense of relief from knowing his antagonism extended beyond just my ambitions.

"No. He liked music back then. I used to play the fiddle for him when we were—" She shifted from wherever she was going. "—together."

"He doesn't like music now," I said.

"People change," she said. "We all do. In good ways and bad. That's part of life."

"But why does he hate the idea that I want to be an artist?"

"It's not that you want to be an artist," she said. "It's that you don't, in his eyes, want to make a responsible living."

"Like he does?" I asked. "He's a great provider."

"That's not fair," she said. "He's worked very hard."

I heard the front door open. "I'd better get back to my homework," I said.

———

TWO DAYS LATER, even with Jillian's agonizingly slow pace, there was no mistake about the identity of her avian subject. It was a chick, recently sprung from an egg. And there were cherry blossoms scattered around one lush, red cherry. She hadn't sketched anything in first, as she usually did, but was painting the objects cold.

I was still staring at the canvas when Jillian walked past me and sat on her stool.

If I was going to be mocked, I wanted to get her to admit it to my face. Not that she was facing me at the moment.

"Why?" I asked.

"Why what?" she asked, squeezing a dab of alizarin crimson onto her palette.

I couldn't think of the right *why* version of my question. *Why . . .*

. . . are you mocking me?

. . . are you turning that song into a painting?

. . . do I keep discovering new ways in which life can suck?

I pointed at the canvas. "That's from the song. . . ."

She nodded. I wanted to stroke her hair. Or sniff it. I was getting seriously worried about my urges.

"You took it well," she said.

"Huh?" The unexpected statement didn't immediately register in my mind. Had she just *praised* me?

"I could see you wanted to play something else from the record. It must have been hard, standing there while everyone laughed at the song."

"Not everyone," I said.

"Not everyone," she said.

I chewed on that for a bit, then digested it. To my amazement, I wasn't the one who ended the silence.

She tapped her canvas, between the blossoms and the chick. "So, if you were painting this, what would be happening?"

The change in direction nearly spun me out of the conversation. I hadn't expected anything resembling social discourse with Jillian. My whole planless plan seemed to have been to get her to admit she'd been mocking me. Though I have no idea what purpose that would have served, other than to justify my indignation.

Jimby's words came back to me.

"Then I'd let her hit me with the ax."

"Why?"

"So she'd feel guilty. Then we'd get to know each other and fall in love."

But I hadn't been mocked—or axed. Instead, it looked like I'd been invited to brainstorm a meaningful interaction of objects in a still life. Objects I seemed to have inspired.

I stepped to her side and studied the painting. I was close enough that I could hear the slow rhythm of her breath. I forced myself not to look at her, and tried to focus on the question. Though I feared the great blankness would continue to block my creativity, an idea came to me easily enough.

"I'd have the chick eating the blossoms and laying cherries," I said. "Sort of a recycling thing."

Oh, crap. That was kind of crude. *Hey, why don't you make your bird shit out some fruit? That would be sweet-ass bitchin' awesome!* What a great way to ruin our first conversation.

Jillian laughed. "That's not quite what I had in mind. But it's definitely creative."

I felt like the governor had lifted me, personally, from the electric chair just as the switch was being thrown. Jillian had acknowledged my creativity. We were playing ball in my court now. I grasped the thin tendrils of confidence that were drifting through my spine.

"Being creative is easy," I said. "Execution is hard. I can see amazing things in my mind when I look at a canvas." I froze again. That sounded too much like I was bragging. "Maybe not amazing. But interesting."

Jillian waited for me to go on. I finished my thought. "I just can't make them look the way I want. I don't have that gift. You do."

"Give it time," she said.

I'd given it years. I didn't bother saying anything. It seemed that art, craft, athletics, or any other area that involved mind–body cooperation, required some sort of skill that nobody could teach you. The way Robert's dad could prune a tree. The way Paul could play the keyboard. The way Ms. Ryder could keep control of a classroom. The way Doc Watson could play the guitar. Even the way my mom could make a loaf of French bread. They might have been taught some of the tricks or basic techniques, but there was something they could do that most people couldn't. They were born that way. I guess it could be summed up as natural talent. A *gift*. Jillian had that sort of skill with art. She could render an object in astonishingly lifelike detail. I felt it would be far easier for her to learn to add imagination to her existing skills than it would be for me to add her kind of talent to my imagination.

But maybe that was just because, for me, imagining things was pretty easy. I almost couldn't stop my mind from doing it all the time. Was that my skill? Did I have a natural talent for seeing things in creative ways? Or was this another example of not seeing things clearly at all. Oh, man—I was actually wondering whether my ability to judge my ability to see things was flawed. This could fall into a recursive death spiral of introspection.

I guess I spent too much time lost in thought as I stood at Jillian's side, because she returned to her work. I lingered, trying to think of something clever to say. But I was afraid I'd do more damage by spewing half-formed suggestions than I would if I slipped away in silence. Or, worse, hovered beside her in silence. Patricia's classification of my social standing still haunted me.

I backed away from Jillian. But we'd had an actual conversation. Jillian and I had talked—briefly—and I'd managed not to say the wrong thing or release the wrong fluid.

As I headed toward my easel, I fought the urge to look over my shoulder and ask, *You're not stoned, are you?*

No. Of course she wasn't stoned. Ours had been a stone-cold-sober conversation. But I was buzzed. I took a seat, stared at my blank canvas, and tried not to make too big a deal over what had just happened. Had this been middle school, I would probably have already started planning our wedding. Now, as a high school senior, I realized our conversation meant a lot less to her than it did to me.

I also realized I'd found an answer I hadn't been looking for to a vital question I'd asked last night. A question that I realized had hung from my neck until now, pulling me down.

Why bother to keep living?

Because, if I'd splatted to an abrupt ending last night at the base of the Saint Simon's bell tower, like a garbage bag full of beef stew, I never would have had this conversation with Jillian.

DOING NOTHING
WELL

THE NEXT MORNING, Jillian smiled at me when I walked into Calculus. By the time it dawned on me that the correct response was to smile back, she'd already turned her attention to the front of the room, where Mr. Yuler was firing up a slide on the smart board.

Don't make a big deal out of it, I told myself. That wasn't easy. My mind launched into a frantic hunt for ways I could move our relationship forward.

I could buy her something! That was a great idea. What would be a perfect gift?

A snake, you asshole.

Yeah, get her a bruise-blue waterlogged snake. Who wouldn't love that? Be sure to spend all your money on it, loser.

Okay, that was my rational side trying to remind me that my wooing efforts had led to nothing pleasant during the past six years.

How about doing nothing?

I'd been doing nothing in all sorts of ways for most of my life. The problem was that I burst out of inactivity and performed some stupid action just often enough to ruin the solid foundation that doing nothing had built. I thought about how, over the years, a half dozen other objects of my lust and interest, none significant enough in my halting interactions with them to mention individually, had been scooped up by more active suitors while I did nothing.

Maybe the key wasn't exactly doing *nothing* so much as avoiding doing the wrong thing.

The problem came down to that very distinction—I had no clue what was right and what was wrong.

But I knew what was right and what was left.

I glanced toward either side of me. Nola's empty seat might have remained full if I'd done something. I could have asked her out.

But she had a boyfriend.

So? Maybe she'd offered me an opening when she complained about him. Maybe he hadn't treated her very nicely. Maybe he was the one who'd told her she was fat. Maybe every moment of shoulder contact was a great big whopping hint jammed in my face, and a hope on her part that I would step up to the plate and ask her out. Maybe I was just too insecure, clueless, and socially inept to realize what was happening. So I'd done nothing. If I'd responded, would she still have tried to kill herself? There was no way to know.

On my other side, there was Lucas. He'd acted boldly. But not smartly. If he'd done nothing, his father might still be alive. But would he have been better off? Unlike my aborted and ill-advised bell tower dive, Lucas's thwarted escape might have been the right move, if only he'd done a better job of actually escaping. I had no idea how bad his life at home had been. He'd kept that well hidden. But it had been bad enough for him to attempt a drastic solution.

These contemplations occupied me all the way through Calculus class. When the bell rang, I sprang from my seat so I could walk near Jillian. Or maybe even walk to Physics with her.

Do nothing.

I gripped the desk and watched her walk to the door, hoping she'd glance back—and fearing that any such glance would turn me into a pillar of sweat. She didn't look my way.

Butch tapped me on the shoulder. "I think somebody likes you."

"I doubt it."

"I don't," she said. "I saw the smile she gave you."

"It was nothing," I said. Though I hoped I was wrong.

"It was something," Butch said.

I waited until Art to take a shot at doing more than nothing. After Jillian got settled at her easel, I walked over to her and said, "Hi."

That single word was terminated with a small intake of breath, as if I had half-choked on an apple seed. The gasp was provoked by the memory that I'd used the same approach with Nola in the hallway outside Calculus class, after the first time she'd leaned on me. Following which, I had done nothing.

I clenched my teeth and tried to accept the likelihood that I wasn't carrying around some sort of monosyllabic curse that caused everyone I greeted to attempt some form of self-destruction. In my universe, there was no such thing as curses.

"Hi."

She spoke back, using exactly the same word, though hers was dipped in honey and dusted with brown sugar.

The ball had been lobbed into my court. Easy, slow, drifting up and then dropping in a perfect parabolic arc.

Every time I ever tried to smash a lob to put away a point on the tennis court, I drove the ball into the net or out of bounds. *Lob it back.*

As I tried to think of something that was safe without being inane, she spoke again. "That album you brought in . . ."

"*Southbound?*" I said.

"That was my stepfather's favorite CD." Jillian's eyes drifted away from me, as if she were seeing into the past. She smiled like she'd heard an amusing joke.

"What's so funny?" I asked.

"He didn't like 'The Riddle Song,' either," she said.

"I think Ms. Ryder is unique in that respect," I said. "It takes a special nature to love those lyrics."

"I'd have to agree."

I realized why the background she'd painted looked so familiar. It was the same shade of green as the *Southbound* cover. "So you like that music?" I asked. "I mean, the rest of the album." It would be so super awesome if we had something personal in common. There were a couple other Doc Watson albums in the crate. I could invite her over to listen to them. Imagine that—Jillian and me, sitting on the cool concrete floor of the basement, shoulder to shoulder. I nearly lost her next words as I nibbled at that image and contemplated whether it would be better to play each album through from start to finish or skip around.

"I liked my stepfather's music as much as you like whatever

music your parents constantly played when you were little," she said.

"Got it," I said. My deflation at the loss of a common bond was balanced by the realization that we were having another conversation. I had the strange feeling I was hovering above my body, observing myself engage in a social interaction. "But if you hate the music, why did it get your attention?"

"My stepfather was a good man," she said. "He played the guitar. He even played some of those songs."

"Oh." I couldn't help noticing the "was." But I didn't press for details.

She picked up her brush. "I should get to work."

"Me, too." I sat down at my easel and started sketching out a space scene of a vast universe filled with tiny stars and two large, glowing suns caught in orbit around each other. I myself glowed through the rest of the period. Yeah, we'd done nothing more than exchange a handful of sentences. But we'd *talked.* And I hadn't destroyed the magic of the moment by saying something stupid.

Right before the period ended, I turned toward her again and said, "No baby?"

"What?" She stared at me as if I'd said something stupid.

"You have the cherry blossoms and the chick from the song," I said, figuring she'd misheard me. "I just realized you need to add the baby." I didn't mention to her that, in my version, the baby would be eating chicken.

"I'm not good at babies," she said.

"You did an awesome Buddha," I said. "If you can do that, you can do a killer baby. Just make him a lot younger. Buddha looks pretty young, already. He's sort of ageless. Or you could do a back view of the baby, so you don't even see the face. That's the hard part." I realized I was starting to babble.

I guess Jillian had picked up on that way before I did, because she didn't even bother to answer me before she scurried out. I couldn't blame her. After she left, I saw she hadn't put her brushes away. As I cleaned the brushes and capped her paints, I played back my words, wondering whether I'd said something stupid. Maybe she just didn't want any more suggestions. I know I don't like people telling me what to add to my art, or how to change the stuff I write for English.

At lunch, as I listened to myself contribute my small share of the conversation during those rare moments when both Butch and Robert paused for breath, I wondered why it was so easy to talk with them, and with Jimby or Nicky (who had taken to joining our lunch table at times), but so hard to talk with Jillian.

Maybe all I had to do was treat her like them.

But that was impossible. They were my friends. She was— What? My obsession? My passion? My goal in life? It all seemed so tricky. One moment, she wants my ideas. The next, she's not interested.

Still, this was a new concept, and one worth exploring. Treat her like a friend . . . even if I desperately wanted us to be much more than friends. I kept my eye on the cafeteria entrance the whole period, but Jillian never showed up.

After school, I was in my room, folding my laundry, when I heard a knock on the front door. Then I heard Dad shift out of his war-room chair. I guess he was getting it. That was fine. I wasn't expecting anyone to drop by.

"Cliff!" he shouted a moment later.

He offered no further explanation or message. When I went

down, I found Jimby standing on the porch. Dad had walked off, leaving the door open, without inviting him in.

I stepped outside. "What's up?"

"I wrote it!" he said, thrusting out a handful of notebook paper. "Read it. Okay?"

"Yeah, sure. Let's go around to the backyard."

We went and sat, and I read Jimby's short story.

"Wow," I said when I was finished. It was hard to speak. My throat felt funny. I took a breath, swallowed a couple times, then managed to kick out three more words. "This is great."

I'd expected something about zombies or dinosaurs. But he'd written a story about a boy, James, who was born badly deformed. James used his hands to propel himself around the school on a cart made from three skateboards fastened side by side. Most of the kids made fun of him or ignored him. He was really smart, but they couldn't see past his deformity. Then, one day, there was a fire. The halls filled with smoke. Everyone was terrified. But James, who was close to the floor, stayed calm and led his classmates to safety.

"This is very good," I said.

"Really?" Jimby said.

"Really. It's great. I love the way that what everyone thought was his weakness turned out to be his strength." I paused to consider my next words. He'd done an amazing job. But there were a couple things he could do to strengthen the story. I wanted to give him some tips, but I didn't want him to see them as criticism, and I didn't want to do any of his work for him. I also needed to make sure I didn't step on his voice. This story was all his, unmistakably so for anyone who really knew him, and it needed to stay that way. "Definitely a great story . . ."

"You aren't just saying that, are you?" he asked.

"No. I read a lot of stuff. I just read a whole book of awesome stories. So I know what I'm talking about. This is good. How did the fire start? You don't mention that."

Jimby scrunched his face a bit, then shrugged. "I don't know. It just started."

"What if—?" I stopped. I wanted to suggest that one of the kids who tormented James had started the fire. But I needed to stay clear of telling him what to do. "Some of the kids in the story are pretty mean."

"Yeah," he said. "Like Bovis Bunt. He's terrible."

I waited for him to give my hint more thought.

"He did it!" Jimby shouted. He grabbed my arm with both hands. "Yeah. This is great! I got it. I'll have Bovis start the fire. Then he gets saved by James and feels sorry for being such a big, mean, stupid bully."

"That's perfect," I said. "I love it. You'll make the story even stronger."

"Bovis gets burned first. And all his hair burns off. But James still saves him." Jimby snatched the story from my hand. "I gotta go." He rushed off toward his house, then spun back and said, "Thanks for the help, Cliff. You should be a teacher!"

"Yeah, right . . ." I waved. "Catch you later."

Hah. Yeah. Me, a teacher. That put a smirk on my face. I thought about our short-lived and short-tempered Government substitute, Mr. Strawbroke, being torn to pieces by a class full of thugs. Or Mr. Tippler yelling at us and then going out to get smashed. Or Mr. Xander, who inspired enough hatred that he'd almost been killed. But then I thought about brainstorming with Jimby for plot ideas and guiding him toward ways to strengthen his story. I thought about Mr. Piccaro's passion for novels, Ms. Gickley's efforts to teach me patience, and Ms. Ryder's enthusiasm for making Government less puzzling and more interesting.

My smirk faded. But the thought remained. Me, a teacher . . .

syncongruenicidence

———————————

LIKE A FRIEND. Conversation. Talking. Casual. No agenda. No expectations. Talk. Chat. Just like that.

Damn, now my stream of consciousness was spewing out unintentional hack rhymes. But my plan was solid. I waited until Art, when we could talk without distractions or interruptions. Fourth period seemed to take four days to arrive, but I was finally there, seated by my easel.

I decided to try starting a conversation from my home court. As Jillian walked past me, I said, "You told me you didn't like your parents' music. So, what do you like?"

"Lots of stuff," she said. "Especially Mack and Mary."

"Holy shit!"

I flinched at my own outburst. But Jillian seemed more startled than offended.

"I love them," I said, racing toward an explanation. "They're awesome. The best group ever. Their new album is a total killer."

Slow down. I was in danger of splattering her with my enthusiastic fanboy gushing, along with an inevitable spray of saliva.

"They are definitely awesome," Jillian said. "They played at Saint Jasper's a while back."

"Did you go?" I asked.

"It was too expensive."

"I had tickets," I said.

Her eyes widened, as if I'd told her I'd spotted a unicorn. "How was it?"

"I didn't go," I said. "I couldn't find anyone to go with."

"I would have gone," she said.

"Really?" It was more an exclamation than a question.

"But I guess you wouldn't have had any reason to ask me," she added.

I felt like someone had taken a high-pressure hose that was hooked up to a tank of new concepts, jammed it straight into my skull, and opened the valve all the way. I had to digest this information. And I had to throttle back my babbling. But there was one thing I needed to know.

"You'd really have gone with me?" I asked, trying not to sound too desperate or needy.

"Sure. Why not?"

Why not?

Two small words never loomed so large.

I didn't offer an answer. Anything I could think of seemed too dangerous. I was simultaneously kicking myself over the missed opportunity of the concert and embracing the joy of hearing that Jillian, unlike Patricia, saw me as a perfectly acceptable concert companion. I'd been elevated to *Why not?* status. Maybe it was Patricia, and not me, who was seriously flawed.

"What did you do with the tickets?" Jillian asked.

"Can you keep a secret?"

She nodded. I told her.

"That was sweet," she said.

"Thanks." *Why not?* and *sweet.* I was rising rapidly in the universe.

"Well, I'd better get to work." She headed for her easel.

Did I detect the slightest hint of regret in that last statement? She needed to get to work but didn't want to, because she was enjoying talking with me. Sweet me. I decided to embrace that as a valid theory. Why not?

The instant I got home, I searched online to see if Mack and Mary were playing anywhere near here. I would sell a kidney, if I had to, to get tickets.

No luck. The college had been the last stop on the East Coast leg of their national tour. I checked for other local events. There was a teen concert at the Crab Locker this weekend, featuring some band I'd never heard of, but the idea of taking Jillian to that dance floor, or near that stage, dredged up too many unpleasant memories, even though she didn't seem like the sort of girl who would dump the guy she went with if a better offer came along.

As I was closing the browser, Dad walked up behind me. "You're not going to any concerts," he said. I hated the way he always seemed to be checking on me when I was online or on my phone. "Do you think we have money to throw around?"

"I was just looking," I said. I'd turned my monitor around several times, so it didn't face the hall. Each time I'd done that, I came home to find it turned back.

"You are nothing but a drain," he said. "That's not going to last forever. You'd better shape up, or the day you turn eighteen, there might be some big changes around here."

He'd already hinted that he wouldn't support me if I tried to study art. Now it seemed like he was threatening I'd be on my own as soon as he could legally get rid of me. I couldn't help picturing myself being literally kicked out of the house with a firm boot in the rear. As the image grew even less grounded in reality, I saw myself flying toward goalposts. I needed to remind my father that I wasn't some sort of leech, sucking the blood out of the bank account and giving nothing back.

"Hey, I'm working," I said. "I earn money."

"You're working at a crap job for kids," he said.

"Two jobs," I said. At least he could show some appreciation that I was working hard.

"Crap times two is still crap," he said.

Maybe it had been a mistake to mention work. "I'm saving for college." I figured it wouldn't hurt to remind him that he'd dipped pretty deeply into my original college funds, and that I was willing to pay for everything myself, if necessary.

"To study what?"

"I'm not sure yet."

He smirked. "Good plan. You can major in shrugging and maybe minor in dumbfuckery."

I opened my mouth, then shut it. There wasn't anything worth saying, and I'd had enough of a smackdown for one day. He shook his head and walked off, leaving me alone with the looming question.

To study what?

I'd love to study art. And then what? Nobody was leaving me a fortune so I could do what I wanted, like Butch's dad. On top of that, I now had another problem to deal with. I'd accepted that college was going to be rough and slow, and that I'd be working a lot of hours. But until now, it had never occurred to me that I might also end up homeless. I thought about how bad Lucas had looked, and smelled, after less than a week on his own.

The day you turn eighteen . . .

"He'd never kick me out," I said. But I didn't find my reassurances to be very convincing.

THE NEXT DAY, after Government class ended, I caught up to Jillian in the hall and spoke the words I'd endlessly rehearsed, rethought, and rephrased throughout the day. "Hey, want to get something at the diner?" I might not be able to afford front-section concert tickets, but I could manage to treat us to some fries. Though I'd been careful not to mention any specific food in the invitation, out of fear it might be one she didn't eat.

Time ticked past in billionth-of-a-second increments. Seven or eight billion ticks later, she said, "Sure."

Sure? Just like that?

Stay calm. Don't overreact.

I wondered whether it would be okay to respond with, *Great!* Maybe that was too enthusiastic. But I couldn't be too casual about it. I had to let her know I was glad, without stumbling into eager-puppy territory. What about *Nice?* That was neutral enough. Or was it a little too laid back?

While I was sorting through my choices, Jillian rummaged through her purse, then said, "Wait. I think I left my pen in class. I'll be right back."

I watched her disappear inside the classroom. As the door

closed on her, it opened onto a painful memory. "She'll be right back," I whispered.

A minute crawled by. Then another.

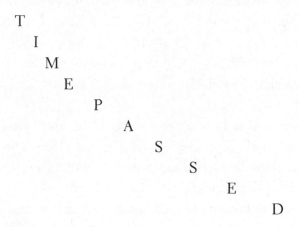

"No way . . ." I said. But when it came to getting the wrong outcome, my life seemed more filled with "way" than "no way."

I took a deep breath, which didn't help at all, then went into the classroom. My eyes fell immediately on the open window. Like before, the half-drawn shade twisted in the breeze.

No way.

No sign of Jillian.

A voice rose from beneath her desk. "Found it!" Jillian popped up, holding her pen.

Stupidly, I pointed at the window and said what was on my mind. "I was afraid you'd bailed on me. . . ."

"Why would I do that?" she asked.

"I'm kidding." I tried to install an appropriate lighthearted expression on my face.

"I'm sorry I took so long. I got distracted when I came in." It was her turn to point at the window.

I went over and looked out. In the front yard of one of the houses across the street, on Vorhees, a boy, maybe two or three years old, was playing with a puppy and laughing hysterically every time he got his face licked. Boy and dog both seemed to be having a ball.

"I can see where you could get lost in time, watching that," I said. I dragged myself out of the past, closing the door on memories of Maddie. "Ready?"

"Ready."

My body was next to hers as we walked to the diner after school, but my mind was rocketing all over the place. This would be the first time we'd be face-to-face without the crutch of easels, brushes, or canvases.

What if she hates everything I love? What if she loves everything I hate? What if she's a whole lot smarter than I am? What if she's a whole lot less smart?

The tormenting tug-of-war between extreme opposites pulled at my brain all the way to the diner.

"You're pretty quiet," Jillian said as I opened the door for her. "What's on your mind?"

I couldn't tell her, *I'm terrified I won't like you.* I gave her the universal answer. "Nothing."

We sat across from each other. I'd debated that part to death, too, and decided I'd let her sit first, and then look for clues about what she expected me to do. She didn't slide very far in when Molly led us to the booth, so I took that as a cue to go to the other side.

"Fries and a Coke?" Molly asked, looking at me.

I gestured toward Jillian. "After you."

"Sounds good," Jillian said.

"Me, too," I said. "Thanks, Molly."

I stared down at the menu in front of me on the table but realized I couldn't use that as an excuse to delay conversation, since we'd already ordered. "How do you like Rismore?" I asked. That seemed safe.

"It's nice. But it's a lot different from Atlanta. I'm still getting used to it. Everyone's in more of a hurry."

"You should try New York," I said. "People in the city are *really* in a hurry."

"I haven't gotten there yet. But I'd like to."

I was about to offer to take her there, on an adventure, and be her guide, but I realized that would be rushing things. I settled for telling her, "It's easy to get there. You can take the train. Or a bus."

After a brief discussion of local transportation options, another silence settled on us. Luckily, as I was struggling to think of a safe topic, Jillian asked, "So, what's there to do around here for fun?"

I had no trouble answering that. Before I'd exhausted the local highlights, our fries came—hot and crisp like they always are. I owe undying gratitude to whoever came up with the idea of immersing sticks of starch in vats of boiling oil—even if I spend far too much of my time on the frying end of the process. Jillian picked one up, blew on it, and bit off a half-inch piece. She chewed, swallowed, then licked her lips and popped the rest in her mouth. As she looked up, I realized I'd been staring at her mouth. I dragged my eyes away, then realized they'd landed on her breasts. I looked back up as another french fry slipped between her lips. Feeling my face flush, I found safe haven in the tableside jukebox.

I flipped through the listings. "Hey, they have 'The Riddle Song.'"

"You're kidding," she said.

"I am."

She smiled, and joined me in looking through the songs. We settled on a Beach Boys number, "Surfin' Safari," which seemed just right for the retro look of the diner.

We sat, talked, and snacked. She didn't tell me all that much about herself, and I didn't want to risk asking personal questions. But to my relief, she also didn't reveal anything that destroyed my hopes that we would establish some sort of relationship. And she didn't mention any boyfriends. It was a terrifyingly normal experience in many ways, not counting the thirty conversations I had with myself each time I was about to utter a sentence, and the constant pressure to look at her without staring at her.

After we left the diner, we walked together as far as the Green. "I'm going that way," Jillian said, pointing south, to West Rismore Avenue. Yeah, I know that doesn't make sense, but the road runs west after going south for two blocks, and cuts through the western part of town, eventually ending at the community pool.

"I live that way," I said, pointing in the direction of the high school. "Other side of the football field."

"Well, bye . . ." she said.

"Bye . . ."

Despite telling myself in ten thousand ways not to make too much of one shared meal, I floated home.

Mom was in the kitchen, preparing a chicken casserole for dinner. "You look happy," she said.

"I treated myself to some french fries." I glanced over my shoulder to make sure Dad hadn't heard. He'd yell at me for even this small an indulgence. Especially if he knew I'd picked up the whole tab.

"It's good to treat yourself once in a while," Mom said.

"It's definitely good." There was something I'd been meaning to ask her. "That Doc Watson album, *Southbound*, was it yours or Grandpa's?"

"His," she said. "I gave it to him for Father's Day, way back—" She paused and looked off into the distance. "—after my sophomore year in college."

"Why that album?" I asked.

"A lot of my friends listened to it. Especially the guitar players. Why are you asking about it?"

"Just curious." I explained about the assignment, but not about the outcome.

"I'm sure it got a lot of attention," Mom said. "Did your classmates like it?"

"They went wild," I said. I washed my hands and started peeling carrots. I can't cook, but I can help out by doing the easy stuff.

It was the start of Memorial Day weekend, which meant I finally had time to finish *Geek Love*. The story was memorably disturbing in a mind-bending way, based on a staggering concept. If nothing else, it showed me some ways that a father could be a whole lot worse than mine. I'm not going to spoil things by telling you what the guy did. But it was jaw-dropping. And that was just the beginning. Things got even stranger after the opening. I would love to be able to paint something that was as stunningly creative as the ideas in that book.

The long weekend also meant I wouldn't see Jillian again until Tuesday, unless I got in touch with her, or accidentally wandered over to her house and rang her doorbell. But I didn't want to rush things. So I settled for spending three days thinking about her during every waking minute. And during some moments when I wasn't awake.

But one of those waking moments stands out especially in my mind. Monday afternoon, walking home from Cretaro's, I passed a carnival at Saint Teresa's, the local Catholic school. I wasn't hungry—Toby in the deli had slipped me a steady stream of goodies to snack on—but the smell of deep-fried dough and charred sausages was too enticing to resist. As I wandered through the midway, I heard a cry that made me cringe.

"Knock down three, you win!"

I looked over at my old nemeses, the hypernarrow cats. There were no snakes hanging from the sides of the booth. But there were dogs. Really cute husky puppies. I'd bet Jillian would love a dog. She'd spent all that time watching the puppy from the classroom window. My pocket was nicely padded with tip money. I went over and paid for the three balls.

I hit a cat on the first throw.

I hit a cat on the second throw.

I missed the third one by a whisker.

"So close, sport," the guy said. "Try again. I know you can do it." He gathered three balls between his hands and held them up.

I was already pulling more money from my pocket when I somehow managed to see myself—really see myself, and what I was about to do.

"No thanks," I said.

"Tell you what. First one's on me." He chucked a ball at a cat right in front of him, knocking it flat. "One down. Two to go. You know you can hit two. You just did it." He held out a ball in each hand.

"I got lucky." I turned my back on him.

"You can't walk away a loser," the guy said.

"You're absolutely right," I said as I walked away.

Maybe there was some hope for me after all.

Sextets and the
Single Girl

I DIDN'T HAVE to worry about what to say to Jillian when school started up again. Though I'd narrowed the possibilities down to a mere fifty or sixty topics, all of which were appropriately casual enough to bridge the gap since our time at the diner. She came up to me before Calculus and said, "That was nice, last week."

"Yeah. We should do that again sometime." I flinched internally at the "sometime." Did that make it seem like I could wait? Was it too late to add "soon"? Or to suggest a different outing?

"We should." She headed for her seat.

I noticed she hadn't offered any temporal quantifiers, or expressed a desire for an immediate replay. I figured I'd hold off asking her out again right away. But we talked for five or ten minutes in Art, mostly about Mack and Mary, before we got to work. I wanted to move my easel over to her table, but I was afraid that would seem pushy. When the bell rang, I thought about walking with her to the cafeteria. I felt I still hadn't mastered the proper balance of doing nothing. So I waited while she headed out.

But when I reached the cafeteria, Jillian waved at me from her table, then pointed at the empty seat next to her. I took one hand off my tray and pointed toward my friends. She nodded, picked up her tray, and we converged on my usual table.

"It's about time," Butch said. "Grab a seat. We're not physically dangerous."

"Thanks. I love your hair," Jillian said.

"I spend hours not doing anything to it," Butch said. Her smile indicated she appreciated the compliment.

"Wait until you see mine," Robert said. "It is going to be spectacular. It just needs to get a little longer."

"Shouldn't take more than five years," I said.

"You have an awesome accent," Jillian told Robert.

"Don't praise him," Butch said. "It will only lead to bad things."

"I have a wonderful ability to accept praise without letting it go to my head," Robert said.

As Butch seized the opening and veered off into a discussion of what she thought was really in Robert's head, I introduced Jillian to Jimby and Nicky. I was pleased how well she fit in with my friends.

When lunch ended, Butch pulled me aside. "Much to my amazement and delight, you actually seem to be involved in a normal, healthy boy–girl relationship of some sort."

"Some sort," I said. "That's the problem. I'm not sure how she sees us."

"You've dated, right?"

"Sort of. We went to the diner. But we haven't done anything that felt like a real date."

"So ask her out. Formally. Really. Step up to the plate and swing for it," she said.

"I will. I'm just trying to think up the perfect date."

"There is no *perfect*. At this rate, you'll be asking her out to your retirement party."

Despite Butch's Yoda-like observation that there was no "perfect," I spent the rest of the day trying to come up with the perfect idea. A scary movie would be good, if she was the type to grab an arm for comfort. A dance would be perfect, if I didn't already know how imperfect a dance could be. A meal? Would a fancy dinner, even if I could afford one, really be that different from the diner? If only Mack and Mary were playing around here. We'd talked enough about music that I knew the other bands Jillian liked. I'd already determined that none of them was touring nearby.

So I ended the day without an idea, but I did get another book. The title seemed like a good match for my life: *Stranger in a Strange Land*. Much to my delight, it bore the I DIDN'T GIVE YOU THIS sticker.

Thursday, in Art, I noticed Jillian's first painting, with the Buddha and the onion, was in the corner, leaning against the wall. "Hey, want a frame for that?" I asked.

"I'd love one," she said. "Do they have them here? I didn't see any in the supply closet."

I explained about the woodshop, then picked up the painting. "Let's go look for one."

We headed into the school. "I have to warn you, Mr. Xander is a scary guy. I think one of his parents was an ogre."

"I'll just have to use my charm," Jillian said.

"I'm not sure his heart could stand that," I said. *Uh-oh. Too much?* I risked a glance in her direction. She was smiling. Maybe I had a little bit of charm myself.

As we passed the teachers' lounge, who should come out but Mr. Yuler.

He pointed at my hand. "Painting?" he asked.

"Yup," I said. But I kept walking. I was pretty sure he'd like Jillian's artwork, but I didn't want to take a chance that she'd get trashed like I did. And I really didn't care about his opinion when it came to art, whether he was praising something or belittling it.

Now I was smiling, too.

"What's so funny?" Jillian asked.

I shared the story with her. Then she charmed Mr. Xander, who, it turned out, kept a secret stash of extra-special frames for students he liked. We picked out a stunning frame made of walnut burl and headed back to the Art House.

We were now definitely spending a lot of school time together. I'd even moved over to the empty seat next to her in Physics. I was pretty sure it would be safe to suggest another visit to the diner. But Butch was right. It was time for me to step up to the plate. By the end of the week, the best idea I'd come up with was miniature golf. I figured I'd wait until school was over and ask Jillian out when we were leaving Government.

As I was getting up from my seat, Ms. Ryder said, "Cliff, can I see you for a minute?"

"Sure." My mind launched into a search for transgressions.

I headed toward Ms. Ryder's desk. I couldn't tell anything from her expression. Maybe I'd accidentally copied something in my last paper. I try to be really careful about citing my sources, but I'd rushed to finish the report the night before it was due.

Was my mind drifting in class? Had she caught me staring out the window, or at the clock? There are times when I don't pay as much attention as I should.

Jillian flashed me a sympathetic smile and patted my back as I walked past her. What if I got detention? I felt an urge to ask her out right now. But if I stopped to talk with her while Ms. Ryder was waiting for me, I'd definitely get in trouble.

I remembered something else. Earlier this week, I'd made it to class right before the late bell. That wasn't the first time I'd cut things close.

"What did I do?" I asked when I reached her desk. I searched her eyes, trying to gauge how annoyed or disappointed she was with me, but found no clues.

"Just a moment. I want to talk to you in private." She waited until the classroom had emptied, then pulled a small envelope from her purse. "I can't use these. I figured I should give them to someone who would enjoy the show. They're for tomorrow."

I took the envelope and looked at the pair of tickets inside. They were for a production of *Romeo and Juliet* at the college. It was part of a tristate tour featuring several big-time Hollywood actors. "Wow. Thanks."

"You're very welcome."

As I was about to ask, *Why me?* she added, "For you and a friend."

I froze. Those were the words I'd written on the Mack and Mary tickets. Did she know? Was I that transparent?

"Are you sure you can't go?" I said. "These are great seats. It looks like the third row."

"They're definitely great seats," she said. "But I have to go to a development training session. They announced it after I'd already bought the tickets. At least I'll know someone is enjoying the play. It's short notice, but I'm sure you'll have no trouble finding a friend to ask." She glanced toward the door, where Jillian hovered.

Yeah. I guess I was that transparent. On top of which, Ms. Ryder had a front-row seat for everything that happened in class. I thanked her again and walked over to the door. I held up the tickets—and flinched as a memory punched me in the gut.

But Jillian wasn't Patricia.

"You, me, and Billy Shakespeare?" I said, handing one of the tickets to Jillian so she could read the details.

"Sounds perfect," she said. "Can you get off work?"

"No problem."

Huge problems: what to wear; how to get there; whether to bring her flowers and, if so, what kind; whether to wear cologne (I didn't even own any); what to say; where to look; and on and on. Jillian had told me that her mom let her use her car sometimes. But it would feel even less like a real date if I asked her to drive us.

I will spare you the details of my thoughts over the next thirty or so hours and sum things up with: slightly dressy, the bus, no flowers, no cologne, let her lead the conversation, try not to stare at her breasts.

I couldn't switch shifts at Cretaro's, so I just told my boss I couldn't come in. She didn't seem upset. It's nice to know I'm somewhere far below irreplaceable in the supermarket food chain. When it was time to head out for Jillian's house, Mom was in the hallway, holding something.

"Take this," she said, handing me a handkerchief.

"I don't have a cold," I said. "And those things are gross."

"*These things* are essential," she said. "Every gentleman should carry one. Especially when he is going on a date."

"I'm not—" I bit back the lie and glanced into the living room, where Dad was napping on the couch. Why was I hiding this from Mom? She wasn't the one who mocked everything I did and hammered me about my lack of worth. And was it really even a date? I still wasn't sure. I hadn't planned it. And Jillian had seen Ms. Ryder hand me the tickets.

"Just take it," Mom said. "You'll thank me later."

It was easier to take the handkerchief than to argue that I didn't need it, or to explain that my plans weren't a big deal. Even though they were. I put the handkerchief in my right front pocket. "Thanks."

She reached out and straightened the back of my collar. "Have a good time."

"I will." I opened the door.

"Wait." She put a hand on my shoulder as the warm air from outside pressed against me.

"What?" I asked.

"Where does she live?"

"Off West Rismore, near the pool."

"Want a ride?"

"That's okay. You're tired."

"It's hot. That's a long walk. You don't want to show up like a ball of sweat."

"Good point." I realized Mom would know a lot more than I would about what makes a good or bad date. "Thanks."

"I'll get my keys."

When we reached the car, she said, "Don't worry. I'll drop you off at a safe distance. She won't discover you have parents."

I laughed. "I guess it would be okay if you met her someday."

"But not today?"

"Right."

"Understood."

Mom dropped me off across the street from Jillian's house. "Have a good time. Be yourself."

"Thanks. I'll try." I crossed the street.

PLAY TIME

JILLIAN ANSWERED THE door. That was good. I was afraid I'd have to get grilled by her parents, but I guess she wasn't any more eager than I to cross that bridge.

"Hi," she said. She was wearing khakis and a black short-sleeved button-down top. It wasn't dressier than my clothes, or less dressy. I'd gone with a dark blue polo shirt. I unpeeled a second layer of stress from my stack of worries, now that I knew I hadn't made a wardrobial error. Maybe I should start painting pictures of onions. . . .

"Ready?" I asked.

"Almost. I just have to grab my purse. Come meet my mom."

I entered the den. Her mother was sitting on the couch, looking through a scrapbook. She seemed younger than my parents, but I'm terrible at guessing the age of adults. There were photos on the wall behind her. I saw some of Jillian, including a series of school photos that proved she'd been pretty from the start. I also saw photos of two different men. I made note of all of this. Jillian had mentioned a stepfather. I guess the first marriage had ended without any major battles, or there wouldn't have been photos of two men. Unless one was an uncle or something. But only one of the men looked at all like her, and they weren't together in any of the photos.

I realized Jillian was talking.

"Mom," she said, "this is Cliff. We're in the same Art class."

"And Calculus," I added. I'm not sure why. I guess I didn't want her to think I was some sort of poser who spent his day walking around with a sketch pad and couldn't do serious math.

Her mother didn't look up. I was used to being invisible and inaudible to girls my age, but hadn't expected to become stealthy around adult women until I got older.

"Mom." Jillian raised her voice slightly. "Cliff's here."

She looked up. I held out my hand. She took it briefly and said, "Nice to meet you, Cliff."

I responded with similar words. She returned her attention to the scrapbook, which was open to what looked like vacation pictures.

"I'll be right back." Jillian touched my arm as if to reassure me that I wasn't being abandoned.

She left the room. As I stood there, wondering whether to try to make conversation, Jillian's mom said, "Don't let her fall in love with you."

What? That was so far out of left field, it curved back into right field. I ran the memory through my mind, trying to find a different set of words that sounded similar. There wasn't one that made any sense. I had to have totally heard her wrong, but I wasn't going to ask for an instant replay.

"Uh, okay. I'll try not to."

"All set." Jillian came back in, rescuing me from I'm not sure what. She gave her mom a kiss, and we headed out.

"I hope she didn't ask you anything embarrassing," Jillian said.

"Not at all."

It's hard to get embarrassed at stuff you don't understand. I pushed it aside. The whole encounter, with that cryptic warning, was too weird for me to digest at the moment, especially when I had a minefield of other issues to tap-dance through. I looked back at the house and tried to imagine what my mom would say if she were alone with Jillian. It would be something nice. I didn't want to think about the sort of crap my dad would greet her with, or shovel out on me after she left.

We caught a bus right after we got to the stop, a half block from her house. It wasn't crowded. We'd have no trouble sitting together. More fears allayed. I stepped past a pair of empty seats, so she could slide in first. The bus pulled away from the curb. There were only six or seven stops before the college, four in town, then two after a ten-mile stretch of highway.

As I was wondering whether this was a date, Jillian said, "So, this is a date? Right?"

"Right. I guess. I mean, yeah. If you want it to be."

She slipped her arm through mine and leaned against me. "I want it to be."

Nice. I pushed back guilty memories of Nola and allowed myself to enjoy the contact with Jillian. Her hand rested on her leg. I thought about putting my hand on top of hers. Just a friendly, casual touch. But Nola's words drifted through my mind. *"Why do guys want to touch girls?"*

The bus dropped us off right in front of the theater. When

we got seated, I pointed to the word "Tragedy" in the program and said, "Spoiler alert."

"Maybe this time will be different," Jillian said.

It wasn't. The young lovers perished. But they did so quite magnificently and eloquently. There was a reception in the lobby afterwards, so people could meet the cast, mingle, and sip watery red punch.

"I'll get us a drink," I said, heading to what I realized could be referred to as the punch line, though I didn't share that joke with Jillian. I might not know a lot about girls, but I did know their affection wasn't won through bad jokes.

As I turned toward Jillian with our drinks, I saw her talking with the guy who'd played Romeo. He was in his early twenties, and was often featured in the entertainment news in the presence of assorted models, celebrities, and bad singers. He smiled, said something to Jillian, and put his hand on her shoulder.

Something wet splashed over my right hand. I looked down and saw I'd crushed one of the cups as my fists clenched, and dented the other. I tossed the crushed cup into the trash, rinsed my hand at the water fountain, and hurried over to Jillian.

"Here," I said, handing her the cup.

"Thanks." She took the cup and turned away from the guy. "Let's go."

"What did he want," I asked after we'd crossed the lobby.

"He invited me to a party," she said.

I felt like someone was trying to yank my balls out of my body by way of my throat. "Did you tell him you're in high school?"

"I told him I was with someone," she said.

Wow. She hadn't ditched me for Romeo, even though there was no way I could compete with him. I guess I'd assumed I'd always get dumped the instant a better choice came along. Maybe it was Shelly, like Patricia, who was flawed. But what did that say about my dating choices? I hoped there wasn't a pattern. Jillian seemed perfect.

We had to wait awhile for the bus, but it was nice sitting on the bench, looking at the stars, and talking about the best parts of the play. I was almost sorry to see the Rismore bus in the distance as it turned onto College Avenue. But I was pretty sure this wouldn't be our last date.

"I'll be riding this a lot," Jillian said when the bus pulled up to the curb.

"You're going here?" I asked. I'd been afraid she'd be flying off to California for college, or Neptune.

"Commuting," she said. "They have a five-year program for engineering. What about you?"

"County, for now. I'm still not sure what I want to do."

We had no trouble finding seats together. Not that I was worried. As the bus passed the Green and turned onto West Rismore, Jillian said, "Let's walk."

"Sure. That would be great." I pulled the cord to signal the driver to let us out. The air had cooled off a bit. And even if I worked up a sweat, it would be at the tail end of the date. She'd had several hours in the company of damp-but-not-soaked Cliff.

As I walked with Jillian and marveled that nothing had leaped from the shadows to ruin our first real date, she put her hand in mine. Our fingers interlaced. I liked the feel of her palm against my bare flesh, even if it was only the flesh of my hand.

"They were doomed from the start," she said.

"It's just a story," I said.

She was quiet. I got the feeling she had more to say. It took a minute for the next words to come.

"Do you believe in curses?" she asked.

"Curses?" A shiver ran down my spine as her mother's warning came back to me, along with an image of the star-crossed lovers lying dead in a tomb at the end of the play. "What do you mean?"

"Bad luck you cause yourself," she said. "Because of things you do."

"Not really." I wondered what this was leading to, and remembered my own dismissal of any cursed connection between my words and Nola's fate. "I don't believe in stuff like that."

"Neither do I," she said. "But I don't believe in coincidence, either."

"Like what?" My mind raced through every interaction we'd had, wondering how any of them fit with coincidence or curses. Nothing came close.

"My father died when I was six. He was in a train crash." Her voice couldn't hide the lingering hurt.

I thought about the guy in the photos who had Jillian's smile and her eyes. "That's rough." Since she'd mentioned she had a stepfather, I figured her first dad wasn't around all the time. But I never would have guessed he was dead. I waited to see if there was more.

"My stepfather got caught transporting heroin," she said. "One of his sketchier friends offered him a lot of money to make one run. It was the only time he'd ever done it. We needed to cover the rent."

"Oh, man," I said. "I know how rough it can get when there's no money." I tried to picture my dad selling drugs. I think he was more the type to rob a bank or mug someone if things got really desperate.

"He was supposed to go to the county prison, but they sent him downstate. He got stabbed four days later."

"How old were you?" I asked.

"It was last year," she said. Her grip tightened.

Ouch. Fresh wounds. That was so much for one person to cope with. Jillian was watching me, as if waiting for the right time to tell me more.

Bad things happen in threes. Two deaths would be a tragedy, but probably not evidence for a curse.

"What else happened to you?" I asked.

Jillian stopped walking and faced me, but didn't let go of my hand. "My little brother," she said. "He was born seven months after Dad died in the train crash."

"The baby in the photo?" I realized I hadn't seen any little-kid debris in her house. No toys. No discarded socks.

"Johnny," she said. There was no joy in her voice. No sound of big-sister pride.

I waited.

"He died when he was three months old."

"That's brutal," I said. "I can't even imagine what that would be like." I remembered the way she'd reacted when I suggested adding a baby to the painting. Worse, I remembered exactly the words I'd used. *"You did an awesome Buddha. If you can do that, you can do a killer baby."* No wonder she'd fled the Art House.

"He was in his crib, playing with a stuffed bunny rabbit my aunt made him." The rest came in isolated sentences, bracketed with painful stops. "I picked him up. I did it all the time. He looked so happy. I put him on my shoulder and rubbed his back. He fussed a little at first, but then he got so quiet. I didn't know. The rabbit had button eyes. One of them was loose."

She couldn't finish.

"He choked?"

She nodded. Then, as we both swallowed huge portions of silence, said, "He died in my arms."

No way. I am so glad that was a thought and not a blurted exclamation. Holy shit, she'd been smacked and slammed by life. I could see where her mom might think Jillian's love was a death sentence. I'd even understand it if Jillian thought that way herself a little.

"That must have been terrible."

She nodded.

"It wasn't your fault."

"I should have noticed."

"You can't blame yourself."

"Every man in my life, everybody I loved . . ."

She dangled the thought, like a noose.

Don't let her fall in love with you.

I had context now for that bizarre warning. I hoped her mother didn't blame Jillian. It was one thing to feel that love led to curses. It was another to blame the beloved. Jillian's love was no more to blame for those deaths than my presence at the next desk was to blame for Nola's or Lucas's tragedies, or my presence at home was to blame for my father's unemployment. I left those thoughts unspoken. Jillian didn't need rational responses right now. She needed understanding.

"Damn. That's a lot to live through," I said. "You should write a book." I flinched. That sounded so stupid and insensitive.

"Nobody would believe it," she said. "It's too much."

"Yeah," I said. "You're right." It was okay in a book to have a dead parent, or a dad in jail, or a dead sibling, but all three would be way too much.

"And then I'd have to do something destructive," she said.

"Like dating the wrong guy?" Oh, hell. I can't believe I said that.

To my eternal relief, she smiled and gripped my shoulder with her free hand. "I'm too smart to do that. But you're right. That's how it would play out in a book. I'd date a guy who hit me, because I felt I needed to be punished."

"At least you didn't have a dog," I said, trying to lighten the air a bit more. "They rarely make it through a book alive."

Instead of smiling again, she gave me a look of such bottomless pain, I knew I'd stepped into another unseen pit.

"Oh, no . . . ," I said.

There was a nod buried somewhere in the convulsive sobs that followed. It was obvious, at least in Jillian's case, that life was far more painful than fiction.

She let me hold her as she cried. My God, even racked with tears and wrapped with tragedy, she felt right in my arms. But after all my years of wanting and lusting to hold a girl this close, body pressed to body, there was no passion at the moment—just compassion.

Eventually, she pulled away. "I'm sorry," she said.

"Don't be." I wanted her back in my arms. I wanted to embrace and swallow all her sorrow. I wanted to be her comfort. I settled for handing her my handkerchief, and reminding myself to do something amazingly nice for Mom.

"I needed to tell you." She dabbed the tears from her cheeks.

"I'm glad you did."

"I don't let myself get close to guys. A date or two, maybe . . . but I never let myself get close."

"You can't go through life like that." I thought about how I'd avoided any attempt at dating after I'd been hurt by Shelly.

"I know. . . . There aren't any real curses. Right?"

"Right."

We didn't talk much the rest of the way to her house. When we reached her front door, I put my hands on her shoulders and said, "I'm not going away."

"I know."

"No curses."

There was a kiss—brief but full of promise. Lips slightly parted, her hand against the back of my neck. I realized I was inhaling through my nose the very breath she exhaled, as if she were giving me a gift of life. Then, too soon, it ended.

I headed home. *I have a girlfriend.* The thought tried to fit itself into the rigid self-image I'd constructed over the years. I'd built a walled fortress from the large and small hurts thrust on me by others or brought about by my own actions. Or inactions.

I have a girlfriend.

I think.

A girlfriend who's afraid to fall in love.

I decided not to add that to my stack of worries. Not tonight.

BACK IN SCHOOL on Monday, Jillian's first glance toward me was loaded with uncertainty. I realize she might have regretted revealing so much of herself, her past, and her fears. Maybe I wasn't the only insecure human on the planet.

I smiled, trying to send a thousand reassuring messages in one simple expression. She seemed relieved. We talked in Art, but kept away from any mention of death and curses. We shared a bag of Doritos at lunch. We both thanked Ms. Ryder for the tickets when we got to Government class.

The day went perfectly. Until it ended in bloodshed.

BATTLE

⇒—————————————⇐

"FRIES?" I ASKED when Government ended.

"Sure," Jillian said.

As we cut across the front lawn, I heard a loud whoop of triumph. I glanced back just in time to see Jimby vault out of the front exit, clutching a handful of papers. He kept looking around as he walked down the center path toward the street.

"Hang on," I said to Jillian. "I think Jimby's trying to find me." I waved at him.

He stopped when he saw me, held up the papers, and shouted, "Cliff! I got a B-plus!"

"Awesome!" I shouted back.

"She said I did a good job!" He broke into a happy dance. I hate to say it, but even Jimby, loaded down with a backpack and holding a story, danced better than I did.

Some of the kids on the lawn turned toward him when he shouted, but they lost interest right away. Jimby's displays of exuberance were familiar enough to be unremarkable. As he was stomping the cement in celebration and I was grinning at the sight of his pleasure, I saw Clovis and his crew spill out of the front entrance.

"Oh, no. This is bad." I waved at Jimby again, trying to get his attention, but his gyrations had shifted him enough that he was facing away from me.

"Jimby!" Jillian shouted.

He kept up his dancing and whooping, right in the middle of the sidewalk, shouting, "B-plus! B-plus!"

"We better get over there," I said to Jillian.

"Out of my way, retard," Clovis said when he reached Jimby. There was plenty of room on either side for him to walk around, but I was pretty sure that wasn't going to happen.

Jimby froze. I knew how much he hated that word.

"You deaf?" Without waiting for a response, Clovis gave Jimby a shove.

Jimby staggered back and toppled down on his butt. I relaxed a little, relieved that Clovis hadn't punched him. He'd be okay. We knocked each other around harder than that when we played touch football. Or basketball. Even checkers, one time.

He started to get back up.

Stay down, I thought. I dropped my backpack and ran toward them.

Not having the good fortune to have this page in front of him, Jimby wasn't instantly aware of my thoughts.

He pushed himself up and screamed at Clovis, "I'm not a re-tard! You're a stupid bully. I should have let you burn up in that fire!"

Clovis recoiled and wiped his face. Oh, hell. Jimby gets a bit wet when he shouts. I rushed toward them, shifting from a jog to a full-speed sprint, but not in time to stop Clovis from punching Jimby in the stomach.

He went down again. Then he rolled on his side and puked, splattering Clovis's shoes.

"You disgusting brain-dead piece of shit!" Clovis shouted. "I'm gonna kill you!" He kicked Jimby in the face. I saw a spray of blood shoot from Jimby's nose.

I dived forward and tackled Clovis.

It wasn't exactly like diving headfirst into a tree, but it was closer to that than to a leap into a pit full of pillows.

Even so, Clovis went down.

We tumbled across the ground. I rolled free, figuring I was better off on my feet, where I could move around and avoid a choke hold or armlock. If Clovis got his arms around my neck, I'd be in trouble. I had a feeling he didn't recognize the concept of tapping out.

He was still on the ground. That should have been my chance. I could have hit him hard as he was rising. But this wasn't a movie, and I'm not a fighter. I hesitated as I contemplated my best move. Before he even got fully upright, Clovis proved his aggressive instincts were better-honed than mine. He charged forward, springing at me from a crouch. His first punch caught me on the shoulder. The next clipped my chin.

I was dazed for a moment, but mostly by the realization that I wasn't badly hurt. The punch had jolted me, but it hadn't knocked me down.

"Watch out!" Jillian shouted.

Good plan.

I backpedaled and watched Clovis's hands. He went into an exaggerated windup like a Little League pitcher and threw a looping right at my head. I blocked it with my left arm. And learned that you can't really block a looping punch that way. I took most of the impact on my forearm, but his fist still managed to continue the loop and jolt my cheekbone.

Despite the jolt, I was able to thrust my right fist straight out, hitting him in the stomach. He grunted and stepped back, more surprised than injured, I imagine. But I'd landed a punch.

I will repeat that.

I landed a punch.

My whole life, I'd never been in a serious fight. Somehow, I'd managed to avoid battle until now.

Clovis threw another looping right.

This time, I ducked.

That would have been a totally brilliant defensive strategy on my part, if he hadn't followed the right with a left to my chest. Of course, thanks to my decision to duck, my chest had been replaced as the point of impact, altitudinally, by my face.

That one caught me straight in the jaw, briefly giving me a view of several minor constellations. I went back and down. But I tucked my chin in and rolled over my shoulders.

Holy crap. I'd never done a backwards roll, either. This was a day for potentially bone-snapping firsts. I hoped it didn't turn into a day for lasts. Like last day on earth. Or last day with all my teeth. My brief exercise in gymnastics brought me next to Jimby, who was on all fours, watching the fight.

"Get out of here," I said.

"You sure?"

"Yeah, I got this covered."

"We can gang up on him."

"That wouldn't be sporting," I said. More to the point, it might bring the rest of the Thug Nuts into the fight. They seemed content, for the moment, to leave things one on one.

I figured it would also be a good idea to get Jimby to a safe spot before Clovis reached us. I pointed at Jillian. "Do me a favor. Keep an eye on her. Things could get rough."

I caught her eye, then pointed at Jimby. She nodded.

"Don't worry," Jimby said. "I'll protect her."

I had to protect her, too, from something far less solid than a fist, but far more damaging. As much as she tried to push herself away from it, I knew that somewhere deep inside, she believed that any guy she cared about would suffer. If I got badly hurt, which seemed to be Clovis's plan, she might never talk to another guy. Not that I ever wanted her to talk to *another* guy. But if I got beat up, and she felt it was her fault, it's possible she'd leave me. I couldn't let that happen. I needed to survive. More than that, I needed to win. Somehow.

I got up and wiped my forehead with my arm, trying to keep the flood of sweat from blurring my vision. Clovis came in hard. In the peripheral world that was trying its best to distract me, I realized we were ringed by a mob of cheering students. Much of the shouting seemed to involve enthusiasm for my efforts and delight at any damage I dealt to Clovis. The volume definitely rose whenever I landed a blow, or even came close.

That helped.

I also realized that whatever beating I'd taken so far from Clovis, it wasn't the first thumping I'd received. I'd been smacked plenty of times, both physically and emotionally. The Pit had walloped me pretty hard. So had Patricia and Mr. Yuler. Even Christopher and Brad, without knowing it, had smacked me in the gut with a spiked baseball bat.

Life had beaten the crap out of me in various ways over the years. I'd slipped on wet rocks once, when wading in the Black River, up near Hacklebarny State Park, and had gone down hard. That hurt a lot worse than a punch from Clovis. I'd fallen off bikes and skateboards. I'd tumbled down hills and slammed my fingers in plenty of doors.

As much as I liked to imagine myself traveling through life as a sensitive artist, I guess, deep inside, when it really mattered, I was one fucking tough dude.

I could handle this.

I kept swinging, dodging, counterpunching, and doing various pugilistic stuff I couldn't even find terms for. I had no idea how long we'd been fighting. I was panting. Sweat drenched my back and rolled down my face, stinging my eyes. Clovis was heaving for air, his breath rasping like someone having a bad asthma attack. His face was ruddy. The glare of rage was tinged with a coating of confusion. In his world, I was supposed to go down at the first punch, if not sooner.

But I guess the reality was that, unlike movie characters and comic book action heroes, both of us pretty much sucked at fighting. I, because I chose not to seek out fights. Or, to be brutally honest, because I feared them. Clovis, because he chose intimidation and weak opponents in lieu of true combat.

As he hauled back his fist for another of his increasingly predictable looping rights, I landed a solid left jab to the side of his face. My hand felt like I'd slammed it against a steel beam, but Clovis spun halfway around. The crowd cheered.

I risked a quick glance to my right. Jillian had an arm around Jimby's shoulders, both to comfort him, I'd imagine, and to keep him from leaping to my aid.

When I stepped toward Clovis to follow up my jab with a right, he lunged forward and gave me a hard shove with both hands. I staggered back as I fought to regain my balance, and bumped into the wall of flesh that ringed our arena. Past

Clovis and beyond the crowd behind him, I saw fragmented flashes of a dark suit and yellow necktie moving our way. Principal Strichtman was coming down the front steps.

We were a zero-tolerance school. It didn't matter whether someone came at you with a machete. If you fought back, you got suspended. If I got suspended, my dad would really make me suffer.

Just then, Holy Moses, the crowd behind me parted. I felt hands on my shoulders. My classmates were dragging me into the sea of spectators. To my right, Jillian whispered something to Jimby.

He nodded. His nose had mostly stopped bleeding. But it had flowed heavily enough to stain his shirt, which was also splattered with vomit.

Jimby stepped into the open area and dropped to the ground at Clovis's feet.

The crowd closed in around me, swallowing me into its anonymity like I was a marble dropped into a bowl of pudding.

The principal burst through the other side of the human-walled arena.

Jimby rolled on the ground, clutching his face and howling. "Don't hit me again, Clovis. Please don't hit me. You can have my money. All of it."

As I stood propped there, hands above my knees, and dragged oxygen into lungs that had almost quit working, I frowned, puzzled by Jimby's actions. The frown became a grin when I realized what was happening. This was perfect.

Clovis's jaw dropped. Befuddlement clouded his face. At that moment, Jimby was the smartest person in the room. Or the arena. Or maybe even the universe.

The forces of justice, in the form of a half-dozen teachers and administrators, including one excessively rough and visibly angry eight-fingered shaved-headed shop teacher, swooped in on Clovis and dragged him off. He screamed inarticulately about the frame-up being perpetrated against him, flailing his arms as he pointed alternately at Jimby and in the direction of my disappearance from the front lines.

"Tell them!" he shouted at his lackeys.

They remained mute. I could already see them sizing each other up, figuring out who would rise to the top.

A hand, cool and soft, rested against the back of my neck. "You okay?" Jillian asked, her words entering my ear on currents of a warm breath that sent a tingle through my flesh.

"I've battled floors and doors that hit harder," I said. "Not to mention some fairly jagged river rocks."

She hugged me, kissed my cheek, and whispered, "Well fought, Romeo."

I flinched at the pain, but sucked it up. Meanwhile, in the center of the former boxing ring, one of the teachers was trying to convince Jimby to go to the nurse, but he told her he was fine.

I went up to Jimby after the teacher left and asked the same question Jillian had asked me—without the erotic presentation. "You okay?"

"I'm super duper," he said. "I can act. Right, Jillian?"

"Right," she said. "You were perfect."

"I was pretty smart," he said.

"You sure were." I threw him a hug, not caring at all about the contact transmission of blood and vomit. "Smartest guy in the fight," I said.

We'd always been blood brothers at heart. This just made it official. We were blood and guts brothers.

Nicky came toward me as the bulk of the crowd dissolved.

"You did a great job blocking his fists with your chin. I'm glad you finally decided to back off and give him a chance to rest. I was getting tired just watching the two of you."

He stared straight into my eyes as he said that, and punctuated the last sentence with a small nod. Despite the joke, his face remained serious. I got the message. He would have stepped in if he felt I needed to be rescued from the risk of serious injury.

"Thanks for letting me take a beating," I said. "It would have been totally gay if you saved me." I flinched as I heard myself say that. I must have had all my good sense punched out of me.

Nicky put a hand on my shoulder. "You only get to make that joke once. And only because the way you fight was pretty close to the most stereotypical, derogatory meaning of that word. Really, it was painful to watch you flail your arms out there. You give 'straight' a bad name. Do I have to teach you everything?"

"Just the manly stuff," I said. "I definitely need guidance in that area."

"Not all of it," he said, flicking his gaze in Jillian's direction. "You seem to be on the right track."

"Well done, Rocky," Butch said, coming up to us and punctuating her sentence with a punch.

"Ouch!" I rubbed my shoulder. If I could hit like her, the fight would have lasted about five seconds.

Robert joined us, too. "Milk shakes," he said. "That's what the doctor ordered."

"Your treat?" I asked.

"Never," he said.

"Just checking," I said. "Let us wash up first. Come on, Jimby, I have an extra shirt in my gym locker."

Jimby and I, Spartans through and through, went to the

locker room to wash off the worst of the blood and vomit. Then I hobbled with my friends toward the diner, refighting the battle a dozen times in my mind.

Unlike my usual brain trick of imagining disastrous outcomes for any physical activity or encounter, this time I landed a couple awesome blows. Which wasn't all that far from reality.

After

I DIDN'T GO in through the front door when I got home. I wanted to delay dealing with my parents' reactions for as long as possible. I guess I also had a vague hope that another hour or two of healing time would make me look less like someone who'd tried to head-butt a meat grinder. I slipped in the back and grabbed a pack of peas from the freezer, before going to the patio.

The cold felt good against my cheek. I sat there, letting myself get numbed, until Jimby plopped down on the seat opposite me at the picnic table. "You're a good friend, Cliff."

"Right back at you." I was still pretty exhausted from the fight. I think I might have dozed off before Jimby came by. I didn't really remember hearing him walk over. "I know I can count on you. And you can count on me—anytime, anywhere."

He flashed me a grin. "Don't get mushy."

"I won't." I shook the bag of thawing peas. "But I think these are."

"Want to wrestle?" he asked. "I've got some new moves."

"I'm a little sore," I said. "How about we just throw the baseball?"

"Super! I'll get my glove." He ran off to his house.

I looked down at his paper, which he'd been carrying since he retrieved it from the battleground. He'd showed it to me at the diner, but I couldn't keep from reading the comments over and over. In green pen, next to the grade, his teacher had written, "Very good work. You have exhibited a great deal of creativity."

Hot damn. Good for him. And good for me, I guess. I'd given him a shove in the right direction. But he'd done all the work himself. I was amused to notice he'd even changed "Bovis Bunt" to "Bovis Burnt." It looked like I wasn't the only one who could screw around with characters' names.

Jimby had been mainstreamed as much as possible in school. But I knew there were teachers who worked with students like him. Kids who needed a little extra help, but weren't really in bad shape. I wondered how hard it was to do that. I didn't even know if it took extra years of college beside what you needed for a regular teacher's degree. I could look that up later. Right now, it was just an idle thought. I didn't even know whether I could get a college degree.

When Jimby got back, I grabbed my glove from under the table and hoisted my battle-bruised body off the bench. "You really think I'd be a good teacher?"

"You already are," he said.

"Thanks." I held my arms wide out. "I'd be a pretty good flying, samurai-sword-swinging zombie hunter, too."

"Watch out," he said, tossing the ball to me. "You say too much made-up stuff like that, people will think you're stupid."

"Good point."

"But if you write a story about that," he said, "people will see that you're smart."

"I'll keep that in mind."

We tossed the ball for a while. But I was too beat to play for long. So Jimby headed home, and I got back to icing my face and reliving the glory.

There was no way I could hide the damage from my parents. When I went to the kitchen for dinner, Dad, who was sitting by himself at the table, took one look at me and said, "Lose a fight?"

"No. Won it."

"So there's a bigger loser out there? I guess anything is possible."

I didn't bother answering that, since it wasn't really a question, and I'd had enough battles with bullies for one day.

Mom let out her usual bruise-reaction gasp when she walked into the kitchen. "You're hurt!"

"I'm okay," I said.

"Were you fighting?" she asked. "You don't get that banged up just from a fall."

Dilemma.

I could tell her I was protecting Jimby. She'd appreciate that. But Dad would shower me with hatred and disdain for taking a beating to protect someone he felt was subhuman. And he would toss that hatred on top of the pile he already had for Jimby. I didn't want that.

"I stood up to a bully. He got in trouble. I didn't."

"He couldn't have been much of a bully, if you beat him," Dad said.

I ignored him. "It's not as bad as it looks," I told Mom. "Nothing's broken. I'm not in trouble. And I have no plans to do it again."

That seemed to satisfy her. Though she did tack on a reminder that, "Violence never solved anything," before dropping the subject. Maybe she was right, but it sure felt good when I landed a punch.

I looked at the baked chicken, broccoli, and rice on my plate. I wasn't hungry. But if I picked at my food, Mom would think I was sick. So I forced down enough of it to keep her from rushing me to the emergency room or sending me off to bed.

After dinner, I went online and looked up some stuff about different types of teaching. There was special ed, of course. I wasn't sure if that's exactly what I had in mind. There was also something called "intervention," where you help kids who've fallen behind. But if I wanted to work with kids like Jimby, maybe that didn't even require a specialty. It would be easy enough to find out more. I had plenty of teachers I could ask.

While my mom didn't want me to fight, and my dad didn't think I could fight, I found out the next day in school that, as far as my classmates were concerned, there was a bit of glory in being a bully thumper.

"Good job," Christopher said when I walked past him. He offered me a fist bump.

I was briefly puzzled, but as I bumped fists with Christopher, Brad said, "You're a tough dude."

"Thanks."

I received two more fist bumps and three high fives on my way over to my friends, and a kiss on my bruised cheek from Jillian when she joined us. Throughout the morning, Jimby and

I both got a lot of praise for our part in ridding the school of Clovis. As did Jillian, for coming up with the plot.

It seemed that everybody except the administration knew the real story. Maybe they did, too. Anyone who saw me could tell I'd been in a fight. Normally, teachers are supposed to try to find out what happened if they notice a bruise, but everyone gave me a free pass.

It wouldn't surprise me if the principal was glad to get Clovis out of the school, and out of his office. But I couldn't help thinking about what would happen when Clovis returned. I wasn't afraid of a rematch, so long as it was a fair fight. That was the problem. I didn't trust him to fight fairly. Especially now that he knew I wasn't all that easy an opponent.

IN ART, I moved my easel across from Jillian. "Okay?" I asked.

"Perfect," she said.

I stepped behind her, leaned my chin on her shoulder, and studied her painting. I remember how she'd sketched in, and then rubbed out, an image of a train on her first canvas. That had to have been connected with the death of her father. She'd backed off from painting it. I guess the memory was too painful. But she'd added something new that I'm sure was even more brutally painful an experience.

I pointed at the beginning strokes of what was obviously a baby. "It's not easy, is it?"

She shook her head. I felt her shoulder stiffen, as if she wanted me to move away, or at least drop the subject.

"Sorry. I'll shut up," I said, stepping back.

"No. It's okay." She put down her brush and turned to face me. "It's hard, but I need to do it. I have to accept the past. I guess this is my therapy."

"You'd started to paint some other things from the past," I said. "Right?"

"Yeah. Some of them were happy memories. Those were easier to do. My stepfather had gotten interested in Buddhism. At least, until he found out most practitioners were against hunting and fishing. He loved going to Lake Hartwell for bass. But Mom got him a small Buddha statue one year for Christmas. That was a happy memory."

"A Christmas Buddha?" I asked. I could appreciate the irony of that.

"Yeah. He laughed about it."

"Sounds like he was an awesome guy." I thought about her first painting. "Did he give you gloves?"

Jillian smiled. "Me and Mom. Matching gloves. Three years in a row. I don't think he enjoyed shopping."

"I can see why you painted them," I said.

"I saw a therapist for a while after Johnny died. She's the one who got me to start painting. But I wasn't ready for the most painful memories. I couldn't face the train," she said. "I didn't have any kind of anchor. Nothing to hold on to. Mom tries to be there for me, but she's hurting worse than I am. And her pills kind of make her sleepy a lot of the time."

"I'm glad art helps you," I said.

"Art, and someone who understands," she said.

I wasn't sure what to say to that, so I just put my arms around her.

When I went back to my canvas, with the universe and the

twin suns, I stared at it for a while and thought about some of my recent wounds. Would it help to paint them? I grabbed a piece of paper and sketched a slice of strawberry pie forming out of the smoke rising from a smoldering joint. I tried to picture how it would look beneath the twin suns. It didn't feel right. I crumpled the paper and tossed it into the trash can. I sketched a pair of concert tickets. I crumpled that sheet. I started to sketch a blue snake slithering out a window. I stopped. The pain of those experiences seemed dull and unimportant. I'd survived a fight, defeated a bully, and found a girl I could talk with. Her tragedies, which I'd learned of in one searing, condensed moment of revelation, were far harsher than the juvenile traumas I've now spent thousands of words recounting.

But I couldn't stop worrying about my next encounter with Clovis. Suspension for fighting was only a week. He'd be back. I hated the idea of looking over my shoulder for the rest of the school year. And I hated the idea that Clovis would be the mechanism Fate chose to destroy the happiness I'd just found by putting me in the hospital, or in a coma.

As I carried my lunch across the cafeteria, I imagined Clovis tackling me while my hands were full, sending me flying across the floor.

"You look distracted," Butch said when I sat down. "Is all the fame going to your head?"

"This isn't the end of it," I said.

"You're not alone," Jillian said. "We've got your back."

Robert laughed. "I wouldn't worry about that rematch if I were you."

"What do you mean?" I asked.

"Have you noticed anything missing?" Butch asked.

"Not really."

She pointed across the cafeteria, to the empty table where the Thug Nuts usually sat. I realized I hadn't seen any of them in school today. "What happened to them?"

"They were stupid enough to make a video when they were booby-trapping the woodpile," Butch said. "It shows them talking about how they're going to crush Mr. Xander. The police arrested all of them last night."

"The police? Wait. I know the Thug Nuts are stupid. But they aren't stupid enough to post a video where other people could see it," I said.

Robert grinned. "No. But they were stupid enough to post it where someone who's smart enough could get his hands on it and anonymously pass it along to the right people."

"Brilliant," I said.

"I know," Robert said.

For once, Butch didn't argue with him.

WINDING DOWN

WE STILL HAD two weeks of school left, but at the same time things were winding down academically, they were heating up romantically. Wednesday was Senior Cut Day. I hadn't made any sort of plans. Butch was against what she called "organized group anarchy." Robert was against easily spotted acts of rebellion. I was neutral. But when I got to Calculus, Jillian said, "Meet me by the side door of the Art House, third period."

"Why?"

"It's a surprise."

Various parts of my body tingled at the mention of any surprise from Jillian. After I'd walked her home from school yesterday, and we were saying good-bye on her front porch, she'd surprised me with a very deep, wet kiss, which I'd eagerly reciprocated.

When I met her at the Art House, after surviving two periods of intense fantasies, she was holding a shopping bag.

"Here, muscles," she said, handing it to me. "You carry it."

I took the bag from her. Whatever was in there was about as heavy as a half-dozen softballs. "What is it?"

"Picnic," she said.

What a magic word.

She headed up the street. When we reached the light, she turned toward the Green. I realized she didn't really know her way around town.

"Wait. I have a better idea," I said. I pointed the other way, past the Crab Locker. "Have you been to the state park?"

"Not yet. Is it nice?"

"It's way beyond nice. I think it's my favorite place around here."

"Then let's go."

As we passed the Crab Locker, Jillian stopped and read the sign in the window. "There's a dance Saturday!" she said. "I love to dance."

"Then let's go," I said, echoing her previous words but faking my enthusiasm. *Jillian is not Shelly*, I reminded myself. And she'd already blown off Paul when he tried to hit on her in Government, her first day here. Not that he would be playing there. I saw it was going to be a fairly big-name band. They were pretty well known, at least in New Jersey.

"We just have to hike up this road, and we'll be at the overlook," I said when we reached the entrance to the park.

"It's beautiful," Jillian said.

As we walked along the road between the fields, I heard a familiar voice.

"Cliff! Hey, Cliff!" Christopher waved at me from the meadow by the overlook. Brad was with him.

"Hey, guys," I said, waving back. Then I turned to Jillian.

"There's a clearing in the woods over there. It has a fallen tree we can sit on."

"You don't want to join your friends?"

I thought about the last time I'd talked with them. It had led to a painful experience. But that was because I'd been unaware of what was really going on. They hadn't intentionally hurt me. This time, I had a full understanding of the situation. And I had a girlfriend. I hefted up the bag. "Sure. Why not? But I hope you have a ton of food in here."

"Why?"

"They're probably totally wasted," I said.

"No kidding," Jillian said. "I can tell that from here."

Maybe that's why she could paint things in such detail—because she could see them clearly. We joined our two very popular, very stoned classmates and had a great time. We even shared our pie.

We stayed in the park after Christopher and Brad left, and picked up where that kiss had left off. I slipped my hand beneath her shirt and placed it against her back. Flesh is magic. I wanted to touch her breasts, but I was afraid to spoil what I had by trying for too much.

Nola's words still haunted me. *"Why do guys want to touch girls?"*

THURSDAY, AFTER SCHOOL, Jillian and I went to a movie. While we were waiting for the ads and previews to end, I said, "You remember when you walked past me that first day, in the Art House, and I said 'sweet-ass'?"

"It caught my attention."

"I wasn't talking about your body."

"No?" She awarded me with a pout. A very cute pout. "That certainly makes the memory less interesting."

"I mean, I could have been. But I'm not like one of those guys who are crude around girls. Or women. Or—"

"Hush," she said. "I was only teasing. I know what you mean."

We watched the movie. She put her hand on my arm during one of the scary parts. I had, of course, picked a scary movie in hopes of that. I'm not a perv or a stalker, but I'm a guy, and there's a part of us that is always calculating a way to touch or be touched. It's not my fault I was born with nerve endings and testosterone. When the scary part was over, she rested her hand on my leg. I'm not sure what happened on the screen after that.

And, yes, there was a dance Saturday. And, yes, Jillian and I went. As much as I had tried to use a dance to get my hands on Shelly, I was now more concerned with not getting my hands on Jillian the wrong way—which was difficult because I wasn't totally sure which way was wrong, in her eyes.

I didn't know what she wanted, but I knew exactly what I wanted. I wanted to hold her so close, there was no way to tell where I ended and she began. I wanted to slide my hands down her back and cup that sweet ass in my hands. I wanted to grind my hips against her. I wanted all of that and more. I settled, happily, for less. It was still the best dance I'd ever been to.

Especially near the end, when the lead singer said, "You've been a great audience, and I have a surprise for you. A couple of our good friends are passing through town on their way home from a national tour."

He paused to let that sink in.

"No way . . ." I whispered to Jillian.

"They've agreed to join us for a song or two," he said. "I'm pretty sure you'll all recognize them. Let's give them a big hand."

"It can't be . . ." Jillian said.

It was.

And they played a slow song.

Yeah. I got to hear Mack and Mary, and I got to do it while Jillian was in my arms. It wasn't a whole concert, but it was perfect. I realized Jillian was rewriting my life. All the bad things I'd experienced were unwinding in wonderful and affirmative ways. I felt like a counter-clockwork orange.

So, all in all, life had become amazingly good. I had a girlfriend, I had other good friends, I'd moved up the popularity ladder a couple rungs, and I even had a slight bit of an idea about what sort of real career I could think about pursuing if I could somehow make it all the way through college. My birthday was coming. I'd finally be eighteen, and able to get my license. After all these years of being driven, I'd get to drive. I'd even figured out the perfect argument to convince Dad it made sense to spend some of the savings he controlled on a car for me. If I had wheels, I could get better-paying jobs. He couldn't argue with that.

In a novel or a movie, this moment of happiness is the point where everything would fall apart, and I would be crushed by disaster, break up with Jillian, and spend the rest of the story trying to repair our relationship and win back her heart. As you can see from the size of what remains, that won't be the case. Which doesn't mean there aren't bad and brutal things ahead. The worst is yet to come.

[AB | pro | se]
DUCTION

ON FRIDAY, WHICH was the last full day before graduation, I got slipped a surprise from Mr. Piccaro on my way out of Calculus. "I'll catch up with you," I told Jillian.

He'd written, *May this help you get lost in time,* on the wrapper. When I tore it open, I found not a time-travel novel but a blank journal. Inside the front cover, he'd written, *May this help you find yourself.*

"Lost and found," I said.

He didn't slip off like a spy. He hovered near me like he was watching a friend leave for a new life in a foreign country. "Last one, I guess," he said. "Unless you get held back."

"Unlikely, though tantalizing," I said, offering him a handshake. "So long, and thanks for all the books."

He smiled, letting me know he'd caught the Douglas Adams reference. "It's been a pleasure."

I thought about everything he'd given me during the past school year. "Was there a lesson?"

"Probably. But that's between you and the authors. Good luck. Stay in touch."

"Speaking of that . . . If I had questions about teaching, would it be okay if I asked you?"

He smiled like someone who'd just scored a goal in a tough soccer game. "Any time." With that, he slipped off.

"A book?" Jillian asked when I caught up with her.

"More like a kit," I said. I'd told her about Mr. Piccaro a while ago. I realized I'd need to find a new source of books. "Instead of the diner, want to go to the library?"

"I can't," she said.

"Why?"

"I've got stuff to do."

"What kind of stuff?"

"Stuff."

There was something evasive in her tone. I didn't press for an explanation. She wasn't my property. She could do what she wanted. But my irrational fear that something would go wrong because everything was going so well got a tiny boost from that exchange. She didn't talk much at all during Art, either. On top of that, Robert and Butch seemed unusually quiet at lunch.

"There are no curses," I muttered as I got up from my desk in Government at the end of the day. "Everything is going great. There's no reason that would change." School was over for the week, and I had a birthday to celebrate tomorrow. Not that my parents would do much. Mom would get me a present. Dad would scowl and remind me that he could now legally kick me out of the house.

Jillian dashed off the instant the bell rang. I tried to think of anything I might have done to annoy her, but nothing came to mind. Last night, I'd put my hand on her breast when we were making out. It was halfway accidental, and more to the side than right on top. I moved it as soon as I realized where it was. Okay, not instantly. But I didn't linger long enough for her to pull my hand away.

"Star-crossed lovers," Ms. Ryder said as I went past her desk.

"What?" Did she know something I didn't?

She held up the entertainment section from last Sunday's paper. "There's a nice review of *Romeo and Juliet*. I saved it for you." She pointed to the headline: SHAKESPEARE'S STAR-CROSSED LOVERS DAZZLE AND BEGUILE AT ST. JASPER'S.

"Thanks."

"They said Juliet stole the show."

"I agree." We talked a bit more. I understood. She'd missed the play and wanted to at least get a secondhand taste of what it had been like.

After I'd shared all the details I could remember, I thanked her for the newspaper and headed out.

"Cliff," she said as I reached the door.

"What?"

"Thinking back, I imagine I probably shouldn't have asked you to play 'The Riddle Song.' It's not really a crowd-pleaser."

"That's for sure."

"I had the feeling anything I tried to do at that moment would just have made things worse."

"I think you're right."

"Sorry."

"That's okay. It worked out pretty well, in the end."

I headed down the hall toward the gym.

Might as well go home. . . .

The school was pretty much empty now. I spotted Nicky leaning on the wall by the water fountain outside the locker room door. I waved. He obviously saw me, but he didn't wave back. At least he stayed put. If he'd dashed off, too, I'd know for sure I'd done something wrong.

"Hey," I said when I reached him. "What's up?"

"We need to talk," he said.

I was going to make a joke of some sort, but as my brain was shuffling through the various branching humor paths that could be used to construct a reply, I noticed his expression was scarily serious, like he was searching for the person who'd keyed his car or egged his house.

"Uh, okay," I said. "What do you want to talk about?"

"Not here." He dropped an arm across my shoulders, bent it just enough to trap the back of my neck, which wasn't much bend at all, given the size of his muscles, and started walking down the hall.

I went along with him. The only other choice would have been a slow decapitation reminiscent of pulling a piece of warm taffy apart. My brain abandoned a hunt for humor and began a search for anything I could possibly have said or done that might have angered my friends.

Nothing.

Wait!

This morning, when Butch held out her wrist for me to smell her new perfume, I'd said, "Fruity."

I'd meant "fruitlike." But what if Nicky had been walking behind me at that point and thought I was calling him names?

I could try to explain that to him, but I realized he could be pissed about something totally different, and I'd only be making things worse. Maybe he'd decided my "gay" comment after my fight with Clovis was unacceptable. It would be smart to wait and see.

But what if he started to choke me? Some people get angry slowly. Others snap unexpectedly and lash out. His anger could be building with each step.

Oh, hell. What if Jillian didn't like that I'd sniffed Butch's wrist? But she knew Butch and I were just friends.

Nicky led me down to the basement. I realized he was taking me to the band room. There was no light coming through the space at the bottom of the door. The hallway was dark, too, as if someone had turned off most of the lights. This was starting to resemble an organized effort. Not that Nicky needed help if he wanted to squash me.

Every rubout scene from every mob movie I'd ever watched ran through my mind. I wondered whether I'd get a baseball bat across the kneecaps or a bullet in the back of my head.

Nicky reached past me with his free hand, turned the knob, and pulled the door open. "You're about to get what you deserve," he said.

He pushed me inside the dark room. I tripped, fell, and hit my knees. I heard him coming in behind me.

The lights blazed on.

I hunched down and raised my hands to cushion my head, bracing for another beating.

"Surprise!"

Jillian, Butch, Robert, and Jimby were there, standing beneath a banner that proclaimed, HAPPY BIRTHDAY! Butch was holding a cake, complete with unlit candles. The others were holding presents.

I looked over my shoulder at Nicky. "You almost made me shit my pants," I said.

He shrugged. "Hey, 'almost' only counts in hand grenades and horseshit. I'm glad you bought it. Happy birthday, bitch."

Jillian dragged a small cooler from under the table and pulled out a two-liter bottle of cola. She'd also brought party cups with HAPPY BAR MITZVAH, MIKEY on them. "They were on sale," she said.

Butch got a Zippo from her pocket and started lighting the candles.

My folks had thrown parties for me when I was little. But my last few birthdays had been lonesome affairs, and nobody had ever done anything like this. I could feel myself dangerously close to choking up, like those people on TV who'd just won the lottery or survived a tornado. I didn't want that. I pushed against my emotions and got control.

Butch stepped forward with the cake. "Baked it myself," she said. "From scratch."

"And cooked all of this up?" I asked.

"With some help." She nodded toward the others.

I thought about how I'd been sidetracked in Government. "Ms. Ryder, too?" I asked.

"Yup," Robert said. "She was happy to assist us in your delay, but unwilling to actively participate in an unsanctioned use of school property. But I promised her a photo. And I think I got a great shot of you cringing in terror."

"No Internet," I said.

He flashed me a grin. "Of course not."

"Thanks, Butch," I said. "Thanks, everyone."

"It's Penelope," she said.

"Penelope?" The syllables felt foreign on my tongue. "No nickname? You're going with your real name?"

"I'm tired of that game," she said. "I'm heading off to college soon. I need to find out who I am, and I think that starts with not trying to be someone else."

"I don't know if they're ready for a force of nature like you up in Syracuse," I said.

Butch—I'll refer to her that way for the remainder of this story, so as not to confuse things—gave me a funny grin. "It's Rutgers," she said. "I switched."

"What? That's where Robert is going."

"I know." Butch and Robert exchanged a meaningful look.

"Seriously?" I asked. I realized I hadn't seen her with Judah in ages, and Princeton had been out for at least two weeks.

"Maybe. Maybe not," she said. "I guess we'll find out."

I thought about Butch, her long, silky hair, her compact body, and her amazing mind. She'd been briefly unattached, and I'd been unaware. I doubt, had I known, I would have chased after her. But that didn't keep my mind from going where it wanted. That's another dark secret about me. I suspect it might be a secret every guy harbors. Whenever I hear that any hot female is suddenly available, even if she's a movie star, model, or singer who would never in a billion years even glance at me or cross my path, I fantasize briefly about the impossible possibilities. I guess, just like schadenfreude is the flicker of a smile you get when you hear about someone else's suffering, there should be a word for the flicker of hope you feel when you hear about someone's availability.

"Don't worry," Jillian said, draping an arm across my shoulders. The scent of her shampoo brought me back to the real world and reminded me that, thanks to her, my life right now was far better than any fantasy. "They'll still let you hang out with them. You have your charms."

"But forget about the front seat," Robert said.

"That's enough revelations for one party," Butch said. "Let's get back to you, and that wonderfully humiliating tradition I've been looking forward to all day."

Robert had brought his father's guitar. "I spent all evening learning this," he said. He strummed what seemed to be random chords while everyone sang "Happy Birthday."

Butch held the cake toward me and said, "Make a wish."

I glanced at Jillian, blushed, pushed my mind away from the biochemical frenzy the wish had sparked in my groin area, and blew out the candles.

Cake is just as awesome as pie, especially when shared with friends who are aware you are there. And when the icing has been applied by someone who appreciates excess.

I think everyone says, *No, I don't want a party*. But, the truth is, a party is nice. And a surprise is even nicer. Especially if you've never had one.

"Open mine first," Robert said, handing me a present.

It was a half dozen of those pine tree deodorizers you hang from a rearview mirror. "For when you get your car," he said. "I don't know what kind of make, model, or year it will be, but I'm sure it will require many of these."

Robert held up another present.

"Two?" I asked. "What did you do with the real Robert?"

"It's not from me," he said. "Ms. Ryder asked me to give it to you."

It was a book. *The Water Is Wide*. It looked like it had something to do with teaching.

Nicky handed me a plastic card. It was a gym membership. "Free pass. Use it as often as you want. A friend of my parents' owns the place, and I work there sometimes as a trainer. You just have to promise not to wear a shirt."

As I stared at him, he said, "I'm kidding, dimwad. Nobody wants to see your scrawny body."

Jimby laughed and said, "Keep your shirt on, Cliff."

"How about we drop the subject of my torso and get back to the presents?" I said.

Butch gave me a book of poems by Gerard Manley Hopkins. I wasn't familiar with him. "Something to balance the macho street brawler side of you," she said. "We don't want you launching into a life of thuggery, just because you're good with your fists."

Jillian also gave me a book. *The Artist's Way*. "Every artist should read this," she told me.

"Here," Jimby said, handing me something that turned out to be enveloped in five or six feet of wrapping paper. It was an Incredible Hulk action figure. I think it came from his collection, and reflected his view of me, which made it all the more meaningful.

"Thanks," I said. "This gets a special spot on my desk."

We ate cake and drank soda. The guys mocked me in the affectionate way that North Jersey friends do. Eventually, people drifted off.

And then there were two.

I looked around the band room—empty except for Jillian and me. Were we going to make out? This wasn't exactly the perfect place. The main character in *Stranger in a Strange Land*, Valentine Michael Smith, who grew up on Mars, is an amazing kisser because he gives the kiss his total concentration in a way that people raised on Earth can't do. I wanted more of those deep wet kisses and gentle neck bites we'd exchanged, but I knew I'd be distracted, waiting for someone to walk in and catch us in an unsanctioned use of school property. Even so, the thought of snuggling with Jillian, and maybe testing how much further we could go, set my blood racing.

As I followed that line of thought, Jillian faced me and took my hands. "My mom had to take the train into the city. She'll be gone until late this evening, birthday boy."

"Then we've got your place to ourselves." I tossed that line out as a joke and added an exaggerated wink so Jillian would know I wasn't trying to take advantage of her.

"Exactly," she said. She didn't wink. She didn't laugh. She leaned forward and kissed me, then said, "Let's go."

COMING OF AGE

"**WE HAVEN'T BEEN** going out long," I said.

"Are you trying to talk me out of this?" Jillian asked.

"No!" I sorted through my feelings as I stood in her living room. Nice girls didn't sleep with guys this easily. Or did they? Jillian was a nice girl. "It's just—I can't believe I'm so lucky." I flinched at the word "lucky." Guys always talked about getting lucky, which was another just slightly less crude way of saying they got laid. I didn't want to imply anything demeaning.

"Shhhh." She pressed a finger against my lips. "I'm not a slut. I'm not a whore or an easy piece of ass. I'd never rush into sleeping with someone. I like you a lot. But I can tell from the way you fight to keep your eyes from straying, and the way you tense up when we touch, that one thing fills up most of your mind most of the time. Right?"

"Guilty." I shuddered at the idea that my lust was so badly hidden. Before I could say anything in my defense, she went on.

"You are so obsessed with this that it would stand in the way of any kind of real relationship between us. And I very much want a real relationship with you. You're a great guy. You're smart and sensitive. You stand up for people. You can be funny without being crude. You love nature. You're nice to waitresses. We're good together. Maybe even great. We need to take this step. As much for me as for you. So, shut that sweet, hot mouth of yours. Okay?"

I nodded, enjoying the feel of her finger sliding across my lips as my head bobbed in agreement. I thought about slipping my lips over her fingertip, but I was now totally terrified of any false move that would cause her to change her mind.

She took my hand and backed toward the steps. I followed, like a balloon on a string.

We went up to her room.

My heart was slamming its fists against the inside of my chest in a drum roll that seemed destined to end with an explosion. I know that's a terribly constructed metaphorasimile or whatever, but my brain was totally drowning in unbound electrical discharges, and functioning at the lowest lizard level. If a fly had zipped past me, I might have snagged it with my tongue.

Jillian began to unbutton her shirt. She took her time. I wanted to rip it wide in a dramatic act of masculine bravado, turning buttons to bullets that ricocheted off the walls. But this didn't seem like the time for macho acts of wardrobial destruction. This seemed the time to avoid doing anything that might make her think she'd made a terrible mistake.

Unassisted, she got the shirt—that awesome, pure-white, breast-cradling shirt—unbuttoned. She flipped it over her shoulders, then dangled her arms back so the shirt slid off, a silent angel falling from grace. Or toward it.

Her bra was beige, and lacy at the edges. I'd seen a thousand of them in the catalogs that I'd snitched from the mail, wrapping the bodies of impossibly constructed women. But Jillian was nothing but possibilities at the moment. I leaned forward, sure I would botch this part. I'd never had an opportunity to explore the mystic or mythic workings of a bra clasp.

To my relief, she smiled and reached behind her.

The bra fell.

Her breasts were the most beautiful natural wonders I'd ever seen. There are no words. I'd seen chest-loads of bare breasts in photos and videos. But these—they were here, in the room, in my life.

Jillian slipped into bed, lying on her back. I lay next to her, to her right, on my left side, trying to hide my trembling. I reached out across her body and placed the palm of my right hand against her left breast. I knew my own body, in all its textures and firmnesses. I knew Jillian's face, neck, shoulders, hands, arms, and back. But I'd never felt flesh like this. It was warm and firm, but soft. It seemed to press back against my hand, through some sort of biological magic.

My god. If I died now, my life would be complete.

But I lived.

I moved my fingers slightly, feeling the indescribable wonder of Jillian's breast. I slid my palm across her flesh, traveling in slow circles. She shuddered, and moved her head closer to me. I felt her soft hair against my left arm. She kissed my shoulder, then bit it gently.

Unsure what was allowed, I raised myself up on my side and kissed her right breast gently, delicately, as if I were the guardian of a shimmering soap bubble. I paused, waiting to see whether she'd tell me to stop. She slipped an arm beneath my side and caressed my back.

Something else beckoned.

I slid my right hand down her stomach, over the indent of her navel, and beyond.

My fingertips met the tightness of her pants across her waist. I pressed gently downward, feeling the taut muscles of her stomach yield to the pressure. My hand slipped past her belt, below her waistband but above her panties.

I felt soft cotton beneath my fingers, and rougher denim against the back of them. I eased my hand out and slipped my fingers beneath the elastic.

I hesitated. She didn't stop me. I felt nails grip my back. Sweet pain.

I slid my hand forward, over supple flesh and firm bone. As my wrist brushed the hard curve of her right hip bone, my mind tossed out a thought of Scylla and Charybdis. But I wasn't voyaging between Homeric monsters. I was navigating toward paradise. I could picture what lay ahead in the small part of my mind that wasn't chanting *ohmygod!ohmygod!ohmygod!* My hand reached the precipice. I cupped my fingers over the edge, toward the warm mysteries that Jillian offered me.

And that was how I wish it had been.

And that is probably enough for any of you dick jockeys out there to get yourselves off. I don't blame you. I got pretty firm writing it. Go wash your hands. Or change your shorts. Or if you're a real perv, be a good guy and wipe off the underside of the library table you just spooged. I'll wait.

Yeah, I lied to you again. Just like at the start. But that's only two lies. And they came pretty far apart. Besides, lie or not, you know you're going to read that part again and share it with your friends. And, in many ways, it's not a lie. It's a fantasy. It's one of the thousand ways I'd imagined I would come of age. Except for not happening, it was totally real, and belongs here as much as anything else I've told you.

Ready for the truth? Here's how it happened after we reached her room. Really. And I'm pretty sure when you hear the truth, you'll understand why I had to share the fantasy first.

"You're not the only one who's been wanting this," Jillian said. She pushed down against her belt on either side of her hips and dropped her pants without unzipping them. Then she slipped out of her panties. They were pink. She left her shirt untouched.

I pushed off my own pants and underwear in one move. I wanted to leap on her and end my virgin years. But something that had been drilled into us by a series of self-conscious health teachers all through middle school and high school wrapped its latex arms around my horny crotch.

"What about . . ." I groped for the right way to say it.

"Protection?" she asked.

"Yeah."

"I'm on the pill," she said. "Mom put me on it when I turned fifteen. She said it was for my acne."

"Acne?" I asked. "The pill helps acne?" There was so much I didn't know. But I guess it worked. Her skin was unblemished.

Jillian nodded. "The truth is, Mom got pregnant when she was seventeen. She decided that this was one experience she didn't want to become a family tradition."

What about a condom? I knew about sexually transmitted diseases. But I didn't have one. That was for sure, unless self-inflicted friction burns counted. And I didn't care if I caught something. Not right now. Not when my groin was screaming for me to get to work and release eighteen years of hormonal pressure.

Still, there'd be a price. I knew that. If I had sex without a condom and didn't suffer in some dreadful way, I'd be telling a tale with no redeeming values.

Screw it. The hell with morality and redemption. I'd willingly take whatever came.

Jillian dropped onto the bed and held her hands out to me.

I climbed on top of her, propping myself with my arms so I wouldn't put too much weight on her.

"Cliff . . . ," she whispered. It wasn't a statement or a question. It was my name. As if to affirm that it was right for me to be here.

"Jillian . . . ," I whispered back, as afraid in the reality of this moment as I'd been in my fantasy of spoiling everything by an action or inaction.

This is it.

I was about to leave my virginity behind me. I thought about the HAPPY BAR MITZVAH, MIKEY cups. Today, I was about to become a man.

I shifted my hips until we were in line. Jillian, below me, was a mix of warm flesh and sharp bones. Right now, I would have died for her. I would have cut off my arms and legs. But not my penis. That guy had a mission.

I raised my hips slightly and maneuvered. I was flying on instruments now, coming in for a landing on a mysterious island paradise.

This is it!

I let myself slip between her legs.

This is really it!

I started thrusting with my hips.

Is this it?

All those stories, all those years of hearing about sex. Metaphors, similes, hyperbole. I wanted angels to sing. I wanted chrysanthemum fireworks to explode in the sky. I wanted trains to shoot through tunnels and waves to crash on a sandy shore.

It was . . . sort of nice. Better than jacking off, but nowhere near the realm of trains and angels. I realized Jillian hadn't made a sound yet. From movies, I knew that women were supposed to moan in ecstasy if you did it right. They shouted "Yes!" or screamed your name. They called on God. Were those movies all a lie?

Jillian spoke my name. But it wasn't a scream. "Um, Cliff?" she said.

"What?" I asked, keeping up a steady humping motion.

"Don't you want to come inside me?"

"Uh . . ." I slowed my movement and tried to isolate the sensations I was receiving from my groin. I felt the roughness of pubic hair and the friction of some sort of fleshy contact. But it seemed pretty likely I was thrusting myself downward between her legs. Okay, not just likely. That's what was happening.

I was thigh-humping Jillian. They were awesome thighs, but that's not what they were designed for.

"Cliff?"

"Oh, yeah. Sorry."

As I spoke, she reached down and guided me inside her.

That, as some of you know, and all of you can surmise, was much better.

Much, much better.

Explosively, delightfully, angel-and-train-and-chrysanthemum better.

When it was over and we were lying side by side, breathless, moist, and content, I figured I should confess my lack of experience. "That was my first time."

Jillian laughed, slid out of bed, and pulled on her pants. "I figured." It was a gentle laugh, incapable of bruising even the most delicate ego.

"Was I okay?" I asked.

"You were the most amazing stud who's fucked me today," she said. "Of course, the day isn't over."

It took a second for me to process that and figure out she was pulling my leg. In my defense, I'm pretty sure there was no blood available at the moment to carry oxygen to my brain. As I stepped into my pants and stared at her shirt-encased breasts, which had remained fabric bound during the entire time we'd been in bed, I felt a warmth and firmness chasing away the spent feeling in my groin.

I realized, though we'd just had sex, I still had never seen her without her shirt, except in my fantasies. I reached out and touched a breast, gently. She sighed and leaned toward me. The firmness in my groin got more definite. "Do we have time to do it again?" I asked.

She looked at me like I was asking her to pick a card. Any card. "Seriously? You're ready to go again?"

"Yeah. I've got a lifetime of lust bottled inside me," I said. "You might never get out of here."

Another laugh. "We'll see."

She slipped her pants back off. And her shirt. She let me remove the bra. I suspect she would have been quicker at it. I know whatever I lacked in dexterity, I made up for in enthusiasm.

Later, when I finally got out of bed and started to put my pants on, Jillian stared at me, right at crotch level, and frowned.

Before I could feel embarrassed or worry that I was underendowed or deformed in some way, she tilted her head to the side and moved her lips, as if mouthing four words. I realized she was reading my inverted tattoo.

AND SO IT GOES.

"Maybe you should change 'so' to 'in' as a reminder," she said.

"I don't think that will be necessary," I said. "I'm a fast learner."

"Yes, you are," she said. "And a cute one."

And that, my dear, sticky-handed friend, is the way it happened my very first, and second, and almost third (but for that whole willing-spirit, weak-flesh thing) time.

Oh, and by the way, Venus is also the evening star.

AFTErGLOW

WHEN I GOT home, I went down to the basement, dug up the David Bromberg album, and put on "Wallflower."

As it played, I danced.

Slowly. Happily. Unself-consciously. By myself, but no longer alone.

InTROSPECTIOn,
ReDUX

SO. I CAME of age. Big-time. And we are almost back where we started. The narrative, at this very moment, has reached the night before that morning where I first grabbed your attention with an act of violence. I had my payoff. You got to watch. Now you get yours, as the end unfolds, merges with the beginning, and all things come full circle. I only wish I could get to watch you reach your climax, the way you saw me reach mine. I've been working pretty hard, trying to get you off. Literarily.

But symmetries are elusive, if not mythical. As are coincidences, and most hunts for meaning.

Enough. I've become a man of actions, not words. Let us go where we need to be. Back to the start. Yes.

COMING OF RAGE

MY PHONE RANG. It was Jillian.

I'd been awake for at least an hour, but I just got dressed. Before that, I'd lain there, thinking about last night, reliving the amazing moments I'd experienced with Jillian, and wondering how my life could have taken such an astonishing turn.

"Hi," I said.

"I'm pregnant," she said.

"Pregnant?" I saw my life turn into a series of double shifts in front of rancid deep fryers, punctuated by periods of being cried at and puked on by some nubby little bundle of flesh I was supposed to bond with and adore. I saw myself becoming an angry parent, mocking my kid and his ambitions when I should be showering him with love. Hating him because he took away my freedom. And I hated myself for picturing all of that.

Jillian giggled. "You idiot. Did you sleep through Biology?"

"So you're not pregnant?" I asked. My heart rate fell back into double digits.

"Probably not," she said. "I mean, there'd be no way to tell, this soon."

"So that was a joke?"

"Got ya," she said. "You really are cute, birthday boy."

I would have gotten angry if I weren't already planning our next get-together.

"Yeah, you got me. I'm easy," I said.

"I'm not," she said. Her tone was suddenly serious.

"I know," I said. I heard footsteps coming down the hall. I didn't want to share any part of Jillian with Dad. I lowered my voice. "You don't leap into bed with just anyone. You gave it a lot of thought. I hope you don't feel you made a mistake."

"No. I feel good. Better than good."

"Me, too."

"Come over later?" she asked.

"Sure."

We exchanged good-byes, and I hung up.

I heard a crash. Dad punched my half-open door, so it slammed against the wall.

"*You got some slut pregnant?*" Dad yelled. His face was a shade of crimson you rarely see outside of cartoons, and his knuckles were red from punching the door. I guess I'd shouted that word loud enough for it to carry down the hall.

"No!" I looked around, as if a calming answer lay somewhere in my room. "She was kidding."

"So you're screwing around?" He stepped in and slapped the phone out of my hand. It hit the wall, then fell to the floor.

"It was a joke!"

"Joke?" He jabbed his finger out, poking me hard in the shoulder. "Your whole life is a joke. I lose my fucking job. I bleed myself dry, paying for everything you and your mother want, and you run around taking chances with some tramp?"

Nobody calls my girlfriend names. I wanted to grab him by the neck and throw him out the window. But I knew that was a fantasy.

"She's on the pill," I said. "She's not a tramp. And you haven't paid for anything in ages. Mom and I earn all the money."

Damn. Wrong answer.

Dad hit me with an open hand, rocking my head so hard, I thought my neck would snap. The smell of blood welled inside my sinuses.

"Idiot!" he shouted. He slapped me again. "Stupid loser idiot!"

I put up my hands, open, palms out, as if that would ward him off. He clenched his fists and threw a hard punch, smashing into my forehead. Unlike Lucas, I didn't have a wall behind me to hold me up. I went down as the world spun in wild circles around me. I felt a sharp pain explode through my skull, followed by wet warmth running down the side of my face.

We're back at the start. The beginning. The opening of the story. The edge of the Cliff.

And we're back at the truth. The real truth. I lied when I said the beating was a lie. That's the honest and ugly truth. Shit—who wants to tell the world his father uses him as a punching bag?

Some truths can be cast as lies. And some lies can be cast as truths. I said he got drunk only three or four times a year. True.

And then he'd stay drunk for months. That's why Mom drove us everywhere. And that's why he couldn't find a job. It's why he lost his awesome job in the first place. And why he lost the next job after that.

Instead of a belt buckle, I'd had my face gashed with his Bucknell ring. Close enough. True enough. Painful enough. Blind in one eye? Yeah—for now, as blood ran from a gash in my forehead. Three lost teeth? Happily for me, and my damn fine teeth, that part was pure fiction.

And all those places where I said Dad smacked the table or hit the roof? Pretty much true, except he spared the table and smacked the child.

I spewed out a shitload of clues for you.

Dad would really make me suffer.
After being smacked down repeatedly . . .
Dad would definitely hit a wall or two.
I couldn't help picturing a fist crunching into my
*   face.*
Dad would kick him right back out. . . .

It was all there. His violence, his anger. My growing immunity to beatings. Mom's overreaction to every bruise. She'd seen only the mild stuff. The things he could get away with under the guise of strict parenting, tough love, or boyish roughhousing. Poke. Prod. Shove. But I'm sure she lived in fear of him doing worse to me, and in denial our lives were all that bad.

I wanted to spill the sorry truth out for you from the beginning. But I was ashamed. I was beaten in too many ways. I guess, after constantly hearing what a loser I was, I blamed myself for a lot of his anger. As much as I needed help, I was incapable of asking for it. Until now. Until someone helped me see my worth. Until someone let me be her anchor. And let herself be mine.

So, now you have no idea what to believe. And you probably don't want to believe that this version is the truth, because it sucks to accept that anyone would use his kid for a punching bag. And because it is true too often in our sad and violent world. If we ever meet, I'll show you the scar on my forehead. I'll let you touch it, Thomas, and erase your doubts.

Here is all I have to offer as I try to tie together the threads I've dangled and make my exit. I hope it's enough. Either way, here it is: If I were, in my heart, in my core, a liar, would I have told you the pathetic, fumbling truth of my first attempt at making love? Would I have confessed that Maddie climbed out a window to avoid me, or that someone I thought was a friend wouldn't want to be seen with me at a concert?

Brother. Sister. Whoever you are, taking this journey with me—the only unconfessed lie that lay hidden throughout this voyage came at the start. And its nakedness has been uncovered. Its half and quarter truths have been revealed.

But there are still shards of shattered narrative to sweep up from that first meeting. What else is true? Alexander Graham Bell's invention saved my life. But not by interrupting the beating with a phone call. How realistic would that be? Punch, punch, ring, ring. *Hold on, I have to take this. Hit yourself for a minute until I can come back.*

No.

After my father landed that first solid punch to my forehead, knocking me down, I grabbed my phone from the floor and thumbed 911. Before I could say anything, Dad stomped the phone hard enough to kill the call. He would have stomped my hand, too, if I hadn't snatched it out of the way.

All those times he'd slapped me, I thought he'd lost control. Now, as I saw the crazy anger in his eyes, I realized how wrong I was. Those slaps in the past hadn't hurt as much as they might have, because he'd kept some control. He knew he couldn't get away with doing any real damage. He'd been like a drunk taking small swigs from a hidden flask to tweak his blood alcohol to a tolerable level. Now that he'd drawn real blood, there was no reason for him to stop.

This is what he'd wanted all along—to make me hurt outside as much as he himself hurt inside. And he was on his way to getting his wish. He was far stronger than Clovis. And this wasn't a school yard fight. This was a merciless beating. I curled up and wrapped my arms around my head as he pummeled me and screamed obscenities.

"Stop!" I yelled.

That only seemed to fuel his anger. All I could hope was that he'd get tired, or regain some control, before he killed me.

But there are some things in this world you can't take back once they've been set loose. A 911 call is one of those. Even if you hang up, or crush the phone, they have to check it out. So I wasn't saved by the bell. I was saved by the call. The police were at the door less than two minutes later.

I'd protected my abuser all these years. Hid my bruises when he wasn't careful where he hit me. Made up stories. Maybe that explained my creativity. I was an amazing liar, and obviously awkward at navigating my way through the spills and bruises of life. And he was sly enough not to lash out with too much fury when Mom was there.

It wasn't always bad. He played the Perfect Dad role pretty well at times. We went on nice vacations. I got excellent presents when times were good. Guilt is Santa's biggest helper. But whenever Dad lost a job, and had more free time at home to drink and brood, I knew there'd be pain. I took it all, and never told anyone.

This time, my face bleeding like the severed head of a goat, my father reeking of cheap gin, I wouldn't have needed to say anything when the police were drawn inside by my screams for help and his cries of rage.

But I did. I said everything. As I spilled my guts, I felt like I was vomiting demons and razor blades. The cops stared at me with a mix of sympathy and weary familiarity. They stared at Dad with a look that said they'd be happy to shoot him in the back of the head and dump his corpse in an alley.

If I thought having sex after so many years of lusting for it was explosive, it was nothing compared to ripping myself away from beneath the boot of the man who beat me. The vast, uncertain future I'd always feared if I ever spoke the truth now seemed manageable and far from terrifying. Just as I was no longer a virgin, I was no longer a victim.

"He asked for it!" Dad shouted when I'd reached the end of my torrent of accusations and lay there, gasping for breath. "He's always been a loser. Always pushed me. I think he likes getting hit."

They took him out first, handcuffed and thrashing.

"You're finished!" he screamed as they dragged him down the hall. "I want you cleared out of my house before I get back."

So I was homeless at eighteen. And so beaten, I couldn't even think about what to do or where to go when all of this was over. And then, as they were leading me down the stairs, those same stairs that played such a violent role in our first encounter, one final lie came true. Three steps down, I fell, dropping like someone had hit me with a sledgehammer.

BeD, anD THe ResT

I WOKE IN the hospital, confused. Dad hit me only once in the head, not counting the slaps. The blow hadn't been hard enough to knock me out. My arms had pretty much taken the rest of the pummeling.

Mom was there. Sitting in a chair by the side of my bed. Keeping vigil. For a disoriented, fuzzy moment, I couldn't separate my identity from images and memories of Nola. Had I gorged on a fistful of pills that dark night when I nearly gave up on life?

"What happened?" I asked.

Mom sprang from the chair. "Don't try to sit up. The doctors think you've had multiple concussions," she said. "There was a blood clot. It got knocked loose."

"Will I be okay?" From what little I knew, clots could do terrible things to your body. I listened to my own voice. My speech wasn't slurred. I flexed my fingers. My hands seemed to be okay.

"You'll be fine. You were lucky the police were there. You passed out on the stairs. But one of the officers caught you. They took good care of you. I never knew—" She gasped as anguish seized her voice, then continued, measuring each word. "I mean, I knew he was rough. That's how his father was. And his father's father. But I had no idea it was this bad. If I knew he was hurting you, I would have done something. Multiple concussions. Why didn't you say something? Why did you hide it?"

Concussions? Even in my current half-dazed state, I found an explanation easily enough. The fall into the Pit. My fight with Clovis.

"Those weren't from him," I said. "I fell. The Pit. Remember? Then I got into a fight." It made sense now, why I'd been so sleepy those days. And why I'd felt nauseated.

"You don't have to lie. Not anymore." She threw her arms around me. "I'm so sorry."

"I really was in a fight. You can ask Jimby," I said. "I was protecting him. Robert and Butch can back me up. You have to believe me."

"I do. But this morning, what happened, there's no excuse for that."

She was right. "I think Dad's in jail."

"Yes, he is." She held me tighter.

"I don't know what's going to happen to him," I said. *Or to us.*

"Things will work out," she said.

"Did he ever hit you?" I was pretty sure he hadn't. But he could have hidden things from me as easily as he'd hidden them from her. If he'd ever hit her, he deserved to rot in jail.

"Never."

There was an odd rise in pitch at the end of that word. I stared at her.

"Once. It was a long time ago. Just once. It was an accident."

I waited. It took her a moment to start.

"I was sort of a free spirit back then," she said.

"Free spirit?" I contemplated various interpretations of that phrase.

"I had a boyfriend when I met your father," she said. "Ross was an artist. Brilliant. Wild. Passionate about life. All my friends were artists, poets, and painters."

"So you dumped this guy for Dad?"

"Not right away. But your father was very persistent. He was charming, funny, and thoughtful."

I could see the persistent part. I guess I inherited something from him, after all. But I couldn't picture the charm. "So what happened?"

"I foolishly decided it would be okay to meet both of them at an outdoor concert. I wanted them to be friends. All my friends got along with each other."

"Knowing Dad, that doesn't sound like the best plan," I said.

"It wasn't. Your father and Ross got into a terrible fistfight. I can't even remember who threw the first punch."

"And Dad beat him up?" I asked. I could testify to the force of his punch.

Mom shook her head. "No. He got beaten pretty badly."

"And you fell for the loser?" It gave me more pleasure than I'd care to admit to stick that word on Dad.

Mom nodded.

"So it became Beauty and the Beaten," I said.

"That's what it became."

"But you said he hit you once. . . ."

"It was after I'd graduated. We were—" She paused, then apparently decided I wasn't in a judgmental mood. "—living together. This was before we were married. One of the guitarists from my old band decided to take a shot at really making a living with music. He asked me to join him. I wanted to give it a try. The idea of earning a living doing what I loved was so powerful. Your father was dead set against it. I guess the fact that the guitarist was Ross's brother didn't help. We argued. I turned my back on him and started playing, to drown him out. He got louder. I played harder. He came around and tried to knock the fiddle from my hand. I was swaying when he swung his hand. He wasn't aiming at me." She left the next part unspoken.

"That sucks."

She rubbed her cheek. I didn't think she was even aware of the motion. "He was so sorry. And it was an accident."

"There's no excuse," I said. "Never."

"I know. I moved out that night. We talked a lot before I agreed to come back."

I guess I could forgive one terrible mistake that he made long ago. But he'd made a series of mistakes after that, with me as the recipient. I tried to picture the funny, charming man she'd described, but all I could see was drunken anger and resentment.

"Did Dad ever love me?" I asked.

"Your father loves you," Mom said. It was an instant and automatic response. I waited for the truth.

"He loved you when you were little and he was sober," she said.

I shook my head. "Booze can make you do a lot of things. But I don't think it can make you hate what you love."

"I know he loved you . . . ," Mom said.

I allowed her to cling to that fiction, but couldn't bring myself to validate it with a response.

"I love you," she said. "Don't ever doubt that."

"I won't."

I thought about when we used to visit Dad's father. He'd give Mom a hug but pretty much ignore Dad. And me. We'd stopped going there after Grandma died. Something always came up. If I tried to come to grips with all of the past, right now, I'd drown. For the moment, I had to deal with the present and future.

I wrestled with the idea of Dad in jail. He'd never hit her after that one time. Maybe he'd be able to stop hitting me. "I could tell the police I started it," I said. "I'd brought up money and shoved it in his face. That's when he'd lost it."

Mom stepped back. I think a thousand thoughts flashed through each of our minds. I can't speak for her thoughts, but I know mine. I could save him, maybe, from jail, if I could figure out the right story.

What did I want? Did I want him locked up? Did I want him free, getting help? Was vengeance more important than family?

He was my father.

But if I hadn't used the phone, he might have killed me this morning.

But he was my father. He wasn't a criminal. Fathers who don't belong there get killed in jail.

I saw Lucas being punched in the face by his dad. I saw Robert trying to slip out of a hug from his father, but not trying hard enough to actually escape. I saw Butch sitting with her dad, doing the Sunday crossword puzzle together, and sharing a bowl of popcorn. I envied Robert and Butch as much as I pitied Lucas. I saw myself walking through the corridors of school, hearing whispers about a father in jail.

"I need to think," I said.

Mom put her arms back around me. "I know."

"Are you going to see Dad?"

"I have to," she said. "It won't be easy. But I can't hide from what happened. I need to deal with it."

I thought about Jillian, and all she'd had to face. "You're strong. You'll be okay."

"I hope so."

"Can you get me something before you go?" I asked. I thought about the gift Mr. Piccaro had given me. I couldn't ask Mom to go all the way home. But I could ask her for a surrogate.

"What do you want?"

"A notebook," I said. "And a couple pens." So I could lose myself in time. Or find myself.

"I'll check the gift shop. They should have that."

She brought me what I needed. Unlike Jillian, I didn't have the skill, or the desire, to draw accurate images of my pain. But I had the words.

I started writing, creating a half lie, at first, to try to purge the demons with a fictional telling, based on the truth, painting my pain with words instead of pigments. Four paragraphs into the heated narrative, as I slammed down with my father at the foot of the stairs and wondered whether to give him a broken back, I knew I needed to go with the truth and not try to invent parallels and parables for the story of my life. A made-up story, as much as I loved it when handed a novel, would be like my sketchy paintings of blurry dragons and half-recognizable game controllers. Truth would be like Jillian's isolated objects, each depicted in painstaking detail. I would paint my demons with words, holding true to what happened, suspending them against a neutral background. Sentences would be my objects, meticulously drawn and carefully placed.

So, here we are, just several hours past the place where we started our journey, but many lifetimes wiser after the two months we spent together. I'm glad you came along. I hope you feel I fulfilled my promise of a story worth hearing. I can tell you this—despite the bumps, it was a story worth living. I hope you agree. And I hope you find, or have found, your own Jillian. You deserve that.

As much as I hate to leave you, I'm not going to linger. Time has passed since our previous present. The notebooks and journal are nearly full. The pens are nearly dry. There's just one last essential scene to share. But first, before I share that moment with you, let's leap ahead briefly to the true chronological ending of my story.

Here's where I am now, in space and time, in the real world, as I prepare to write that final scene. My father didn't go to jail. But he didn't come home, either. Mom wouldn't let him. I haven't seen him since that day. I know at some point, I have to deal with that and make peace with my past. Whether the message is *I forgive you*, or *I'll never forgive you*, I need to deliver it to him face-to-face. I think I need to make a trip to see my grandfather, too. But not quite yet. I want him to understand the legacy he created. And let him know it's reached a dead end. If I ever become a father, I'll be like Robert's dad, or Butch's. Not like mine or Lucas's.

My amazing, brilliant friend Jimby said it perfectly, way back when I was wondering how I could get the attention of the dazzling light who entered my universe: *Nobody has the right to kiss you without permission. Or touch you in bad places. Or hit you.*

Those are words to live by. Though I know there's a lot more to being a good parent than not hitting. But I'm getting wordy, and that will do neither of us any good. Let's complete our visit to the present.

Summer is half over. I'm an official high school graduate. I made it out of the hospital in time to walk onstage, get handed my diploma by the principal, and toss a quick bow to the cheering crowd. Since then, after a full week of doctor-prescribed rest, I've been working hard, driving to a construction job that Butch's parents helped me find. Yeah, driving. I got a car. What kind? To describe it, to even hint at the color of the body or the curve of the chrome, would be to reveal too much of my soul. Or, perhaps, too much of the limitations of my budget. Instead, I'll let you craft your own wheels. Think of the kit you've labeled WHAT I'D LOVE TO DRIVE. Make it in that image, rev it up, and take it for a ride. Don't forget the air fresheners. Or your friends.

Mom has been working hard, too. She's a manager now, at the bakery. She's working a lot more hours, but she gets to start later in the day. The cop who caught me on the steps when I fell stops by there all the time. He buys a lot more rolls than anyone would need. She thinks he wants to ask her out. She's not ready for that. Not yet. Maybe someday.

But she's found time for more happiness in her life. All these years, she'd kept her fiddle. It was stuck in the back of her bedroom closet. Now she'll take it out and play sometimes. It has a crack on the face, near the bridge, but that doesn't seem to hurt the sound. I told her she should form a band. She said she was too old for that, but I could see she liked the idea. Mostly, she plays happy tunes, like Doc Watson instrumentals. But when she plays a haunting ballad or a lament in a minor key, I think she's painting away bad memories with her bow.

We decided, if we scrimped and watched our spending, I

could go to County full-time. I didn't think that was necessary. Mom insisted. I'm glad she did. I'll be taking classes in education. And maybe creative writing. I might even take an art class, though I've accepted that it's unlikely I could ever have a career as a painter. I guess part of maturity is learning to see not just yourself as others see you, but seeing your art that way, as well.

But let's get back to the hospital. To the true ending. And beginning.

When Mom left the room, after delivering the notebook, I used the phone by my bed to call Jillian.

"Bad news," I said.

"You're pregnant?" She giggled.

God, I loved her laugh. Maybe I loved all of her. My mind and groin were still too rut filled and hormone washed to sort out all of that. But I knew she was the best thing that had ever happened to me. I hoped we kept happening to each other for a long time. Maybe even a lifetime.

"No. Not pregnant." I touched the bandage on my forehead. "But I'm not as pretty as I used to be."

"That's okay. I'm not as shallow as I used to be," she said.

"Seriously, I'm sort of banged up right now."

"What happened?"

"It's a long story," I said.

"I have time. Tell me."

And so I did.

[Please take a moment to savor the fact that you just finished reading an entire freakin' novel, before moving on to the mostly unnecessary page or two of author's notes. Feel free to skip, instead, directly to a satisfied sigh and the terminal snap of a closing cover.]

AUTHOR'S NOTES

I share one trait with Cliff. (Or, at least, one I'll admit to.) There are things that I want you to know that I know.

"Euler" is pronounced *Oiler*. "Yuler" is pronounced however you want.

Ms. Percivel should have been named Ms. Amfortas, since she was the keeper, not the seeker, of the Grail. But amusing and euphonic trumps scholarly and accurate in my universe. And nobody really cares.

Either "verbal fists" or "oral fists" would have worked in Cliff's initial weight-room encounter with Nicky, but I opted for the former since I didn't want to sully the scene with irrelevant innuendo.

I am aware that Cliff's darkest moment could have been paired with a reference to Dorothy Parker's classic poem "Résumé." But some literary opportunities, tempting as they might be, are best left unexploited.

And there are things I need to say.

I have an awesome editor. I'd read the opening chapter to Susan Chang, on a whim, when that was all that existed of this work, after we'd spent a day talking about wizards, monsters, and spaceships. "That's your next book," she said. Whether we're on a third revision pass or a first paragraph, Susan has never steered me in the wrong direction.

I have an awesome publisher. Kathleen Doherty was enthusiastic about this book from the start. She has been enthusiastic about my work for twenty years. Without that support, I doubt I would have the luxury of spending each day writing. And I know this book would never have been written. I'm very glad it was. I hope you are, too.

I have awesome family and friends. I owe big thanks to Joelle Lubar, Alison Myers, Doug Baldwin, Connie Cook, Shannon Tyburczi, and Jordan Sonnenblick for reading various drafts at various stages. And I owe thanks to the writers, educators, and booksellers who took the time to read and respond to this book back when it was in manuscript form. I am well connected.*

I have awesome readers. Thank you for taking the leap with me.

---

*Yes, that was a literary reference.

Ages 13–17; Grades 8–12

ABOUT THIS GUIDE

The questions and activities that follow are intended to enhance your reading of *Character, Driven*. The material is aligned with Common Core State Standards for Literacy in English and Language Arts (www.corestandards.org); however, please feel free to adapt this content to suit the needs and interests of your students or reading group participants.

Prereading Activities

1. *Character, Driven* is written in the first-person point-of-view, meaning the narrator is also a character in the story. Have students share titles of other novels featuring first-person narrators. Then create a brainstorm list of things a first-person narrator can and cannot understand or share with readers.

2. Ask each student to write a one-page essay describing another novel they have read that is written from a first-person viewpoint. Have them note the title and genre of the novel and include a very brief (two- to four-sentence) plot summary, and an observation of something the reader discovers or

understands particularly well because of the first-person viewpoint.

Supports Common Core State Standards: W.8.3, W.9–10.3, W.11–12.3; and SL.8.1, SL.9–10.1, SL.11–12.1

Developing Reading and Discussion Skills

1. In the opening chapter, readers realize that Cliff is aware that he is writing his words to the reader. What insights into novel writing does Cliff reference? What do you think he is trying to tell readers when he notes that ". . . not every book tells a story"?
2. Describe Cliff's family's financial situation. How does this effect his home life?
3. Who is Jillian? What past experiences with girls make Cliff uncertain (or even afraid) to approach her?
4. Describe the assumptions Cliff admits to making when starting to read a novel, and the concerns this raises for him about his own narrative (the book you are reading) in the chapter titled "Inter Lewd."
5. Describe Cliff's relationships with Lucas and with Nola. What happens to each of these characters as the story progresses? What type of language does Cliff use to explain these outcomes? Does he seem to feel a sense of responsibility, empathy, or another type of emotional connection to these characters? Explain your answers.
6. Why does Cliff think Ms. Ryder is a good teacher? Do you think Cliff is an especially good judge of teaching ability? Why or why not? What other teachers have an important impact on Cliff? What do you think Cliff would list as the three most valuable attributes of a good teacher?

7. Cliff enjoys art classes. Is he a good artist? Does it matter? What other talents seem to emerge as he considers creating new paintings? Why is the discussion of art a dangerous topic in the Sparks household?

8. Do you think there is a relationship between the wordplay Cliff employs throughout the story and the visual-arts compositions he and Jillian paint? Why or why not? How might these creative outlets relate to the emotional journeys of the characters?

9. By the end of the story, Cliff has realized that he has a quality circle of friends. Name at least three of these characters and explain how each of them strengthens Cliff for the challenges to come in the final chapters.

10. As he is struggling with his painful home life, Cliff is also trying to sort out what he will do after high school—what he wants to learn and who he wants to become. How do his plans and dreams evolve over the course of the story? Has Cliff's journey provided you with any insights into your own thoughts about life after high school? Explain your answer.

11. Could you argue that *Character, Driven* is an exploration of the relationship between how the stories we tell enable us to endure, manage, and possibly even change the trajectory of our real lives?

12. Early in the novel, Cliff struggles with the issue of describing himself to the reader because ". . . the truth is, nobody sees himself clearly in a mirror or photo." Then, in the final chapter, he admits to buying a car but that "[T]o describe it, to even hint at the color of the body . . . would be to reveal too much of my soul. . . . Instead, I'll let you craft your own wheels." What is the relationship between these

two statements? What might Cliff (or David Lubar) be encouraging readers to do with respect to their own lives?

13. Do you think the narrator's name is really "Cliff Sparks"? Why or why not?

14. Could the theme of *Character, Driven* be reflected in the cliché "You can't judge a book by its cover"? How might this common expression be applied to Butch, Nicky, Jimby, Jillian and, ultimately, Cliff himself?

Supports Common Core State Standards: RL.8.1–4, 9–10.1–5, 11–12.1–6; and SL.8.1, 3, 4; SL.9–10.1, 3, 4; SL.11–12.1, 3, 4.

DEVELOPING RESEARCH AND WRITING SKILLS

UNRELIABLE NARRATOR. By the end of the novel, readers come to realize that Cliff has been an unreliable narrator. Go to the library or online to research the literary term "unreliable narrator." With friends or classmates, create a reading list of famous novels featuring unreliable narrators. Divide into two groups to debate the following topic: Resolved. One cannot be a reliable narrator of one's own life.

TIMELINE. *Character, Driven* is written as a series of flashbacks and even-further flashbacks. Make a list of the novel's chapter titles. Beside each title, note the time in which the chapter takes place (e.g., "present," "last April," "sometime last year"). Note any patterns you detect in terms of the relationship between content, timeframe, and the nonlinear style of the story.

EPIC WORDPLAY. From chapter titles to the body of the text, the novel is filled with wordplay, such as puns and double entendres. In the character of Cliff, write an essay explaining how and/or why you came up with your chapter titles.

THE GIFT OF BOOKS. Throughout the novel, Mr. Piccaro quietly gives Cliff books to read. Using a library Web site or other online resource, create an annotated list of the titles Mr. Piccaro shares. Then, write a one-page essay about the relationships, if any, you observe between the title and Cliff's own journey.

FIRST PERSON, DIFFERENT PERSPECTIVES. Cliff second-guesses the ways that he didn't get to know Lucas or Nola better. Perhaps Cliff's friends feel similarly about him. From the viewpoint of Butch, Nicky, or Jimby, write a journal-style essay discussing your friendship with Cliff; any concerns or suspicions you may have about his home situation; and the way your own home or family life influences the way you handle your potential knowledge about Cliff.

SOCIAL ISSUES. *Character, Driven* tells the story of Cliff's journey from mere survival to escape from an abusive situation. Sadly, child abuse is not fiction, and teens suffering abuse may not see a way out. But conversation and awareness can help. Learn more about this serious issue (teens.webmd.com and kidshealth.org/teen are good starting points for research), including warning signs, appropriate ways to offer your support, and resources for victims. Compile your research into a multimedia presentation to share with friends or classmates.

CHARACTERS ONSCREEN. Individually or in small groups, imagine you are creating a film or television adaptation of *Character, Driven*. Write a promotional paragraph and the script or storyboard for the first fifteen minutes of your film. If desired, create a video trailer for your movie.

ARTS CAN . . . From Jimby's story to Jillian's paintings to a performance of *Romeo & Juliet*, *Character, Driven* is a story in which the creative arts perform many valuable functions. Individually, or with friends or classmates, create a poster, mural, or image/word collage depicting the many levels at which art entertains, informs, and more in the novel—and in life.

INTRODUCING YOU. If you were going to write about the last two months of your life, any way you wanted, what tale would you spin? Writing in first-person, with the reader in mind, write a chapter title and the first five pages of your story.

Supports Common Core State Standards: RL.8.4, RL.8.9; RL.9–10.4; RL.11–12.4; W.8.2–3, W.8.7–8; W.9–10.2–3, W.9–10.6–8; W.11–12.2–3, W.11–12.6–8; and SL.8.1, SL.8.4–5; SL.9–10.1–5; 11–12.1–5.

ABOUT THE AUTHOR

David Lubar grew up in Morristown, New Jersey. His books include *Hidden Talents*, an ALA Best Book for Young Adults; *True Talents*; *Flip*, a VOYA Best Science Fiction, Fantasy, and Horror selection; the Weenies short-story collections *In the Land of the Lawn Weenies; Invasion of the Road Weenies; The Curse of the Campfire Weenies; The Battle of the Red Hot Pepper Weenies; Attack of the Vampire Weenies; Beware the Ninja Weenies; Wipeout of the Wireless Weenies; Strikeout of the Bleacher Weenies*; and the Nathan Abercrombie, Accidental Zombie series. He lives in Nazareth, Pennsylvania. You can visit him on the Web at www.davidlubar.com.